BE MY GHOST

Books by Carol J. Perry

Witch City Mysteries

Caught Dead Handed

Tails, You Lose

Look Both Ways

Murder Go Round

Grave Errors

It Takes a Coven

Bells, Spells, and Murders

Final Exam

Late Checkout

Murder, Take Two

See Something

BE MY GHOST

CAROL J. PERRY

KENSINGTON
PUBLISHING CORP.

www.kensingtonbooks.com

KENSINGTON BOOKS are published by

Kensington Publishing Corp.
119 West 40th Street
New York, NY 10018
Copyright © 2021 by Carol J. Perry

Special book excerpts or customized printings can also be created to fit specific needs. For details, write or phone the office of the Kensington Sales Manager: Kensington Publishing Corp., 119 West 40th Street, New York, NY 10018. Attn. Sales Department. Phone: 1-800-221-2647.

The K logo is a trademark of Kensington Publishing Corp.
ISBN-13: 978-1-4967-3136-4 (ebook)
ISBN-10: 1-4967-3136-0 (ebook)

ISBN-13: 978-1-4967-3135-7
ISBN-10: 1-4967-3135-2

First Kensington Trade Paperback Printing: September 2021

10 9 8 7 6 5 4 3 2 1

Printed in the United States of America

For Dan, my husband and best friend

You can't stay in your corner of the forest waiting for others to come to you. You have to go to them sometimes.
—A. A. Milne, *Winnie-the-Pooh*

Chapter 1

Maureen Doherty stood at the window of her corner office on the top floor of Boston's William G. Bartlett Building. "Rain," she muttered. "Pouring down rain. Just what I need." With a sigh, she turned away from the cold, gray outdoor vista and faced her almost-empty desk where a brown corrugated box stood open.

She reached for the framed photo of her parents, Nancy and Frank Doherty, posed in front of their San Diego condo. They smiled up at her. Into the box they went, followed by half-a-dozen brass plaques engraved with her name and "Independent Retailers Ready-to-Wear Buyer of the Year." With the closing of the venerable Bartlett's of Boston department store there'd be no more of those plaques in her future. A framed document certifying her degree in Fashion Merchandising, and a well-worn copy of *Mastering Fashion Styling* were next, along with a manilla folder of tax information. It was only September, so she didn't need to worry about taxes on past income just yet. The immediate problem was going to be *future* income.

The closing of Bartlett's hadn't come as a shock to Maureen. The shutting down of brick-and-mortar stores was happening all over the country. Even the big guys, like Sears and the great independents like Filene's, were gone, so it was no wonder that a family-owned department store like this one was doomed to fail, even after eighty-five years at the same address. It was a good bet that the market for women's sportswear buyers was dwindling too, even for an almost-thirty-six-year-old frequent "buyer of the year."

With another sigh, a "New York, New York" paperweight, a souvenir of one of many buying trips to the city, went into the box, followed by a dusty jade plant rooted in Maureen's maternal grandmother's willowware flowerpot. She made a final check of the desk drawers, pulling them out and closing them one at a time, just in case something had been left behind.

Not much to show for ten years in the same job, she thought, brushing back a stray lock of short blond hair and blinking back tears.

"Maureen? May I come in?" William G. Bartlett III stood in the doorway.

She wiped a hand across blue eyes and smiled at the gray-haired older man. He looked tired. "Of course, Bill. Just cleaning up a few loose ends."

"I understand. This hasn't been easy for any of us." He shook his head. "We held on as long as we could, didn't we? I want you to know how much I appreciate your staying on until the last minute." His smile was wry. "Nothing left to sell now except the store fixtures. The moving crew is having a ball sweeping up all the coins that have been under those old wooden counters since nineteen thirty-six. Probably quite a lot of silver down there."

A bit awkwardly, he handed Maureen a long envelope. "This'll help a little to tide you over for a while. Any plans for the future yet? You know I'll give you a glowing reference, whatever you chose to do next."

"Thanks so much, Bill. No plans yet, but I'll keep in touch," Tears threatening again, she slipped the envelope into her handbag and tucked the carton under her arm. Feeling more than a little sorry for herself because of the "no plans" reality, she pushed the last empty bottom desk drawer closed with her foot—a bit harder than necessary. "It's been a good ten years. I'll miss the old place."

"We all will," he said, and held the door open for her. A coin rolled slowly across the carpeted floor, stopping at Maureen's feet. He bent and picked it up. "A nineteen-eighty-three Bermuda nickel. Must have been under your desk."

Had she really kicked the drawer that hard? She felt a flush of embarrassment.

He turned the coin over. "The queen of England on one side and an angelfish on the other, but no silver." He handed it to her. "Can't be worth much, but here, keep it for good luck."

"I will." Sliding it into her pocket, she gave a wave with her free hand, stepped into the top-floor elevator, and pushed the DOWN button.

Leaving by the employees' ground level exit, she gave a reluctant backward glance and stepped out into the nearly empty parking lot at the rear of the building. It was early afternoon and the rain, by then wind whipped, fell in slanting, stinging sheets. Balancing the carton on the rear fender of a five-year-old green Subaru Forester, she unlocked the back hatch, shoved the box inside, climbed into the driver's seat, and headed for home.

The drive to Saugus on US 1 took Maureen only about half an hour on a good day and she usually enjoyed the ride. This was *not* a good day, weather-wise or otherwise. She turned on the radio. More rain and cooler temperatures were forecast. She switched to the easy-listening station. Cher's "Believe" was a much better choice.

Maureen had sent a few resumés around recently, but so far nothing had materialized. She hadn't looked inside the envelope Bill had handed her but was pretty sure there'd be enough there to tide her over for a month or so. Then what?

She could head out to California and visit the parents for a little while. But *then* what? She'd have to find someplace she could afford and it had to be someplace that accepted dogs. Sort of big dogs. She smiled, thinking of Finn.

"Poor Finn. He's out of work too." She'd acquired the beautiful, lovable golden retriever for way less than he was worth from a guide dog instructor she'd met at yoga class. "He's too friendly. Too easily distracted," the woman had told her. "Nice pet, but a dismal failure as a guide dog."

Cher crooned something about being sad about leaving. That fit. Maureen was sad to be leaving Bartlett's. No doubt about it. She slowed the Subaru to a stop at a red light and Cher almost whispered that it was time to move on. Nodding agreement with the lyric, she turned onto Lincoln Avenue, passed Kane's Donuts, where a grinning jack-o'-lantern proclaimed the fast-approaching October holiday. Maureen stuck her tongue out at the pumpkin. *This isn't a good time to be out of work in Massachusetts with winter coming on*, she told herself. *High taxes, high rents, and high heating bills.*

She turned into the alley behind the two-story house where a cozy second-floor apartment had been her home for a decade. It was a good thing she hadn't signed the new lease Mrs. Hennessey had stuck under her door. The current lease would expire at the end of the month and now there was no way she'd be able to afford even the modest rent on this place. She'd be able to collect unemployment insurance for a while, she had a 401(k), and there was a small savings account. No need to panic.

Not yet.

She drove into her usual parking space, stepped out onto rain-soaked ground, opened the hatch, picked up the box, and hurried to the back door. Wiping her feet several times on the rough fiber mat, she went inside, opened the metal mailbox with her name on it, pulled out a few envelopes and a couple of catalogs, and stuffed them into the cardboard box. Starting up the stairway, she heard Finn's welcoming "woof."

"I'm coming, boy." She spoke softly, sliding the box along the wooden bannister, hoping the landlady wouldn't poke her head out of her kitchen door and invite Maureen in for "a cup of coffee and a little chat." Mrs. Hennessey loved chatting and knew that the old store was closing—everybody knew that. However, they'd never spoken about the possibility of Maureen moving. This didn't seem to be the right moment for that conversation.

Maureen unlocked the apartment, slipped inside, and pulled the door closed. She put the box on the kitchen table and knelt to accept Finn's joyous welcoming tail-wagging, doggy kisses, and happy "woofs." "Looks like we're both out of work now, boy," she whispered. "But don't you worry. We'll be okay, you and me—I think. I guess. Somehow." The golden nudged her leg. "Dinnertime?"

She poured his favorite kibble into his bowl and while he happily ate, she began removing the remaining items from the box, spreading them on the table. "If I was going to stay here I'd make a nice wall arrangement with the plaques and my diploma," she told Finn, "but why mess up the wall with nail holes when I'm going to be moving anyway?" She put the photo of her parents on top of a bookcase, and put the jade plant into the sink for a good soaking.

Last of all she pulled out the envelopes and the colorful catalogs, then pushed them aside. "I can't afford anything from Bas Bleu or J. Peterman," she told the dog, "and I'm sure the rest are just bills." She gave the pile a casual once-over. "See? Utilities, Spectrum, T-Mobile, Discover card—whoops. What's this?"

The cream-colored envelope bore a Florida postmark and a distinctive script return address. *Jackson, Nathan and Peters, Attorneys at Law.* A letter from a law firm. Not good.

"The way things are going for us lately, Finn," she said, "it's bound to be bad news." She laid the letter facedown on the table. "Now I'm almost afraid to look at the one Bill Bartlett gave us."

She opened a box of Lean Cuisine and popped it into the microwave, glancing every few seconds at the two envelopes. When she'd finished her dinner, she put a decaf pod into the Keurig machine. "Well, Finn, shall we open the mail and see what our future holds? Financially and legally?"

Finn gave an affirmative-sounding "woof." He put his head in her lap. "Which one should we open first?" The dog looked up at her with soft brown eyes.

"I know. We'll toss a coin. I've got one right here." She pulled the Bermuda nickel from her pocket. "The queen, we open the one from Bartlett's; the fish, the letter from the lawyer. Here goes."

The coin landed with a clink on the table. "Heads. Okay. Money first." She pulled open the unsealed flap of the white envelope. The amount of the check enclosed was a surprise. Her low whistle made Finn's ears perk up. "Five thousand dollars. This'll help a lot with our future plans." Finn tilted his head to one side. "Yeah, I know." She ruffled his fur. "We *have* no future plans." She added two pink packets of artificial sweetener to the coffee, took a sip, then slit the second envelope open carefully—respectful of the 40 percent rag content with its graceful script designation, *Lawrence Jackson, Attorney at Law*—and withdrew a single sheet of paper.

On the first day Finn had come to live with her, Maureen had read aloud the list of instructions that had come along with him. He'd immediately sat at her feet, eyes focused on her face, ears alert, apparently enjoying every word. She'd soon developed the habit of reading to him often—from newspapers, magazines, advertising flyers, novels. He seemed to like them all. She didn't receive many personal letters, though—

her parents usually phoned or e-mailed—so this would be his first.

" 'Dear Ms. Doherty: In the matter of the estate of Penelope Josephine Gray, this is formal notice that Penelope Josephine Gray died on the last day of July past and that you are the apparent only heir to Penelope Josephine Gray's estate, consisting of certain property in Haven, Florida. Please contact this office at your earliest convenience for further information regarding the administration of the decedent's estate."

The letter was signed by *Lawrence R. Jackson, Administrator of the Estate.*

"What does it mean?" she asked.

Finn blinked. "Woof," he said.

" 'Certain property,' " she quoted the letter. "That could mean anything. A farm. A swamp. A mansion. And who is Penelope Josephine Gray?" Finn lay down and closed his eyes. Maureen read the letter again, this time to herself. The fancy letterhead included telephone, fax, and e-mail address.

What if it was a scam? What if Lawrence R. Jackson was an identity thief? Maureen nearly laughed out loud at that one. Who would want her identity? A single woman with no job and pretty darned close to no home.

She opened her laptop and typed in "Jackson, Nathan and Peters, Attorneys at Law, Haven, Florida."

"The website looks legit," she told Finn. "They've been in business at the same address since the eighties. Not a very big building. Looks more like a house than an office. It says here they specialize in wills, trusts, estate planning, and family law. What do you think?"

"Woof," Finn said.

"You're right. I'll call my folks. They probably know exactly who Penelope Josephine Gray is."

Frank Doherty answered on the first ring. "Hello, sweetheart," he said. "What's going on?" She knew her parents were concerned about the loss of her job, and she'd tried hard to convince them that *she* wasn't worried, that something would come up.

Maybe something had.

"Darndest thing." She read the lawyer's letter to him—by this time her mother was on the line too. "Do you two know who Penelope is?" Maureen asked. "Do we have some kind of family connection to her? Or to Haven, Florida?"

"Never heard of the lady," he said. "You, Nancy?"

"Uh-uh. I don't recognize her name. But I think we've all been to Haven. You'd just finished the eighth grade and we drove down to Florida. Remember, Maureen? It was right after we went to Walt Disney World. Nice little place. We went out on a fishing boat. You caught a fish."

She remembered the fish. "I wanted you to cook it for dinner. We took it to a restaurant and they cooked it for us. So that was Haven?"

"I'm quite sure it was," her mother said. "Cute town. Quiet. Near the beach. A little house there would be nice. I say you take them up on the offer. Whoever she was, Penelope what's-her-name has done you a favor. Maybe she was a customer at Bartlett's and you sold her the prettiest dress she ever owned. Maybe she saw your name somewhere and liked the sound of it. People do strange things. You'll figure it out. Meanwhile, why turn down a trip to Florida, with winter coming on?"

"I'll give the lawyer a call," Maureen promised. "If it sounds okay, I think I'll do it."

Frank Doherty gave instructions for her to keep them informed and asked if she needed anything, as he always did.

She answered that she was fine, thank you, and assured him that she didn't need anything, as she always did.

"Oh, Maureen?" Her mother's voice was hopeful.

"Yes, Mom?"

"Maybe you'll meet someone in Haven."

Maureen smiled at the familiar admonition, said goodbye and immediately googled Penelope Josephine Gray.

An obituary from the *Tampa Bay Times* dated in July was headed with a black-and-white photo of an attractive white-haired woman:

> Penelope Josephine Gray, aged 89, died in her residence at the Haven House Inn. Ms. Gray had been the owner operator of the inn for many years and was known as an active and generous member of the community. She was a member and past president of the Haven Chamber of Commerce, a member of the Haven Ladies Guild. She was a graduate of Smith College. Ms. Gray had never married and had no children.

Everything sounded legit so far.

Maureen tapped Lawrence R. Jackson's number into her phone.

Chapter 2

"Jackson, Nathan, and Peters. How may I direct your call?"

"This is Maureen Doherty. May I speak with Lawrence Jackson please? He's expecting my call."

"Please hold."

"Larry Jackson speaking." The voice was pleasant, businesslike, with a slight southern inflection.

"Good afternoon. This is Maureen Doherty. I have a letter from your office regarding an estate?"

Short pause. A sound of paper shuffling. "Oh yes, Ms. Doherty. The Penelope Josephine Gray estate. Good to hear from you. Will you be coming to Florida soon to claim your property?"

"I don't know. This is all quite a surprise to me," she said, looking at Finn and rolling her eyes. What kind of goof would drop everything and take off for Florida based on a one-page letter from a total stranger? She kept her tone level, courteous. "Can you give me some information about my, um, my property? What sort of property is it? And who is—was—Penelope Josephine Gray? The name isn't familiar to me at all."

"Oh, really? We were not aware of that. I'd assumed you were a relative. Ms. Gray was the proprietor of the Haven House Inn until her recent passing. It's a—um—historic prop-

erty. Built back in the early nineteen-hundreds, I believe."
His voice had turned jovial. "It appears that it's all yours
now, Ms. Doherty. Congratulations."

"Thank you." Maureen frowned. "You called this place,
this inn, a *historic* property. Is it actually an operating inn?"

"Oh yes indeed. It's been operating for over a hundred
years. Haven used to be a very popular west coast Florida
beach resort town, but"—there was an audible sigh—"then
the theme parks came and the big highways passed us by.
Things change." His voice brightened. "But there are still
folks who come to stay at Haven House every year, and it's a
full-time residence for some others. There's even a small
restaurant in the building."

That was encouraging. If she owned an inn, even a cen-
tury-old one, where people actually lived and other people
were regular visitors, it meant she'd have a place to stay—
rent-free—at least for the time being. She made a quick decision—without even tossing the coin. "All right then, Mr.
Jackson. If you can give me directions, my dog and I will be
on our way within a day or so. I presume pets are welcome?"

"Yes indeed. The late Ms. Gray had several cats," he said.
"The inn has a website. Just google the Haven House Inn.
You can get an idea of what it looks like and there are directions on the site. I'll call the inn and tell them to expect you
soon."

"Okay. Anything else I need to know?"

"I don't think so. Oh yes." Jovial voice again. "Did I mention that it's rumored to be haunted?"

Maureen laughed. "I guess most of the old hotels in the
country make that claim. I know they do around New England. Seems to be good for business. Don't worry about it. I
don't believe in ghosts. Do you?"

"Me? Ghosts? Of course not. Well then, Ms. Doherty,
when you get settled, call me and we'll deal with the necessary paperwork."

Maureen agreed, said goodbye, and raced for her laptop. Sure enough, there was the inn—*her* inn—and it didn't look too bad. There was a picture of the front of the place—lots of windows and more than a few rocking chairs on a wide porch that seemed to wrap around the building—some shots of bedrooms, some with four-poster beds and some with lots of white wicker, one with a fireplace, and a photo showing the entrance to the restaurant with the name ELIZABETH'S over the door.

"Who's Elizabeth?" she wondered aloud. Finn had no answer but nuzzled her knee. "Hey, we don't even know who Penelope Josephine Gray is, do we?" She squinted at the screen. If she'd actually been to Haven when she was a kid, she didn't remember ever seeing Haven House. She remembered that fish, though. It had been her first one and she'd been so excited. Smiling at the memory, she scratched behind Finn's ears as she checked the maps on the inn's website. As Larry Jackson had said, there were several sets of directions, including one that looked like an almost-straight shot from Boston over to I-95 and on down to Florida's Gulf Coast.

"Let's start packing, Finn," she said. "We're going to Florida."

There was a little more to it than just packing, but within a few days Maureen had told Mrs. Hennessey the good news about her inheritance, which provided a perfect reason for moving. She'd picked up a map from Triple-A just in case her GPS didn't work, and packed the Subaru's rear compartment and back seat with several suitcases full of clothes—she was, after all, in the fashion business—her computer, laptop, and printer, along with the few things that seemed worth transporting all the way to Florida, including the contents of the box she'd brought home from Bartlett's, a couple of lamps, and quite a few books. One of the stock boys from the store was happy to load all the rest of her furniture into his truck for his own first apartment. Some of her fall and all of her winter clothes were distributed among a group of girlfriends who'd gathered for a wine-and-pizza goodbye party. Each of them promised faithfully to come to Florida real soon and to stay at the Haven House Inn.

It was three-thirty on Wednesday morning when Maureen shared a final cup of coffee and a tearful goodbye with Mrs. Hennessey. She strapped Finn into the passenger seat, stopped at Kane's (they opened early for fishermen) for three cinnamon-sugar doughnuts and another coffee, filled the gas tank at the Shell station, and they were on their way. The rain had stopped, but the skies were mouse colored and overcast. Finn looked back and forth from the doughnut box on the console to Maureen's face.

"What?" she said. "We have a long drive ahead of us. I'll need the sugar. For energy. You wouldn't want me to fall asleep at the wheel, would you?" She could have sworn he rolled those big brown eyes. Mindful of maintaining her size 10 figure—she'd packed a couple of really cute bathing suits—she promised herself that whenever, wherever, they stopped for lunch she'd have a salad. She sipped her coffee, helped herself to a doughnut, and headed for the Southeast Expressway and Route I-95.

Maureen, with the aid of Garman, Triple-A, and a toss of her new lucky coin, had selected the famous South of the Border motel—just south of the North Carolina border—as her halfway point. It was pet friendly and she'd wanted to stop there ever since that eighth-grade trip to Walt Disney World had taken them past the place. Nancy and Frank Doherty had jointly vetoed the idea. "Tacky," Nancy had declared.

At seven o'clock in the evening, after sufficient highway rest station breaks for Finn and herself, the promised salad for lunch, and two more doughnuts for energy, Maureen saw the huge sombrero marking the entrance to the place. She drove slowly past the Ferris wheel, the merry-go-round, the giant pink flamingoes. The old childhood thrill came back. It was everything she'd imagined it might be—wonderfully, deliciously tacky. Check-in was quick and efficient. She bought a couple of postcards to send to her parents and Mrs. Hennessey. She fed Finn, put his food and water bowls on the bathroom floor, turned on the television, and told him she'd be back soon.

She'd spied a colorful roomful of old-time pinball machines just off the lobby. That'd be her first stop. *We'll have to get back on the road early*, she told herself, *but I'm going to take the time and a few dollars to experience at least a taste of one of my childhood fantasies. Maybe I'll even stop at Pedro's for a hot dog.*

It was an eighth-grade dream come true. From the arched doorway she spotted the flashing lights and heard the intriguing sounds from a colorful Ship Ahoy machine with great graphics of pirates and ships. The Addams family beckoned enticingly from another. Bones, Spock, and McCoy invited her to visit *Star Trek* once again.

Smiling, she entered the room, immediately drawn to the flashing lights of a true-to-the-original Zoltar fortune-telling machine. It looked exactly like the one she remembered from the old Penny Marshall movie *Big*. She pushed a dollar bill into the slot. "Okay, Zoltar," she whispered. "What do you see in my future? I really would like to know."

After a satisfying moment of blinking, pinging, and chiming, a card inched out from an oblong golden portal. A drawing of a quarter moon and a star were at the top of the pale blue oblong. The text, centered on the card in dark red, followed:

> *With a message from the dead*
> *On a journey you've been led.*
> *Another message from a stranger*
> *Holds an answer, comes with danger.*

A riddle, a puzzle in plain sight.
An answer, a vision in black and white.
You'll know the where but not the why.
Beware the place one comes to die.
ZOLTAR KNOWS ALL

Maureen stared at the thing for a long moment, not moving away from the costumed wizard locked inside his glass booth, turbaned head nodding, plastic eyes watching, pale hands ceaselessly moving over the crystal ball. "Nonsense," she muttered. "Stupid gibberish." Shoving the blue card into her pocket, she hurried from the room, pirates, space explorers, Morticia, and the anticipated hot dog forgotten. Alone in the elevator, she reread the card. *Was* it nonsense? Silly amusement park trivia?

With a message from the dead on a journey you've been led. That part, she admitted to herself, was true.

What about the rest of it?

Finn greeted her with tail wags and kisses. She sat on the floor beside him, her arms around his neck, her face against soft fur. "I don't know what I've gotten us into, Finn," she said. "But it's much too late to turn back now."

Chapter 3

On Thursday morning, by the time the sun rose over the giant sombrero, the Subaru was gassed up, Finn fed, Maureen coffee fueled, and they were on the road again. "I'd like to get to Haven while it's still daylight," she told the dog, "so we can get a good look at our new home."

You'll know the where but not the why.

She opened the car windows, admitting a pleasant, Carolina-woodsy smell. Finn happily stuck his head outside. "I'll call that lawyer first thing tomorrow morning," she promised him. "We'll find out *why* this Penelope Josephine Gray person wanted to give me her inn." She knew Finn wasn't listening—his eyes closed, silky ears flattened by the early-autumn breeze. She wanted that *why* for herself.

They made good time, pausing briefly at a South Carolina rest stop for Maureen to walk the dog, to refill her new South of the Border coffee mug, and to buy a couple of glazed doughnuts for energy. Scenery seemed to fly by. They stopped for lunch just outside Savanah—salad again—where Maureen wished they had time to explore that historic city. *Maybe someday*," she thought. *Not today. Florida, here we come.*

The sun was low in the sky when they crossed the Howard Frankland Bridge from Tampa to St. Petersburg. "We're almost home, Finn," she told the dog, who dozed on the seat beside her. "Just a few more miles and we'll be there."

Following Garman's well-enunciated instructions, Maureen passed a WELCOME TO HAVEN banner. "This is it, Finn. Wake up." She nudged the golden, made a left turn onto Beach Boulevard, heading toward a sunset streaking the sky with improbable shades of turquoise, gold, pink, and magenta. Finn woofed, and stuck his head out the window, sniffing soft, tropical air.

She recognized the inn immediately from the pictures she'd seen on the website. It was bigger than she'd thought it might be. She pulled into a fenced area marked HAVEN HOUSE GUEST PARKING. Remembering her promise to call her parents as soon as she arrived, she tapped their number into her phone. No answer. She glanced at the clock on the Subaru's dash. With the time difference it was early afternoon in California. They were probably out to lunch. She left a message and promised to call later.

Finn was anxious to get out of the car. She grabbed his leash, her handbag, her overnight case, and a bag containing Finn's food and bowls. She'd deal with the rest of the contents of the Subaru later. "Okay, boy," she said, "This'll be your first walk in our new neighborhood. Look. There's the beach at the end of our street." Finn gave a happy "yip," and straining at the leash, he pulled Maureen—not toward the beach, but across a brick sidewalk bordered by a narrow patch of wild flowers, mostly daisies—and started up the front steps of the building. A Halloween pumpkin grinned from the top step. This was a real pumpkin, with a lopsided grin, with a candle inside—not a lighted plastic one like the one at Kane's Donuts. She smiled at the remembered smell of singed orange pumpkin flesh

Several of the rocking chairs she'd noticed in the photos were at the top of the stairs. The elderly occupants—two men and two women—regarded Maureen with undisguised interest. "You checkin' in?" asked a woman, a halo of white hair surrounding a deeply tanned and wrinkled face.

"Yes," Maureen said.

One of the men leaned forward, causing his chair to stop rocking. He was short, well muscled, with a shock of gray hair. The other man had closed his eyes. "I saw your out-of-state plates. Massachusetts, huh? You another one of those ghost hunters?"

She remembered the lawyer's good-humored remark about haunting, and her own observation that old hotels usually promoted the myth. "No. Is there really supposed to be a ghost here?'

Three of them laughed in unison. The fourth one now appeared to be dozing. The white-haired woman wiped tears from her eyes. "Oh boy, dearie, are you in for some surprises."

"You sure you want to stay here?" asked a tiny woman with dyed black hair and a great deal of makeup. "Ms. Gray—she used to own the place. Dead now. Anyway, she tried to keep quiet about some things. Nobody's business. But—you know—word gets around."

"Sure does," Maureen agreed, wondering exactly *what* was nobody's business. Bedbugs? Roof leaks? Bad food? Finn had greeted all four of the rocking-chair welcoming committee with individual hand licks and now pulled Maureen toward a door. "Nice to meet you all," she said. "I'm Maureen and he's Finn. Is there a manager inside?"

"Yep," said the white-haloed one. "Elizabeth. She's probably at the front desk."

So that answers that, Maureen thought. *Elizabeth has a restaurant named for her.*

The sleeping man's eyes flew open. He appeared to be older than the others. "You *aren't* one of them ghost hunters, are you? We already got one of them staying here. Asking damn questions every minute. Runnin' around here day and night with that stupid camera." He dropped his voice. "Pain in the butt. Don't need no more of 'em. Pests." He jerked a thumb over his shoulder toward the far end of the long porch where a lone man sat in a rocker, his back toward the others. "Calls himself a 'psychic detective.' He's over there."

"I'm definitely not a ghost hunter," she assured them with a laugh. "We're here on—uh—personal business." She pushed a massive green door open, noting a bronze plaque beside it designating the place as a "historic landmark," and stepped into air-conditioned coolness. *Nice.* She glanced around the lobby. Homey, in a southern way. White wicker chairs, bamboo tables, bright floral fabrics, hanging plants. Nice—but empty. There was no one at the reception desk, but there was an old-fashioned brass push bell. She gave it a tentative tap, then another. No response. She put her overnight case and Finn's bag on the floor and looked around the room. The neon restaurant sign she'd seen on the website was at the left side of the lobby. ELIZABETH'S. Piano music—a bouncy tune—issued from behind louvred plantation doors. Finn headed straight for it, pulling Maureen along. "Woof," he said.

"Good idea, Finn. Maybe we'll find Elizabeth in Elizabeth's restaurant." She pushed the louvred doors apart and stepped inside. Something smelled very good. This room had a more formal vibe than the lobby—but in a good way. There was a fireplace, and fern-patterned draperies framed tall windows. The sun had set, but the shapes of rocking chairs on the porch could still be distinguished in the pinkish afterglow. Round tables were situated around the room, each one topped with a snowy white tablecloth and surrounded with an assortment of straight-backed dining room chairs. The music came from a piano situated near the fireplace. The tune Maureen recognized as one that had been in the old Muzak rotation at Bartlett's. "Tangerine." There was no one seated on the piano bench. *An old-time player piano*, she thought. *How cool.*

There was a scattering of guests at tables around the room. A tall man wearing traditional waiter's garb—black trousers, white shirt, and red vest—balanced a large tray full of plated food over one shoulder. Another man, similarly dressed, stood behind a wonderful old-style, heavily carved wooden bar where one lone customer sat on a red-cushioned stool. There were the usual restaurant sounds of muted conversation, the clink of glassware and silverware. *A little on the outdated side*, she decided, observing the mismatched chairs and threadbare carpet underfoot. *But not bad. Kind of shabby chic. Looks like they blew the budget on the lobby.*

"Hello. Will you be joining us for dinner?" The woman in a pencil-slim black skirt, crisp white tailored shirt, approached from behind a decorative screen. She didn't wear a vest but carried out the color scheme with a bright red cobbler's apron with the traditional bib top and deep front pocket. Raising penciled eyebrows, she gave Maureen a fast up-and-down look, then glared pointedly in Finn's direction. "Pets aren't allowed in the dining room." Her name tag said "Elizabeth."

"How do you do." Maureen smiled and offered her hand. "I'm Maureen Doherty. I think you were expecting me. There was no one at the front desk, so we just came on in."

"Oh, Ms. Doherty. I'm so sorry." The woman had a firm handshake. "Elizabeth Mack. If I'd known you'd be arriving today I'd certainly have been at the desk to greet you. I wish you'd called ahead."

Acknowledging the somewhat passive-aggressive welcome, Maureen smiled, nodded, tugged on Finn's leash, and turned to head back to the lobby. A sudden smattering of applause and a few shouts of "Congratulations!" and "Hooray!" made her look back. The glittering flash of a Fourth-of-July sparkler came from the direction of the bar.

"What's going on?" Maureen stopped at the doorway. Finn moved close to her and gave a soft, worried "woof."

Elizabeth waved a manicured hand toward the room. "Somebody ordered a 'Celebration Libation.' It happens on birthdays or if they had a baby or they hit the Lotto or something." She shrugged. "Penelope thought it up. Good for business."

The man at the bar had spun around on his stool and smiled, lifting a very large brandy snifter in a salute to the assembled guests. The glass, its purple liquid contents topped with the still-shimmering sparkler, was further decorated with varicolored paper umbrellas, a pink hibiscus blossom, and a small American flag. The player piano swung into "You're a Grand Old Flag."

Elizabeth pushed the doors open. "Well, come along. Let's get you settled." She motioned to the waiter. "Herbie. Take over here for a minute I'll be right back."

With Finn in the lead, Maureen returned to the spot where she'd left her bags. A middle-aged couple now occupied two of the wicker chairs, he in suit and tie, she in a black crepe sheath—which Maureen immediately recognized as a Victoria Beckham number that had sold in Bartlett's boutique department for well over a thousand dollars—gold high-heeled sandals, and an enormous gold handbag. She—reading a magazine. He—texting. *They look as if they're going to dinner in Boston, not here in the land of Hawaiian shirts and Bermuda shorts*, she thought. *Definitely not local folks.*

Maureen smiled at Elizabeth. "Perhaps you can just direct me to my room. We've been traveling for a long time. I'd love to get a shower and a change of clothes. Finn would like to go for a walk—then perhaps I can get a bite to eat in your lovely restaurant."

"Of course." Elizabeth reached beneath the counter and handed Maureen a folder. "Your key is inside. You'll have Penelope's suite, of course. It's on the top floor all by itself.

Kind of a penthouse. Nice view." She dropped her voice. "I hope you like cats. Penelope's two cats have had the run of the place for years—except for the dining room, of course. They have their own door to her room and another to the outside."

Maureen shrugged. "I like cats well enough," she said, "but I don't know how Finn feels about them. Guess we'll find out."

"They've been keeping to themselves since Penelope died. Ted, the bartender, feeds them outside the back kitchen door, I guess. I haven't seen either of them lately."

Finn gave a sudden tug toward the front door just as the well-but-overdressed couple rose from their chairs and hurried toward the dining room. "I think Finn wants his walk now. May I leave my bags here for a few minutes?"

"Of course. I'll put them here behind the desk. No sense leading anyone into temptation." Elizabeth hurried around the counter, grabbing both bags. "Done. Now you'll have to excuse me. Looks as if I need to waylay a couple of autograph hunters." She followed the man and woman toward the plantation doors.

"No problem," Maureen said, wondering if bag snitching was common at her newly acquired inn, and at the same time wondering if someone famous was dining there. "Whose autograph?" she asked.

"Just the writer at the bar," Elizabeth said over her shoulder. "No big deal. They can get his autograph later—just not in my dining room. Take care. We'll be serving dinner until ten."

The dog tugged again, and as the two crossed the porch and stepped out onto the brick sidewalk Maureen couldn't help thinking of what it would be like taking Finn out for an evening walk back in Saugus. "Glad we're here tonight, boy? Nice warm breeze instead of cold, drizzly rain." *Not that*

New England isn't usually lovely in the fall, she reminded herself—*leaves changing colors and all*—but being here, on this pretty street with its old-fashioned iron lampposts lighting her way, carved pumpkins grinning from the front steps of the inn, and the fragrance of flowers everywhere, was for now a welcome change.

There were buildings spaced out along both sides of the street. There were several of the expected gift shops and one of those giant T-shirt emporiums. But many of the storefronts had a look of age about them. She peered into the windows of the Beach Bookshop, where an assortment of Halloween-themed paperback mysteries shared space with a retro-looking Frankenstein trick-or-treat bucket. She crossed the street to get a better look at the Paramount, an old movie theater with a lighted marquee advertising *Rear Window* with Jimmy Stewart, while Finn visited several lampposts and two fire hydrants. Happy sounds—and a slight aroma of beer—issued from the L&M Bar at the end of the street, and where the beach began was a long wooden building whose painted sign proclaimed it the HAVEN CASINO BALLROOM, along with a bronze historic landmark plaque like the one on Haven House. "I'll be glad to see all this in the daylight," Maureen said. "Especially my property." She paused, recalling the mismatched chairs, the threadbare carpet, the sparsely populated dining room. "At least, I *hope* I'll be glad to see it. Anyway, I can hardly wait to explore our new hometown, Finn." Maureen turned and started back along the brick sidewalk. She passed a small two-story white house with a red tile roof. A discreetly lettered sign next to the door read JACKSON, NATHAN AND PETERS, ATTORNEYS AT LAW.

"Look at that, Finn." She pointed to the sign. "Our lawyer is just down the street. That's handy. We'll do some more exploring tomorrow. But first, a shower and some dinner."

They approached the inn, which looked especially attractive from that angle in the glow of the streetlamps, heightened by soft lighting from beneath the sloping roof. Several guests were on the porch in rocking chairs, including the four Maureen had met earlier, seated at the top of the stairs. The autograph-hunting couple, her gold bag reflecting light from one of the grinning pumpkins, sat, chairs close together, apparently sharing a magazine. The only other occupied rocking chair was at the far end of the wraparound porch, facing away from the others. *Must be the "ghost hunter" sitting all alone again*, she thought. *That's sad.*

Finn greeted the quartet, the two men and two women, with enthusiastic tail wags and kisses as though he'd known them for years. They responded with pats and ear rubs and "atta boy" and "Hey, Finn." The six nearby porch sitters made friendly comments and before long Finn had greeted them all. Maureen smiled and gave an all-encompassing wave to the group. "Hi," she said. "I'm Maureen. Welcome to Haven House." She learned that the four, Molly, Sam, Gert, and George, were year-round tenants, two of the other six were town residents who'd just come over for dinner, and four were vacationing Haven House guests.

Finn glanced around and tugged Maureen in the direction of the alleged ghost hunter. "You're right, Finn," she whispered. "It's not right for him to be excluded this way. Let's welcome him to Haven House. After all, he's one of *my* guests."

Finn didn't hesitate. He bounded happily down the length of the porch, pulling Maureen along behind him. The chair creaked, rocking gently back and forth, when Finn put his nose on the man's knee.

"Hello there," Maureen said. "Sorry to disturb you. I'm the new owner here and my dog Finn and I would like to welcome you to Haven House."

The man didn't respond and Maureen dropped her voice.

"I guess he's asleep, Finn. Maybe we'll talk to him tomorrow."

Again, the dog pressed against the man's knee, making the chair tilt backward and rock forward.

The man slid silently to the floor. Even in the dim light Maureen saw that his eyes were open—and unseeing.

Chapter 4

Her first instinct was to scream. She didn't. Instead, she reached for the man's wrist. All the Bartlett's employees had taken a mandatory first-aid class. Maybe he was alive. Maybe she could help. She'd recognized him immediately as the lone customer she'd seen at the bar just before she'd taken Finn for a walk. The man who'd been celebrating something special in his life was the mysterious ghost hunter and writer she'd heard about. His wrist was limp, still warm, but she could detect no pulse. The dog had backed away, and now sat, whining faintly.

There was no point in upsetting the others assembled on the porch. Maureen, as calmly as she could, with Finn, head down, tail between his legs, walked back to the front of the building, and through the tall green door. There was still no one at the reception desk.

Should she call 911? Or leave that to Elizabeth?

She pushed open the plantation doors, almost striking the woman who stood just inside. "Watch it," Elizabeth commanded. "What's your hurry?"

"We have a problem," Maureen said, speaking slowly and softly. "There is a dead man on the porch."

"Oh, God. One of the old people?"

"He doesn't look old," Maureen said. "I'm pretty sure it's the man who was celebrating at the bar."

"No kidding. Conrad Wilson. Where is he?"

"At the far end of the porch. He fell out of his chair. He's on the floor now. I don't think anyone else has noticed. What do we do in a case like this?"

"I'll call for an ambulance." Elizabeth sounded almost bored. "This isn't the first time. Won't be the last." She tapped a number into her phone and shook her head. "Why the hell do they all come here to die?"

Beware the place one comes to die.

"Yes. Hello. This is Elizabeth Mack at the Haven House Inn. One of our guests has apparently died. . . . What? . . . A male. On the front porch. . . . Yep. Better send the ambulance." She put the phone down. "Let's go out there and cover him up before those old harpies gather around him. Wait a sec. I'll grab a tablecloth." She reached into a tall cabinet behind the screen, selecting a neatly folded white oblong. "Come on. They'll be here in a minute."

Maureen followed the woman while Finn, his head still down, trailed reluctantly behind his mistress. Within what seemed like seconds Conrad Wilson's still-warm body was shrouded in a sparkling clean white linen tablecloth, its fine fabric skillfully mended in places., its crisp surface divided into precisely pressed square folds.

"There now, Conrad," Elizabeth said, giving the body a gentle pat in the vicinity of its head. "Snug as a bug. That'll keep those old vultures away." She stood, smoothing her slim black skirt. "You stay here with him," she told Maureen. "I'll go up front and wait for the ambulance and the cops."

"The ambulance *and* the cops?" Maureen asked. "Why?"

"The ambulance in case he might still be breathing. The cops to figure out why he isn't. You stay here," she ordered again, then sighed. "Not my first time at the rodeo, you know."

"But . . ." Maureen began to object. Too late. Elizabeth had dashed away, leaving Maureen—along with a recoiling dog—alone with the neatly linen-wrapped corpse.

"I don't know, Finn," she whispered. "Elizabeth behaves as though it isn't unusual for people to die suddenly around here. Not her first time at the rodeo, she says. Like dying is no big deal in Haven."

Finn managed a feeble, "Woof."

"Yeah. It's a big deal to me too."

Elizabeth had been correct, though, about the rapid response of the police and/or the ambulance. A wail of sirens announced the arrival of one or the other or both at the Haven House Inn. The assembled guests and visitors on the porch, inside the restaurant, or maybe even in their rooms responded immediately to the sounds. In seconds there was a rush—a near stampede—to where Maureen and Finn stood guard over the rapidly cooling late Conrad Wilson.

Elizabeth, accompanied by several men, fast-walked toward them, but Molly and Gert got there first "Lookie, Gert." Molly pointed to the fabric-covered mound. "I bet it's that ghosthunter. This is where he always sits."

"Psychic detective," Gert corrected. "Hi, Maureen. What happened to him?"

Finn, perhaps remembering some of his guide dog training, had placed himself between Maureen and the oncoming crowd, growling a low warning. It worked. When Elizabeth and her uniformed male escorts arrived, two of them carrying a stretcher, none of the curious guests, tenants, or random passersby had come within even a few feet of the body—although the glow from multiple phone cameras added an eerie luminescence to the scene.

"This is Officer Frank Hubbard from the Haven police department," Elizabeth announced. "He'll take over." She nodded in Maureen's direction. "She's Maureen Doherty—the new owner of this place. She found the body."

While the officer herded the crowd away, directing them inside the inn or down to the sidewalk, a second officer stood at the foot of the steps, arms folded, discouraging further entry. The two EMTs went to work immediately. Removing the tablecloth, one shone his flashlight onto Conrad Wilson's eye, then gently closed them, while the other pressed a stethoscope on the man's chest, then shook his head. "He's a goner. A guest, Liz?"

"Yes. Conrad Wilson. Been here about a month."

"Whew. Strong smell of alcohol." The other EMT looked up at Elizabeth. "Drinker?"

"Not that I've noticed," she said. "He had one of Penelope's famous 'Celebration Libations' tonight, though."

The first medic laughed shortly. "Oh boy. I had one of them on my birthday last year. Chock-full of one-fifty-one-proof rum. Those things'll knock you on your ass all right."

"Shouldn't kill you, though," the other replied. "Is the coroner on the way?"

Officer Hubbard answered, "Yep. Just leave the body as you found it. Ms. Doherty? You're the one who discovered the deceased?"

"Yes. I guess I am," Maureen answered, avoiding looking at the now-uncovered body.

The officer faced Elizabeth. "Liz, you got a room somewhere where I can question Ms. Doherty here about all this? Some place with a little privacy?'

"Sure, Frank. You can use my office."

"Good. We'll wait here for the coroner. Meanwhile, can you put the dog somewhere, Ms. Doherty?"

Maureen looked at Elizabeth. "We haven't been to our room yet. He'd probably like to go to sleep."

"Fine. Liz, can you get somebody to take the dog up to his room? I'll let Ms. Doherty go as soon as possible." He bent and patted Finn, who, as soon as the crowd had dispersed, had abandoned his on-guard stance. "Nice dog. What's his name?'

"Finn," Maureen answered. Elizabeth reached for the leash. Maureen waited to see if the golden would object, but he seemed willing. "Okay, Finn. Off to bed with you. I'll be up soon." She handed the leash to the woman, remembering the unattended bags in the lobby. "Could somebody take our bags up too?"

"Sure. Come on, doggy."

Finn gazed up at Maureen. "It's okay, "she told him. "Go with the nice lady." Finn did as he was told, looking back at Maureen a few times before the green door closed behind him.

The long. empty porch with its mismatched unoccupied rockers was hushed except for the faraway tinkle of the player piano, the low rumble of an occasional passing car. And crickets. Actual chirping Florida crickets. She suppressed an enormously inappropriate urge to giggle.

Officer Hubbard stood opposite Maureen, the body, with its cast-off tablecloth shroud between them. Averting her eyes from the corpse, she attempted to break the silence.

"Do you have to call the coroner for every death?" she asked.

"Oh no," he said. "Usually, around here, people die in the hospital, or home in bed after an illness. Normal, everyday dyin'. You know? But when somebody dies all by themselves in a kind of public place"—he nodded in the direction of the deceased—"we need to know who he is and why he's dead. The coroner's job is to figure that out."

"The inn knows who he is. Conrad Wilson. I'm sure he must have provided identification when he checked in," she offered.

"I'm sure it's a pretty simple case. Maybe the guy had a

heart condition or something. But we need to know what he was doing here and why he died."

You'll know the where but not the why.

"And the coroner will figure all that out?"

Officer Hubbard held up a big hand and counted on his fingers. "He has five possibilities to choose from. Natural death, accident, homicide, suicide, or judicial execution. It's got to be one of those."

She thought about that. "Makes sense, I guess."

"It's important," Hubbard said. "Like, for instance, the difference between a suicide and an accident can be important to the family. Lots of insurance companies won't pay off on a suicide, but they might get double or triple if it's an accident."

She nodded understanding. His expression was grim. "Of course, if it's homicide, then it gets to be my business."

"How long will they leave—um—him out here on the porch?" she asked.

"That's up to the doc. Here he comes. We can go inside and I'll take your statement." He gave a half smile. "Don't worry. He probably died of natural causes and they'll take him away and everything will be back to normal at Haven House in the morning."

I have no idea what normal is at Haven House, Maureen thought. "Nothing about this so far has been the kind of normal I'm used to. And truly, I don't know if I can be helpful," she said.

"Just routine," he answered, and repeated, "Don't worry."

There was a fast introduction to the coroner, a busy-looking little man, dressed entirely in black, wearing thick glasses. *He looks as though they got him from Central Casting,* Maureen thought, unable to look away as, in quick succession, the coroner photographed the body, used an electronic scanner to take fingerprints, then encased the hands in paper bags.

"Shall we go inside?" Officer Hubbard suggested again.

"Yes, please."

Together, they hurried away from the sad scene.

The officer opened the green door for her. All of the wicker chairs in the lobby were occupied now, and all eyes were on the two as they crossed the lobby to an office marked MANAGER.

She wished she'd had a chance to shower and change and put on some makeup. She almost wished she were back in Massachusetts and had never heard of Penelope Josephine Gray.

Chapter 5

Officer Hubbard sat in the chair behind the white wicker desk after directing Maureen to sit in a wicker chair opposite him. Everything here matched the lobby décor. A pair of sunshine-yellow file cabinets dominated one wall and a flowering pink plant in a green ceramic pot bloomed beside a floor-to-ceiling window, partly covered by white louvred plantation shutters. A cork bulletin board was crowded with what appeared to Maureen to be notes about menu items. A painting of a tree covered with red flowers was a bright touch.

The officer put his phone on the desk between them and asked if she minded being recorded. She said she didn't. "Mr. Wilson was seated a good distance away from the other folks on the porch," he said. "Why did you approach him?"

"I wanted to welcome him to Haven House. Perhaps to invite him to join the others."

"Were you acquainted with Mr. Wilson?"

"No. I just arrived a few hours ago." Maureen looked at her watch. "I'm not acquainted with anyone here."

"Elizabeth says that you are the new owner of Haven House."

"That's correct," Maureen said.

"Elizabeth says that Ms. Gray left it to you in her will."

Maureen nodded, suddenly aware of how very tired she was. "Yes," she agreed.

"Did you know that Mr. Wilson was investigating the possibility of—uh—ghosts on your property?"

"I didn't know anything about Mr. Wilson at all." Slight annoyance began to replace exhaustion. "I don't know anything about anyone here. And I don't believe in ghosts."

"Of course not. But some people think that reports about a place being—well—being haunted might discourage business." The officer leaned forward, frowning. "Business here at Haven House. Do you think so?"

"I've never given it a moment's thought, one way or another," Maureen said. "I told you. I don't believe in ghosts."

"Mr. Wilson was apparently drinking at the bar in the dining room before his . . . unfortunate passing. Did you see him there?"

"Yes. He was drinking an unusual-looking cocktail. Everyone noticed. It had a sparkler in it."

"The Celebration Libation." He smiled. "You'd not seen him before then?"

"Not his face. I'd seen *somebody* sitting in that chair earlier this evening. I presume it was he."

Officer Wilson shut off the recorder and stood. "All right. Thank you, Ms. Doherty, "That'll do it for now. You must be anxious to get back to Finn."

"I am," she said.

He opened the office door for her and they both moved back into the lobby. "Officer Hubbard," she whispered. "How long do you suppose the—uh—Mr. Wilson will remain on the porch?"

"Not long. Doc'll check his vitals and if there's nothing strange going on, they'll carry him on down to the morgue and finish up with him there. Good night, Ms. Doherty."

"Good night, Officer." There were only a few people still in the lobby, and Maureen hurried past them in the direction

Elizabeth had said led to the elevator. It did. The Haven House elevator was quite a piece of work. Shiny brass accordion-style doors enclosed a polished wood and scrolled metal interior. Maureen had admired similar ones in some of Boston's old buildings. She pressed the UP button. The doors slid open and she got in. *I love this*, she said to herself, watching through etched-glass windows as the cage ascended two stories within its brick-walled enclosure.

She stepped out of the elevator onto soft rose-patterned carpet, taking the folder Elizabeth had given her from her purse, looking inside for the usual slim plastic card entry device. Instead, she found an old-fashioned metal key with an attached long brown plastic fob marked HAVEN HOUSE INN with the number 33. She heard Finn's welcoming "woofs" from behind a white paneled door, a brass numeral 33 affixed to it and a round cat door at its base. "I'm coming, boy," she said, inserting the key. "I'm home."

Finn greeted her with the usual happy kisses and tail-wagging, the leash trailing from his collar. She nearly tripped over the two pieces of luggage. "Oh, poor dog," she said, kneeling beside him. "That woman must have just shoved you in the door, leash and all, along with the bags." She unfastened the clasp, hugging him and ruffling soft fur. She stood, taking a first look at her surroundings.

No white wicker furniture in this room, which was a welcome relief from the extensive use of it she'd already observed downstairs. The furnishings here were what Nancy Doherty might term "mid-century modern." The walls were white, and a long blue couch stretched along one side of the room. Two beige armchairs flanked a wide, un-curtained, floor-to-ceiling window with a narrow balcony outside running its length—not wide enough for a chair—probably just decorative, she decided. A huge oak tree provided some privacy and the branches framed a view of the street Maureen and Finn had walked that evening, a moonlit shimmer of ocean in the distance. At either side of that window were two narrower ones with crank-out panes.

A clean-lined desk, a sideboard, and a kidney-shaped coffee table were of polished blond wood, and a multi-level cat tower stood in front of another, narrower, floor-to-ceiling window. Potted green plants, whose names she promised herself she'd learn later, added color and texture. A wall-hung television above the sideboard was the only nod to the twenty-first century, and on the wall above the couch hung a large colorful painting similar in style to the one in Elizabeth's office.

"Oh, I think we're going to like this place, Finn," she said. "But have you seen any cats yet?"

With a "woof" that sounded dismissive to cats in general, Finn bounded across gray carpet toward an open doorway. Maureen followed. The kitchen was neat and efficient, with white cabinets and appliances, red countertops, a small red-and-white enamel kitchen table with a pair of blond wood chairs with red-and-white–checked cushions. A red apple-shaped cookie jar, an old-fashioned drugstore blender, and a Keurig coffeemaker were lined up on one counter. She opened one of the cabinets, revealing a set of colorful Fiesta-ware dishes and mugs along with assorted glass tumblers. A top shelf reveled four china bowls—two marked BOGIE and two marked BACALL—a larger aluminum bowl marked WATER, and several stacks of canned cat food and boxes of dry kibble. Another cabinet contained some basic "people" food. Beans, canned veggies, boxes of rice and pasta, assorted soups, crackers, breakfast cereal, coffee, tea bags, sugar, and powdered creamer. Yet another served as a modest but nicely stocked liquor cabinet. The refrigerator and attached freezer were spotlessly clean and empty except for a six-pack of bottled water.

"Someone has been really thoughtful," Maureen told the golden. "We'll just add your food to all this and we're good to go for quite a while. Have you found the bathroom yet, Finn? I need a shower. It's been quite a day." She followed the dog into a bedroom with more white walls and gray carpet. The king-sized bed, bureau, end tables, and side chair in the style she recognized immediately from her department store background as gorgeous, blond, hard-to-find, and pricey Heywood-Wakefield. Bedspread and draperies were dark green. More plants in terra-cotta pots provided contrast and texture. Two club chairs in lighter shades of green were located at either side of the door. A full-length oval mirror reflected a large, aged-looking black leather trunk, dotted with labels from many countries, adding an amusing, offbeat touch to the décor.

The adjoining bathroom had pink walls, a claw-foot tub, a glass-doored shower, and a linen cabinet stacked with fluffy pink towels and white sheets. A mirrored medicine chest was centered over the white marble counter and its shell-shaped sink. The one instance of white wicker was the clothes hamper.

Maureen unpacked her small suitcase and Finn's bag, arranged her wallet, watch, car keys, the Bermuda nickel— and, as an afterthought, the blue Zoltar card—on top of the bureau, then took another tour of the suite. *It's perfect*, she decided. *The whole place is just perfect. I mean, except for the body on the porch.*

Chapter 6

Showered, shampooed, and appropriately dressed in one of Bartlett's very best resort wear outfits—white pants with a navy-and-white–striped top—purchased at cost in the going-out-of-business sale, Maureen returned to the lobby, leaving Finn alone in the so far cat-free suite, happily curled up at the foot of the king-sized bed.

All seemed quiet in the lobby. Perhaps the excitement was over. Maybe Mr. Wilson had been transported to more clinical surroundings. It was a few minutes before nine-thirty. Maureen hoped they were still serving food in the restaurant.

"Good evening, Ms. Doherty." Herbie, the red-vested waiter she'd seen earlier, handed her a plastic-coated menu. "Elizabeth said you might be joining us this evening." He waved to the almost-empty restaurant. "Sit anywhere you like. May I get you something to drink?"

"Thank you," she said, selecting an oak chair with a pressed-wood back at one of the round tables. "I'd like a glass of rosé please." Herbie had clearly been informed that Maureen was to be his new boss.

"Yes, ma'am." He hurried across the room toward the bar where the bartender polished glasses and returned quickly, bearing the pink liquid in a stemmed glass on a silver tray.

She wondered if all the customers were so favored. That would be nice.

"May I suggest the crab-stuffed jumbo shrimp with sweet potato waffle fries?" Herbie asked. "Perhaps with a house salad and Elizabeth's own green goddess dressing?"

"That sounds wonderful. Thank you." Maureen sipped her wine. "Do you happen to know if Ms. Gray's cats are all right? I haven't seen them at all."

"I haven't either," he said. "Not since she died. Cute little buggers. I think Ted has been feeding them. Want him to come over and tell you about them?"

"If he's not too busy."

"No problem. Nothing going on here tonight. I mean after the . . . you know. The ghost hunter thing. The place really cleared out after that."

"Is that all over—I mean, is he gone?"

"Yep. The coroner's big van left a while ago." Herbie shrugged. "Poor guy. He seemed like a nice enough person. Good tipper. Kept to himself pretty much. He just kind of sneaked around, day and night, taking pictures everywhere with that fancy camera he always had with him.

"Interesting," she said. "I've never met a ghost hunter."

"Oh, you'll meet plenty of 'em here," he promised. "Well, let me run this order out to the kitchen and I'll tell Ted you'd like to talk to him."

Maureen held the menu up to her eyes, peering over the top, stealing a glance at the others in the room. The man and woman she'd seen earlier in the lobby—the ones Elizabeth had dubbed "autograph hunters"—were at one of the round tables with another couple. Two men in business suits were in deep conversation at another. Other than those few and herself, the big dining room was empty. She lowered the menu. First thing tomorrow she'd call Larry Jackson and find out where she stood financially. For now, she'd enjoy dinner and wine and a good night's sleep in her new home.

"Hello. Ms. Doherty? I'm Ted. Herbie said you wanted to talk to me. Anything wrong?" The bartender was tall and slim with sun-streaked brown hair and brown eyes. His smile seemed genuine, but nervous fingers twisting a corner of his vest gave away his uneasiness.

"Wrong? Why, no. Not at all." Maureen returned the smile. "I'm concerned about Ms. Gray's cats. I haven't seen either one and I'd heard that you might be feeding them."

Ted's relief was evident. "Oh, the cats! When Herbie said you were the new owner and you wanted to see me I thought I was about to get fired. Those little guys are fine. After Ms. Gray died, though, they didn't want to come inside anymore. I feed them out back. They show up every morning. Even bring me a dead mouse now and then. They know their way around outdoors."

"I'm so glad they're okay. Thank you, Ted, for caring about them," she said. "By the way, just in case I meet them, what are their names?"

"Bogie and Bacall. Ms. Gray was a big old-movie fan." He glanced toward the bar. "Oops. Looks like I've got a late customer. Nice to meet you, Ms. Doherty." He gave a brisk salute and hurried back to work.

Questions about cats and bartenders disappeared with the arrival of perfectly browned plump jumbo shrimp snuggled next to round orange crisscrossed fries. The salad fairly shouted, *Crisp! Green! Healthy!* For the next thirty minutes Maureen's full concentration was focused on food, wine, and—finally—coffee and a generous slice of key lime pie. She signaled to Herbie and waited for him to present the check.

He held up both hands. "No charge to you, ma'am," he said. "Everything here already belongs to you."

Startled, she realized it was true. Leaving a generous tip on the table, once again she rode the elevator up to suite thirty-three.

Putting the key into the lock, Maureen heard no welcoming "woof" from Finn. *Odd*, she thought. *Poor guy must be sound asleep.* She pulled the door closed as silently as she could, and tiptoed inside. She stopped short when she heard a muted "woof" from the bedroom followed by a soft, feminine giggle. *Must be housekeeping*, she thought.

"Hello!" she called, and walked into the bedroom.

The woman turned and faced her. So did Finn.

"Oops, sorry," the woman said. "Didn't hear you. I was just talking with your dog. He's much more fun than the cats. Did I scare you?"

Maureen didn't—couldn't—answer. Abruptly, she sat in the closest pale green club chair. Finn approached and nudged her hand with his cold nose. Almost automatically, she stroked his head, her eyes still fixed on the woman.

At least, the figure *appeared* to be a woman. The shape was right. A tall, slim, blond woman wearing a sleekly fitted long, shimmering white gown. Something was decidedly wrong with the image, though—she was entirely black and white.

And transparent.

Maureen squeezed her eyes shut, willing the hallucination—or whatever it was—to go away.

It didn't. When she opened her eyes, the woman was closer, leaning toward her, an expression of concern on her face. "Are you all right? You're not going to faint, are you?"

Maureen looked from side to side. There was no one else in the room. The words were definitely coming from the woman. "Uh . . . no. I don't think so."

"Good. I guess Penelope didn't tell you about me. You *are* Maureen, aren't you?" Again, the soft giggle. "Penelope told me *all* about you."

Maureen could say nothing, only continue to stare.

A riddle, a puzzle in plain sight.
An answer, a vision in black and white.

Chapter 7

Finn turned his head and faced the woman. "You see her too, don't you, boy?" Maureen pleaded. "Don't you?"

"Of course he sees me! Come here, Finn." The dog looked at Maureen, gave her hand a lick, and trotted to the woman . . . the apparition . . . the hallucination—whatever she was.

"Okay. Who—What are you?" Maureen addressed the image.

"Oh, where are my manners? I'm Lorna Dubois. I don't suppose you've seen any of my films," She fluffed pale hair. "Of course not. You're much too young."

Maureen looked away, then back again. *She could be a hologram,* she thought. *Yes. That must be it. Somebody is making a hologram appear in my room.* She stood, beginning an inspection of the walls, the windows, the electrical outlets. Finn followed, giving a curious sniff to each item, each surface she touched. She returned to the pale green chair and sat. "I don't understand," she said.

"I know." The woman sort of floated toward the matching club chair, gracefully lowering herself into it. "I thought Penelope had prepared you for"—she waved a fair hand—"this."

"I've never even met Penelope. I don't know anything

about her. She apparently left this place to me. I don't know why." Maureen fought back tears. "I came here because I had no other options at the moment."

"Oh dear. I suppose then, that it's possible you don't believe in spirts? Wraiths? Manifestations?" The form moved closer to Maureen, whispering, "In me?"

"I *don't* believe in ghosts, if that's what you mean." Maureen spoke firmly. "And I don't know why I have to keep telling everybody that."

The woman giggled again. "Finn believes in me, don't you, Finn?"

"Woof," said Finn. "Woof woof."

"Just because you don't understand something doesn't mean it isn't there." The woman shook a finger in Maureen's direction. "Loosen up a little, why don't you? Open your mind. And you can call me Lorna."

"I'm open-minded," Maureen insisted, then paused. "I mean, I've always thought I was."

"See? There's room in there for new understanding. I'm a ghost. Deal with it."

"You're dead," Maureen spoke slowly. "But you're here."

"Yes."

"Why here? Why in Haven, Florida?" Maureen asked. "Why in my inn?"

"That's easy. I died in Haven. I was doing Summer Stock down at the Haven Playhouse. It was nineteen seventy-five. I was playing Mrs. Boyle in *The Mousetrap*. Agatha Christie wrote it. You know the play?"

"Of course. I saw it at the Charles Playhouse in Boston."

"Good. Well, anyway, Mrs. Boyle is supposed to be 'middle-aged,' but even at sixty-five, I could do the part."

"Sixty-five?" Maureen's eyes widened. "You can't be sixty-five. You look younger than me."

"Oh, darling, I'm not sixty-five now! We get to come back

at our best age. I'm twenty-six." She raised her hands and stroked the unlined face, then smoothed the satin gown over svelte hips. "Like the dress? It's an original *Adrian*. He designed it for Jean in *Red Dust*. I doubled for her in the dust scenes and the water barrel nude shot."

"Jean?"

"Jean Harlow."

"I've seen photos of her. You *do* look a lot like her."

Lorna sighed. "I know. A blessing and a curse. We were both working in Hollywood at the same time. She was a star. I looked *too* much like her. I got to double for her once in a while. On my own I never made it past 'starlet.' I was in a bunch of B movies nobody remembers. I was the dumb blond girlfriend or the star's ditzy sidekick or an extra in a crowd scene." She smiled. "But I was always working." She returned to the club chair opposite Maureen's. Finn lay between them, looking from one to the other as they spoke.

"So tell me, Lorna, how did you—um—pass away?" Maureen realized with astonishment that she was actually having a conversation with a spirit, a wraith, a manifestation. A ghost.

"Tripped over a damned electrical cord and took a header downstage center," Lorna said. "Right smack into the prompter's box. Broke my neck."

Finn whined and covered his eyes with both paws. Maureen cringed. "Oohh. Did you—um—cross over . . . right away?"

"Yep. Didn't feel a thing. But since I was living at Haven House, and all my clothes were here"—she pointed to the trunk—"I decided to stay."

"So I guess you're the reason that ghost hunter was here. Conrad Wilson?"

"I doubt it. I try to stay out of their way. We all do. Snoopy little devils. Running all over town with their fancy cameras, recorders, Geiger counters, ghost boxes." She winked. "But sometimes it's just too much of a temptation to throw a good scare into one of them. You said Conrad Wilson *was* here. Did somebody finally scare him away?"

"I wouldn't know about that." Maureen stood, crossed the room, and studied the labels on the trunk. *Paris. London. Monte Carlo.* "He's dead, though."

Lorna joined her. "Oh, was that him? I saw a little shade go by the window a few hours ago. I thought it was one of the old people." She shrugged. "Look." She pointed to a round sticker. *Monaco.* "That was from nineteen fifty-six. Grace and Rainier's wedding."

"You knew Grace Kelly?'

"No. Not really. I was dating a photographer. He sneaked me in. What a wedding dress! Helen Rose designed it. It took thirty seamstresses six weeks to make it."

"You really like clothes," Maureen said. "So do I."

"No kidding? I sure couldn't tell by what's in your closet— though what you've got on isn't bad."

"Stella McCartney," Maureen said, "and there's lots more clothes in my car."

The apparition clasped her hands together. "Goodie. Go and get them please."

"Tomorrow," Maureen said. "I'm tired. Could you just disappear now please, like the ghosts in *A Christmas Carol*? You know—'you may be an undigested bit of beef,' I don't remember the rest. Something about mustard and cheese. Anyway, poof! Go away." Grabbing her pajamas from a bureau drawer, she ducked into the bathroom.

I'm overtired, she thought. *My eyes are messed up from driving for fourteen hours. I shouldn't have had the second glass of wine. Seeing the dead man was more of a shock than I realized. When I come out of here, that . . . that thing will be gone.* She undressed, slipped into her pajamas, brushed her teeth, and grasped the glass doorknob. She squeezed her eyes shut for another long moment, "Please be gone," she whispered, and turned the knob.

Finn, waiting just outside the bathroom door, greeted her with tail-wagging and a little sideways prance toward the bed—his usual bedtime behavior. Maureen gave him a pat on the head, said, "Nighty-night, Finn"—her usual bedtime behavior. She walked to the bed, pulled back the spread, and climbed in. Finn lay on the floor beside her.

She pulled the covers over her head and lay awake for a long time.

Chapter 8

It took a few seconds for Maureen to figure out where she was. The wide bed felt unfamiliar but extremely comfortable. Early-morning light streamed through a tall window. Finn's familiar "woof" jogged her memory. "Florida. Of course. We're in Florida."

Padding barefoot across cushy gray carpet to the bathroom, she cast a sideways glance as she passed the vintage trunk. Remembering.

"I'll make your breakfast and take you for a nice walk as soon as I get dressed, Finn," she promised, trying to shake away thoughts of the previous night's visitation. "Right after I have a cup of coffee to clear my head."

Someone had thoughtfully stocked a kitchen cabinet with a variety of coffee pods. She selected hazelnut, loaded the machine, filled one of Finn's bowls with doggy chow, the other with water, and waited for her South of the Border mug to fill. The apparition, or whatever it was, had been right about the dearth of clothes in her closet. She pulled on a pair of cut-off jeans and a Red Sox T-shirt. She'd left her makeup kit in the Subaru but made do with lip gloss, mascara, and bronzer she'd carried in her purse. "We'll unload the car today," she told the dog. "At least the clothes and cosmetics."

Maureen made the bed, rinsed her coffee mug, and after a quick walk-through of the suite—determining that there *was* no see-through black-and-white personage anywhere on the premises—she clicked Finn's leash on to his collar, stuck her wallet into one pocket, and put the room key and the lucky coin into another. "We'll take a nice walk," she told him. "Then we'll call that lawyer and tell him we're settled in."

She wasn't surprised to see Molly and Sam, Gert and George, already on the porch. The four rocking chairs were lined up together at the head of the stairs.

"Morning, Maureen!" Gert called. "How are you and Finn feeling this morning?"

"Just fine, thanks," Maureen said. "Good to see you all so bright and early this beautiful day." Finn greeted each of the four with polite hand sniffs.

"Quite some excitement last night, eh?" Sam asked, leaning so far forward in his chair that she thought he might tip over. "You got a good look at the body, didn't you?"

George chimed in, "Could you tell what it was that finished him off?"

Too astonished by the questions to form an answer, Maureen tugged on Finn's leash. "Well, we have to be going."

"Oh, honey, don't mind them." Molly gave Sam a playful punch on his arm. "Nosiest two old geezers I ever knew. But we saw you and the cop and Queen Elizabeth over there and we just wondered what was going on."

"I don't know any more than you do," she told them, still backing away. "Just that the poor man is dead. Gotta go now. See you all later." She hurried down the steps, taking the bottom ones two at a time.

"What do you think of that, Finn?" she said aloud, once she was out of earshot of both the group and any pedestrians in the area. "Did you catch the 'Queen Elizabeth' crack?"

Finn stopped short, spying a white heron standing directly in his path. He took a step back when the long-legged bird, spreading an impressive wingspan, flew to a nearby outdoor pumpkin display in front of the Quic-Shop Market. "Your first Florida bird, Finn," she said. "Looks like we're both in for surprises here."

They passed a pastel orchid house with gingerbread trim and pink and red hibiscus plants in profusion in the front yard. "I didn't notice this place last night. Look at the sign over the door." Maureen pointed and Finn's brown eyes followed the hand motion. "Haven Playhouse. Looks like it's a private home now, but hey, there's still a bulletin board with a 'coming attractions' empty space on it. I wonder if the current residents know that somebody died in there."

Rolling her eyes at her own statement, she looked away from the house. "I mean, if you can take the word of a hologram or whatever that was."

"Woof," Finn said. They'd reached the beach.

"Let's take a run on the sand before we go back and do boring lawyer business." She slipped her sandals off and together they ran toward the shoreline where clear water lapped at the fine sand. "Later we'll come back here for a swim," Maureen promised. "I don't see any 'No Dogs Allowed' signs."

They spent a happy fifteen minutes on the beach. Running on the hard-packed sand at the water's edge felt good. The two had often run in Saugus at the Breakheart Reservation, but the trails there had been hilly and much different from Haven's quartz-like sand. They slowed their pace, Finn chasing an errant sand crab, Maureen picking up a handful of tiny colorful shells. "These look like little butterflies. On the way back let's stop in that bookstore we passed last night and get a shell book." She stuck a few of the shells into her pocket, pushed sandy toes into her sandals, and the two returned to the brick sidewalk, heading back toward the inn.

A bell jangled when Maureen opened the bookstore's door. "Hello!" she called. "Do you allow dogs inside?"

A feminine voice answered from another part of the shop, "Is it a nice dog?"

"Yes."

The woman's white hair was encased in what appeared to be dozens of small pink plastic rollers. A pair of cat's-eye–shaped purple plastic eyeglasses were perched on a petite nose. She wore a long wooly blue/green tartan plaid bathrobe and unbuckled white ankle boots flapped as she walked toward Maureen. "Yes, he appears to be nice," the woman said. "You do too. I just popped into the kitchen for a nice cup of hot tea. Won't you and your pet join me?"

"Well, thank you. I was looking for a book about—"

"Tea first. Business later. Come along."

Maureen hesitated, but Finn tugged her toward the partly open door. The woman had already placed a second flower-sprigged china cup and saucer onto a small round wooden table. "Sit right down, dear. What's your name? I'm Mrs. Peter Patterson." She gestured toward a black ladder-backed chair as she poured steaming liquid into each cup from a flower-sprigged teapot. "Of course poor Peter is long gone, but I still like to use his name. You can call me Aster. Like the flower. Not Esther, like the Bible. Although Esther was right, you know, about the 'whither thou goest.' Peter wanted to live in Florida, so of course I goest with him. And here I am. What did you say your name is, dear?" She held a sugar cube aloft with silver tongs. "One lump or two, dear?"

"Uh, one please." Maureen sat as directed, Finn close beside her. "My name is Maureen Doherty and his name is Finn."

"Ahh. Irish. If I'd known you were coming I'd have served the Irish Breakfast Tea. Lovely stuff." She plopped one sugar cube into Maureen's cup. "But never mind. Drink up. Now tell me, how did Penelope happen to leave her place to you, dear?"

"You know about that?"

"Oh yes. Small town. Word gets around. Guess you had a bit of excitement over there last night."

Maureen took a sip of tea. "Yes. We did."

"The ghost hunter. Poor soul." Aster leaned forward, pink rollers bobbing. "Who do you think killed him?"

"Killed him?" Maureen put her cup down, spilling a bit of tea into the saucer. "Whatever gave you that idea?"

"Pish-tush, darling child." Aster handed Maureen a paper napkin. "Wipe that up, dear. Why else would a healthy young man like that die in his rocking chair unless somebody killed him?"

Maureen dabbed at the spilled tea. "Died in his rocking chair. You knew that too."

"Of course. Everybody knows that. Would you like a shortbread cookie? I made them myself. They were Peter's favorite. Now, personally, between you and me and the lamppost, I think it was that crazy Sam. He's always threatening to kill somebody or other and he hates the ghost hunters," She waved a teaspoon in the air. "Of course, I hate them too. We all do. Doggoned busybodies, bringing TV cameras and all kinds of riff-raff into Haven. A pox on all of them. Conrad Wilson was a pretty famous one, though. He's on one of those creepy ghost shows on TV all the time and he writes articles every month for *Got Ghosts?* magazine. I would have ordered extra copies if I knew he was going to die. Oh well." She stood, put her cup down, softening her tone "But back to business, Maureen. What kind of book were you and Finn looking for?"

"A book about native shells. I'd like to know what you call these." She stood, grateful for the change of subject, and reached into her pocket. *So Conrad Wilson was a writer for a ghost magazine—apparently one who attracted autograph hunters.* Maureen arranged the butterfly-shaped shells on the tabletop. The Bermuda nickel clinked onto the table too, tails up. She reached for it.

"Coquina," Aster said. "Look like little butterflies, don't they? I like your coin. Pretty angelfish. I have some of them in my aquarium. Didn't you notice it when you came in?"

"I didn't, but I'd like very much to see your fish." Maureen slipped the coin back into her pocket and pulled Finn toward the doorway. *And after that*, she thought, *I'd very much like to get out of here.*

Chapter 9

Maureen left the bookshop twenty minutes later with a yellow bag marked BEACH BOOKSHOP. In it she carried a paperback copy of *Florida's Seashells: A Beachcomber's Guide*, a plastic bag containing three shortbread cookies, and the latest copy of *Got Ghosts?* She'd also acquired a smattering of knowledge about angelfish. She had indeed missed seeing the large freshwater aquarium on first entering the shop, located as it was between two of the book-lined aisles. She'd agreed with Aster Patterson that the graceful fish—she'd learned to identify the Zebra, Silver, and Koi varieties—were beautiful and fascinating to watch. Finn had seemed to enjoy the viewing too. She was most pleased, though, that the conversation about fish had diverted Aster's thoughts away from the death of Conrad Wilson and the recurring question: *Who do you think killed him?*

"I guess rumors do fly around quickly in a small town." Maureen spoke aloud to Finn since no one was within hearing distance on the brick sidewalk and he was taking his time about visiting lampposts. "But I have to wonder who started *that* crazy one." She thought of the people who'd been on the porch last night. "Could be any one of them. Gert or George or Molly or Sam. The autograph-collecting couple were there too, and some people from the neighborhood. Oh, and yes, Elizabeth." She smiled. "I mean *Queen* Elizabeth."

Maureen stopped short on the brick sidewalk. She pulled the Bermuda nickel from her pocket. "Finn! Angelfish in the bookstore and Queen Elizabeth at the inn. Both sides of my coin. Heads and tails. Do you believe in coincidences?"

"Woof," said Finn.

"Neither do I. Usually."

They'd reached the inn. The Haven quartet, as she'd begun to think of them, were at their usual posts.

"Hey, Maureen!" Sam called before she'd even started up the steps. "They've got pancakes with real maple syrup for breakfast. Better hurry before they're all gone. Ted made 'em."

"Sounds good." She stepped around a very large grinning carved pumpkin. "I'll take Finn upstairs and hope there are a couple of pancakes left. Then I've got some unpacking to do." She walked between the rockers. George beckoned for her to come closer. She leaned toward the old man, sensing that he might be deaf. "What is it, George?"

"Who do you think offed the ghost hunter?"

She shook her head, shrugged her shoulders. and lifted her free hand in the air, in a pantomime of, "Beats me," and kept on walking straight through the lobby to the elevator.

Once in the suite, she located Attorney Lawrence Jackson's business card and tapped the number into her phone. She gave her name and the secretary put her through to Attorney Jackson at once.

"Good morning, Ms. Doherty," he said. "I was just about to call you."

"You were? You asked me to call when I got settled in and I guess we are."

"Good. Is the suite satisfactory?"

"It's lovely."

"Well then. I hear you had some excitement over there last night. A death on the front porch?"

"Yes. Unfortunately, that's true," she said, hoping he wasn't going to ask her who'd killed the ghost hunter.

"The poor fellow didn't trip and fall there, did he? Is it possible you might need some legal assistance?"

"That hadn't even occurred to me," she said. "Do you think the inn might be liable somehow?"

"Probably not. I have some paperwork to go over with you anyway. What time would be convenient for me to drop by?"

"Anytime would be okay. I have some unpacking to do. I expect to be here all day."

They agreed on two o'clock in the afternoon and Maureen hurried back to the elevator. She couldn't postpone unpacking indefinitely, but the pancakes sounded good.

Pancakes first, she decided. *Then a couple of suitcases full of clothes and maybe my computer get moved from car to suite.* She headed for the dining room. Breakfast was apparently served buffet-style. A line had formed beside a long table at the front of the room. Bartender Ted, today wearing a white chef's hat and jacket, presided over a large professional grill. He flipped the golden-brown pancakes with every bit as much style as he'd displayed the previous evening mixing cocktails.

Maureen picked up a tray—exactly like the brown plastic ones she remembered from high school—and selected a plate, coffee cup, and utensils. She filled a plastic glass with orange juice from a chilled dispenser and joined the line.

"Good morning, Ms. Doherty. Big stack or little stack?" A smiling Ted poured batter with one hand and turned a round cake with the other.

"Little one I guess, to start with," she said. "Your pancakes come highly recommended by some of your front-porch fans."

"I know just who you mean," he said. "We year-round Haven House residents stick together." He placed a perfect stack of five golden-brown cakes on her plate. "Syrup and butter on the table. Maple, blueberry, and honey. Enjoy!"

"Thank you." She looked around the room. Most of the round tables were empty, while several chairs were occupied at most of the others. She spotted Herbie, moving from table to table with a coffeepot.

I don't want to sit all by myself at one of those big tables, she thought, and approached the closest one.

"Excuse me. Mind if I join you?" She recognized one of the couples she and Finn had met the previous evening. They'd explained that they lived in the neighborhood and came to dinner several times a week.

"Of course. Sit right down," the woman said. "How's Finn today?"

"He's fine," Maureen said. "We took a walk down to the beach this morning and he chased a crab and met a large white bird."

"Gert tells us that you're the new owner of Haven House," the man said. "We're the Flannagans. Dick and Ethel. Live right down the boulevard from here. Heard you come all the way down from Boston."

"How do you do," Maureen said. "Yes. I lived just outside of Boston."

"You found the body, that right?" Ethel asked.

"I did." Maureen began to regret her choice of tablemates. She poured maple syrup on her pancakes and cut into the hot, fragrant circles of goodness.

"Guess maybe you don't want to talk about it while you're eating," Dick said. "Right?"

"Right," Maureen agreed. "I sure don't. These pancakes are wonderful. So light they practically float up off the plate."

"Yep. Everybody shows up when Ted's cookin'," Ethel offered. "He's a good bartender too. Everybody likes Ted."

Maureen had no opinion one way or another about Ted except that he was kind to cats and made delicious pancakes. She chewed quietly, sipped her orange juice, and watched while Herbie filled her coffee cup to exactly the right level, leaving room for cream and artificial sweetener.

Maureen had spent enough years in the retail business to know that a good product, properly promoted, could be extremely profitable. The beach location, the Shabby Chic charm of the place, Ted's pancakes, and Herbie's service were small examples that showed the Haven House Inn—rough edges and all—was a basically good product.

She tasted her coffee. It was excellent. Just one more tiny indication that this hurried trip to Florida might have been more than a move of desperation. It might even be the beginning of something wonderful—dead body on the porch and midnight apparitions in the bedroom aside.

Chapter 10

Breakfast finished, Maureen excused herself from the table, wished the Flannagans a good day, and prepared for some serious moving. The couple-of-suitcases and a knick-knack here and there would take forever. This was a good time to empty her car and complete the move to her new home. She loaded one of the inn's wheeled luggage carriers, took several trips up and down in the elevator, and within the hour she'd managed to transfer several suitcases full of clothes, her makeup kit, computer, printer, and fax machine, a small TV set, two lamps, the box of plaques and photos, the jade plant, a carton of books, and a few assorted tchotchkes onto the floor of the mid-century modern living room. Finn sat joyously wagging his tail in the center of the mess. With a sense of satisfaction, Maureen made a final trip to the Subaru, did a fast cleanup with a hand vacuum, and locked the doors.

It was only when she returned to the suite and surveyed the confused jumble of belongings spread on the soft gray rug that the thought occurred to her. She had no appropriate place for her two o'clock meeting with Lawrence Jackson.

She sat on the couch. Finn, tail still wagging, put his head in her lap. "Wait a minute. Penelope Josephine Gray must have had an office somewhere in the building. After all, she wasn't running this whole operation out of these rooms. All I have to do is find out where it is."

She patted Finn and stood. "I have to go down and talk to Elizabeth. I'll be right back. Be a good boy."

It was close to noon when she approached the dining room once again. Almost lunchtime. Elizabeth would be busy and undoubtedly not happy to be interrupted. Too bad. She pushed the plantation doors open.

"Elizabeth?" she said.

"How can I help you?" The woman's tone was frosty, the words delivered with an exasperated sigh.

"I have a two o'clock appointment with my attorney," Maureen explained. "Is there an office where Ms. Gray conducted business? I'd like to use it."

"Oh, that. Well, I've had to take that office over, since I've been more or less running things around here since Penelope passed. We hired some guys to move her desk and file cabinets and everything into suite twenty-seven and a professional cleaning service made sure everything is spic-and-span. Nobody's used it for years. I'll give you the key." Another long sigh. She pulled a stack of menus from the deep pocket of the red cobbler's apron, placed them on a nearby lectern, and motioned to a young waitress. "Shelly. Take over here. I'll be right back." She pushed the louvred doors open. Maureen followed.

Elizabeth didn't go to the check-in desk. Instead, she opened the door to her office. "Come on. It's in the safe." Maureen followed, watching as Elizabeth moved the painting of the red tree aside, revealing a small safe in the wall. She spun a dial, opened the thing, reached inside, and handed Maureen a key marked 27. It was on a brown plastic fob like the one to her suite. "There you go," Elizabeth said. "It's at the end of the hall on the second floor. There's no number on the door. It's marked 'Staff Only.' Good luck."

"I don't get it," Maureen said, holding the key up, inspecting it. "Why keep it in the safe? Why has the suite been unused for years?"

Elizabeth replaced the painting. "We've been using it for storage, mostly. Anyway, it's supposed to be haunted." She shrugged her shoulders. "Nobody wanted to sleep in there. Closed it back in the seventies Listen. Don't tell anybody about this. The damned ghost hunters will want to get in."

"Haunted?" Maureen lowered the key.

"It's nonsense, of course." Elizabeth smiled. "It's a nice suite. Beautiful desk, chairs, bookcase, everything you'll need. I presume you have your own electronic devices? I've had to keep Penelope's." She held the office door open. "I need to get back to the restaurant. When you get settled in your new office, come down and join us for lunch. Ted made butternut squash soup." Maureen stood in the lobby, the key in her hand, as Elizabeth disappeared into the dining room with a gay little wave.

Shoving the key into her back pocket, she headed for the elevator. So the office was spic-and-span. A nice suite. Everything she'd need.

And quite possibly haunted.

Once on the top floor—the penthouse—she hurried to suite thirty-three. Stepping over the piles of belongings on the floor, Maureen welcomed Finn's happy "woof." "Come on, Finn, let's take a look at our new office." She retrieved his leash from a hook behind the kitchen door and lowered her voice. Skipping the elevator this time, the two walked down the one flight of stairs.

"It should be down at the end of this hall," she told the dog, pulling the key from the pocket of her shorts. Finn trotted ahead of her, looking from side to side as though reading the room numbers. "It'll be on the odd number side," Maureen said. "Here we go. Twenty-three, twenty-five—here it is."

Maureen paused at the entrance. "Okay. Let's do this."

The key turned easily. She took a deep breath and pushed the door open.

It was a corner suite. Sunlight streamed through tall windows in two of the white walls. "It's a nice suite," Elizabeth had said. Beautiful furniture, she'd promised.

Elizabeth had understated on both counts. It was a gorgeous room. The furniture, desk, bookcase, table, and even the file cabinet were crafted of rich, lustrous mahogany. Chairs, upholstered in a striped maroon and gray fabric, faced the desk. A couch in the same fabric and a mahogany coffee table dominated one wall. Two long tables, gleaming from a recent polishing, awaited office machines and the desk had plenty of room for Maureen's desktop computer and two screens. The bookcase displayed a few books about Florida, a handsome wooden carving of a manatee, and several black-and-white photos in gold frames.

"Holy cow, Finn! Look at this place." She crossed the room, admiring the rich tones of a fine Oriental rug There was an attractive powder room behind one door. Another revealed what must have once been a bedroom. It was empty of furnishings, and lightweight beige draperies covered the windows. A good-sized closet stood empty except for a dusty-looking stack of identical black leather-covered volumes on a top shelf. She'd find a way to fill the closet, she had no doubt. "Sure doesn't look like a haunted room, does it?"

"Woof," said Finn, backing away from the closet, pulling Maureen toward the exit.

"Okay. Let's go upstairs and get my office stuff. This is a perfect place for my meeting with that lawyer—haunted or not." Borrowing another wheeled luggage carrier from its spot beside the elevator, she headed back to her suite. The computer, screen, printer, and fax machine, along with a few file folders the lawyer might want to see, fit easily onto the carrier. Removing them from the pile made the remaining items seem less daunting and Maureen made a silent promise to put everything away properly before evening.

She left Finn asleep on the bedroom floor, and by one o'clock the new office was outfitted with office machines, books in the bookcase, jade plant on the coffee table, along with a selection of magazines, fanned out decorator-style, and Maureen's plaques and diploma nicely arranged on one white wall. That left her one hour to walk the dog, take a shower, and get dressed for her meeting.

Dog walk first. She hurried back to her rooms and clipped on his leash. "Come on, Finn. It'll be a fast one." Down the elevator again, through the lobby, past the dining room, and out onto the porch. Maureen avoided looking in the direction of the previous night's painful discovery. There was no way, however, to avoid passing by the four rocking-chair sentinels on either side of the front stairway.

Finn, proving his "too friendly, too easily distracted" designation, stopped to greet each one, who, in turn, felt obliged to pat, scratch, rub, and verbalize their sentiments. Maureen fielded a few questions from the group, without actually answering any of them, then jerked the leash. "Come on, Finn. Gotta go. See you later, folks."

Finn did not want to be hurried, and sulked as they walked along the brick sidewalk. "Be a good boy," she urged. "A nice long walk later, maybe a run on the beach." She held a plastic bag with her free hand. "Just do your business, please, and I'll get back to mine."

Maureen had been glad to see on her previous walks that Haven's city fathers and mothers not only had provided handy stations for doggy waste but also even had curbside water fountains positioned at just the right height for its thirsty four-legged citizens. Finn seemed to take uncommonly long to accomplish what needed to be done, and even attempted to dawdle by stalking one of the tiny lizards native to Florida.

By one-thirty, with Finn taking his afternoon nap, Maureen emptied two of the suitcases onto her bed and decided on "business casual"—white silk blouse, black capris, and black kitten heels. With a promise to herself to get her clothes organized and into the bedroom closet before bedtime, she returned to the lobby intending to meet Attorney Jackson there, rather than try to give directions to her oddly marked office.

Maureen stood when the tall man carrying a leather briefcase entered. He looked like a young Jamie Foxx, only taller. He wore a pale tan Hart Schaffner Marks wool/silk blend suit. (The men's department at Bartlett's of Boston had carried the identical one.) "Mr. Jackson?" she asked, extending her hand.

"Ms. Doherty?" he countered. His grip was firm, his smile orthodontically perfect.

"My office is on the second floor. I'm sure you're familiar with our vintage elevator." He followed, waiting while she pushed the UP button.

"Ms. Gray was quite fond of it," he said. "All the brass and wood and etched glass. I expect the guests like it too."

Maureen nodded. "I expect they do. I've only met one or two guests and a few of the residents so far." The brass accordion door slid open. "Here we are. It's at the end of the hall."

The attorney paused at number twenty-five. "Is your office suite twenty-seven by any chance?"

"Yes," she said, "although Elizabeth tells me that we don't call it that." She put a finger to her lips and whispered, "It's a deep dark secret." They'd reached the door marked STAFF ONLY. She inserted the key and pushed the door open. "It makes quite a handsome office; don't you think so?" She sat in a leather swivel chair behind the desk, and motioned for him to sit in one of the striped chairs.

Lawrence Jackson hesitated just outside the doorway for a long moment, then stepped inside, sat in the chair indicated, and put his briefcase on a table beside him. "Yes indeed. Handsome. Now I expect you'll want to have a look at the most recent profit and loss statements. Please be warned. The place is losing money. Has for years." He placed a sheaf of spreadsheets on Maureen's desk. "You'll note that there's still a significant amount of cash in the operating account. But it won't last forever. Ms. Gray was more sentimental about Haven House than she was practical about it. I also have a few papers for you to sign. Transfer of property, bank accounts, tax schedules, and such." He fanned out several official-looking documents next to the spreadsheets. Each had highlighted areas with little "Sign here" stickers on them. Maureen pushed them to one side, still concentrating on the business statements.

Maureen was good at figures. Her job at Bartlett's had demanded it. She'd always worked a six-month plan. She'd known by Memorial Day exactly what her budget would be for Christmas, and had placed orders, planned advertising lineage, accordingly. She studied the papers silently for several minutes. According to what the lawyer had just presented, there was no budget plan at all for the Haven House Inn. Not even for the following month.

She tapped the top paper. "There are several different room rates here for what appears to be the same type of accommodations. How does it work?"

He sighed. "Ms. Gray was a wealthy but softhearted woman. The four old folks you've undoubtedly met by now—Gert, Sam, Molly, and George—they each pay the same rate year round, in high season or midsummer. They pay one-half of the amount of their monthly Social Security checks—and their meals are included in their rent. Some of the dining room staff along with Elizabeth, the manager, live here. They exchange work for rent. Of course they all draw salaries too. Frankly, it's a mess." He glanced around the room, staring for a moment at the closed bedroom door.

"What about upkeep?" Maureen asked. "Repairs? Do we have a maintenance crew?"

"Not exactly. Ms. Gray hired local help along with Sam and George. Some are more—um——professional than others."

"Housekeeping staff?"

He shrugged. "Not exactly. That's mostly Gert and Molly and some high school girls from the neighborhood."

"Isn't there an advertised rate for new guests?"

"Oh sure. It's very reasonable. There are some return guests every year along with new ones."

"Are the rates changed according to the season? Higher during the winter months?" Maureen scanned the pages. "I don't see it."

"Ms. Gray tried that for a while, but it somehow morphed into the low rate year round." He pulled an advertising brochure from the briefcase. "She hadn't changed the layout or the copy or the room rates on these since the early eighties. I think a lot of people seeing these rates figure the place must be a dump."

Maureen shook her head. "I think you're right. Looks like I have a lot of work to do here."

"You plan to stay then? You mean to operate Haven House?" His face showed real surprise. "I thought you'd want to sell it to the highest bidder. There have already been offers."

"Somebody else wants to run it?"

"Oh no. It would be a teardown. As the real estate folks say, 'the dirt's worth more than the structure.' It would be a good site for condos or even a fast-food place." He reached into the briefcase once again. "Would you like to see the offers Ms. Gray turned down? Against my advice, I might add." He handed Maureen a fat brown envelope. "There are several in here."

She accepted the envelope but didn't open it. "Thanks," she said. "I'll take a look at them later." She picked up the papers with the 'Sign here' stickers. "I'll read these over today. Shall I deliver them to your office? I noticed that you're just down the street from here."

"Yes. We're all readily available to you if you need us. As you know, I handle wills, estate planning, that sort of thing. My partner Nora Nathan handles criminal law and John Peters specializes in family law as well as personal injury cases. I'll leave you John's card just in case there are—um—any ramifications due to the unpleasantness that occurred here last night."

"Thank you." Maureen accepted the card. "I don't anticipate any problem. I believe they're trying to locate the poor man's next of kin."

He stood, took another sideways glance at the closed bedroom door, and picked up the briefcase. "I'll see myself out. Good to meet you."

"Yes. Good to meet you too." Maureen stood, extending her hand, but the lawyer had already opened the door and faced her across the threshold of suite twenty-seven. "I expect we'll be seeing one another from time to time," she said. "I'm sure more questions will come up as I learn to find my way around here."

"Feel free to call on me anytime, Ms. Doherty. Anytime." He hurried away toward the elevator. "You have my number."

Chapter 11

Picking up the brown envelope and the documents the lawyer had left, Maureen started for the door. *I still have a mess to clean up on the floor of my suite*, she remembered. *A pile of clothes on the bed too.* She paused, looking back at the closed room, remembering Jackson's several glances in that direction. Were the glances apprehensive? Curious? What?

She opened the door, approaching the closet. She turned the glass doorknob and looked inside at empty shelves except for the books at the very top. Standing on tiptoe, she pulled down one of the leather-bound volumes. Gold lettering on the cover proclaimed GUEST REGISTER. She turned to the first page, lined, and filled with handwritten names, addresses, and license plate numbers. Nothing unusual there. She made a mental note about using the registers for compiling a possible mailing list for new brochures, placed the book back on the shelf, and closed the door.

Maybe the lawyer, despite his statements to the contrary, believed the rumor about suite twenty-seven being haunted. She smiled, locked the door behind her, and headed up the stairs to her top-floor suite. Lawrence Jackson may have had a bit of that *Christmas Carol* undigested beef too, she decided—the kind that produces imaginary old-time movie starlets in the mind of an overtired, wine-and-key-lime-pie–stuffed ex–ready-to-wear buyer. Thankfully, *that* particular figment had disappeared with the light of day.

She was partway up the staircase when her cell phone vibrated. Caller ID said Frank Hubbard. It took a moment for Maureen to place the name. "Officer Hubbard," she said. "Hello. Can I help you?"

"I'm in the lobby, Ms. Doherty," he said. "Could you come down here please?"

"Of course. I'll be right there." What now? At this rate she'd never get that mess in her rooms straightened out. And what about Finn's promised romp on the beach? The brown envelope and the legal documents still in her hands, she decided that they'd be safer in the living room desk. She hurried the rest of the way up the stairs, surprised to hear the hum of a vacuum cleaner from inside her suite. She unlocked the door.

Gert clicked off the machine and gave a bright-red-lipped smile and opened false-eyelashed eyes wide. "Housekeeping," she said brightly. "I've put away your stuff the best I could. Hope it looks okay."

It looked more than okay. The pair of lamps looked right at home on the tables at each end of the blue couch. A crystal vase an old flame had given Maureen, now centered on the coffee table, held a bouquet of wild flowers, mostly daisies.

"I put the suitcases in the bedroom and hung up the clothes that were on your bed," Gert continued. "Your dog is hiding under the bed, by the way. I think he's afraid of the vacuum cleaner."

"It looks wonderful, Gert." Maureen hurried across the room and deposited the envelope and papers in the top drawer of the desk. She smiled, noticing the desk set. There was a brass plaque with her name on it right next to a mounted pen set and a matching clock, which had once graced her desk at Bartlett's. "There's someone waiting for me downstairs or I'd thank you properly for all this. I'll catch up with you later."

"No problem," Gert insisted. "I love cleaning these rooms. Never know who you're going to meet up here." She gave a broad, heavily mascaraed wink. "If you know what I mean."

Maureen didn't know what she meant but didn't have time to discuss it. "Catch up with you later," she said again, and raced away toward the elevator.

Frank Hubbard stood next to the reception desk facing Elizabeth. They each turned when Maureen approached, neither one smiling.

"What's wrong?" Maureen asked. Obviously, something was. "What's going on, Officer?"

"I need to get back to the kitchen." Elizabeth disappeared into the dining room.

Officer Hubbard moved closer to Maureen, speaking quietly. "We have a problem. The coroner's report is—um—disturbing. Is there somewhere we could talk privately?"

"My office," she said. "It's on the second floor." She led the way to the elevator. Once inside, as the cage made its way between floors, again she asked, "What's going on?"

"It appears," Hubbard said, "that Conrad Wilson died of poisoning. The question now is was it self-inflicted?" He looked around, as though he thought someone might be listening. "Or not?" The two stepped out of the elevator. Hubbard followed Maureen to the suite at the end of the hall. For the third time that day she unlocked the door to suite twenty-seven.

"Come in," she said.

He hesitated at the threshold, reading the STAFF ONLY designation on the door. "Isn't this the—um—isn't this suite twenty-seven?"

"Oh for goodness' sake, yes. It's suite twenty-seven." She couldn't disguise the note of impatience in her voice. "It's also my office. Please come in."

Hubbard nodded, following her direction, and sat in one of the striped chairs. "I'll keep the investigation as unobtrusive as I can," he said. "We'll make every effort to disrupt your business here as little as possible. But we'll be interviewing staff and possibly some guests. We may have to rope off certain areas temporarily, search some parts of the inn."

"Oh dear," Maureen said. "This is not good news." She thought of Larry Jackson's offer of a variety of legal services. What if the inn, already in financial trouble, was somehow responsible for Wilson's death? "It wasn't some sort of food poisoning, was it? I mean, did something he ate or drank here cause his death?"

"It was a large amount of a fairly common heart medication. We're not sure how it was administered. We've talked with Wilson's agent—you knew he did both TV and magazines and was working on a book?"

"I knew he was a magazine writer. I'd heard about the ghost TV shows." Maureen thought of the copy of *Got Ghosts?* she'd bought at the bookstore and hadn't yet read. "Did he have a heart problem?"

"According to the agent, Wilson was in excellent health."

"Then you believe something happened here at the inn that caused his death?"

"According to the coroner, the amount of medication in his system caused his death in a relatively short time."

"He looked fine when everyone saw him in the dining room. It had to be after that," Maureen said.

"How long after you saw him at the bar did you discover the body?" Hubbard leaned forward in the striped chair.

"It couldn't have been much more than an hour."

"What did you do after you found Mr. Wilson? Did you touch the body? Attempt to resuscitate?"

"I touched his wrist. Felt for a pulse. Then I went inside to get help."

"You told Elizabeth what had happened." He leaned back

in the chair, shifted his position, looked toward the closed room, then sat upright again.

"Yes."

"Were you aware that Mr. Wilson, in his line of work, always carried a camera and took many photographs around this property? Your property. Did you have any objection to that?"

"I wasn't aware of it," she said. "Others have told me about it."

"Did you have any objection to it?" he asked again.

Maureen struggled to keep her voice level. "I didn't give it any thought, one way or another."

"When you observed Mr. Wilson at the bar, did he have his camera with him?"

Maureen thought about the moment she'd seen Wilson, with the purple drink. The sparkler and the applause. "I didn't notice," she said. "There was a lot going on."

"Apparently Wilson always had the camera with him," Hubbard said.

"So I've heard."

"When you found the body on the floor, did you see a camera?"

"He wasn't on the floor," Maureen corrected. "He was sitting in the rocking chair. He looked as though he was asleep."

"How did he happen to wind up on the floor?"

"My dog pushed the chair. He—he—slipped out of it." She remembered the man's open eyes.

"Was he holding a camera?" Hubbard asked.

"I don't think so," Maureen said, thinking back. "No, I'm quite sure he wasn't."

"Ms. Doherty." Hubbard leaned forward in the chair again. "Do you feel that publicity—perhaps on a national television show—about ghosts in the Haven House Inn would be detrimental to your business here?"

"I just got here a day ago, Officer Hubbard. I don't know anything about running an inn. I don't know what's good for business or what isn't. But I do know that I don't believe in ghosts."

He turned partway around in the chair, so that he faced the coffee table. He pointed. "But you like to read about them?"

She followed the direction of his finger. The magazines on the table were fanned out so that the titles were visible. Current issues of *Department Store Journal*, *Retail News*, and *Dog World* she'd brought with her from Saugus. *The Carolinas Magazine* she'd picked up at South of the Border. At the bottom of the pile was the still-unread issue of *Got Ghosts?*

"Oh, that. I bought it from Aster at the bookstore. I haven't even opened it." She knew it sounded lame the minute she said it.

"Uh-huh," he said, making the fingers on both hands into a steeple shape and peering at her over the fingertips. "Uh-huh."

"Listen," she said. "I have a lot to do today." She stood. "So, if you don't mind . . ."

"Of course." He stood. "I just wanted you to know that we'd be around the premises for a while, conducting our investigation. We'll try not to upset the operation of your business too much. Thanks for your cooperation, Ms. Doherty. We'll be in touch."

Chapter 12

Maureen closed the door firmly behind the departing policeman, then stood quietly, alone in her handsome new office,
for a long moment. When it seemed as though enough time
had passed for Hubbard to have reached the elevator, she
opened the door a crack and peeked out. The corridor was
clear.

A torrent of thoughts bombarded her senses. The inter-
view—if that's what it was—had been more than unsettling.
The apparent fact that the man had been poisoned was
shocking enough. The realization that an actual police investigation was underway in the inn—*her* inn—was somehow
terrifying. Worst of all, except for Finn, she had no support
system in place here. No parents, no helpful co-workers, not
even a friendly landlady. She was alone.

Her mother's often-repeated words came to her: *Maybe
you'll meet someone—a nice man.* She almost laughed aloud
at that. So far—other than Sam and George—she'd met a
lawyer who wanted her to sell the place and thought she
might need a personal injury attorney, a cop with a thing
about ghosts, and a good-looking bartender who liked cats.
She had, of course, during her almost-thirty-six years, met a
number of "nice men"—but never the right one.

She ventured into the corridor and took the stairs down to the dining room, hoping that there was still some of that butternut squash soup left. Maybe some food would help to calm her nerves, to get her thoughts organized.

It was well past noon when Maureen sat at one of the round tables. The lunchtime crowd—if in fact there had been a crowd—was gone and only a few of the other tables were occupied. She recognized the couple Elizabeth had dubbed "the autograph hunters" at one of them and the Flannagans at another but didn't feel one bit like socializing. She looked around the big, almost-empty room, searching for the ubiquitous Herbie. Instead, she caught the eye of a young waitress whose name tag identified her as Shelly.

"Good afternoon, Ms. Doherty." The girl handed her a menu. "Our lunch special today is homemade butternut squash soup and a grilled cheese sandwich."

Comfort food, Maureen thought. *Perfect.* Ordering the special and a glass of raspberry iced tea, she began to relax, to organize scattered thoughts. *First things first*, she told herself. *I need to take a good long look at the figures Jackson gave me. If I'm going to make a go of this place, poisoned ghost hunter or not, I'll need a plan. Planning is something I know how to do. The Haven House Inn has potential. I'm sure of it.* She glanced around the room again, noting the many empty tables. *But just in case, I'll take a peek inside that brown envelope full of offers too.*

By the time she'd eaten half of the absolutely amazing soup and a quarter of the perfectly browned and richly cheesy sandwich, she'd visualized a new brochure, mentally painted all of the porch rocking chairs in vivid primary colors, swapped off about half of the wicker furniture for some repro Danish modern, ordered some light-colored draperies to replace the dark fern-patterned ones in the dining room, and doodled a design on the back of a paper napkin for new uniforms for the waitstaff.

After she'd finished her lunch, Maureen decided that alone wasn't such a bad place to be after all. She felt competent. Even happy. She looked toward the bar, thinking she'd stop by to compliment Ted on the soup and to inquire once more about Bogie and Bacall.

There were no customers seated on the barstools and the red-vested man behind the counter had his back to the room. She glanced down at her rough sketch on the napkin. The vests would have to go. Maybe Ted would have some suggestions about new uniforms. She tucked the napkin into her purse and leaving a nice tip for Shelly she started across the room. The bartender turned as she approached.

It wasn't Ted.

Maureen stopped, flustered. "Excuse me," she said. "Hello there. I'm Maureen Doherty, the new owner of the inn. I thought you were Ted."

"I wish," he said with a bright smile. "Ted's the main man around here. I'm Leo. Sometimes if things get busy, I'm Ted's barback Course, things don't get busy that much here anymore. Elizabeth called me in at the last minute. Ted got called away for something. Can I get you a drink, Ms. Doherty?"

"Just a Diet Coke," she said. "Is Ted okay? I wanted to compliment him on the soup."

"Yeah. Everybody said it was great. Haven't tasted it myself." He dropped his voice. "Actually, Ted's out in the kitchen. Some cops are back there going over the bar inventory and he's the expert on that stuff. Something to do with the dead guy, I suppose. But I guess you know all about that."

"You probably know as much about it as I do," she said. "I guess the police have to do their work. I hope things will be back to normal around here soon." She sipped her drink, wondering what "normal" might actually be like at the Haven House Inn. She turned partway around on the barstool. The Flannagans had left, but the autograph hunters were still there. They'd caught on to the casual dress code—he in jeans and Hawaiian print, she in shorts and a Guy Harvey T-shirt The gold bag had been replaced with an equally large, but less flamboyant, sailcloth one

They're paying guests, Maureen thought. *It's about time I introduced myself and welcomed them.* She left a few bills on the bar, wished Leo a good day, and approached the table where the two appeared to be in conversation.

"Excuse me," she said. "I'm Maureen Doherty, the new owner of Haven House. I wanted to welcome you. I hope you're enjoying your stay with us."

The man stood, extending his hand. "Won't you join us, Ms. Doherty? I'm Alex Morgan. This is my wife, Clarissa."

"Thank you." Maureen shook his hand, nodded to the woman, and sat in a straight-backed varnished oak chair. "I'm so happy to meet you both. Are you enjoying your vacation?"

"We're on what you might call a 'working vacation,' " Alex Morgan said. "We're here on assignment."

"All the way from New York," Clarissa said. She didn't look happy.

"I hope you're enjoying our lovely beach," Maureen said. "My dog and I took a nice walk down by the water this morning and picked up some interesting seashells."

"We've been meaning to do that. Just haven't got around to it yet," the man said.

"We've been busy taking pictures—making notes." The woman frowned. "We're writers."

Maureen breathed a silent prayer that they weren't travel writers, sure that the Haven House Inn, at that moment, would barely rate even one star. "Oh?" she said. "Writers?"

"That's right." The man reached into his shirt pocket and produced a business card. He handed it to Maureen. CLARISSA AND ALEX MORGAN, it read. GHOST INVESTIGATIONS, INC. There was a New York City address and telephone number.

"You're ghost hunters?" The question had slipped out. She quickly rephrased, "I mean, you're here to see if the rumors about the inn being haunted have any foundation in fact?"

"Exactly," he said. "We've tried not to be obtrusive about it. We're not like that phony showboat Conrad Wilson."

The woman reached over and patted his hand. "Now darling, let's not speak ill of the dead—even if he was a no-talent hack."

Maureen searched for words. "I'm sorry. I thought you were fans. Elizabeth said you wanted his autograph."

Clarissa laughed. "Elizabeth? Is that her name? She tried to stop us, but we were too fast for her. We sent him a drink, walked right up to the bar, handed him the magazine and a pen, and he signed it, no problem. Want to see it?" She reached into the commodious bag and produced a copy of *Got Ghosts?*—the same issue Maureen had bought at the bookstore.

"Yes, well, I—um . . ." Maureen stood, searching for words. "I need to get back to work. I hope you'll enjoy the rest of your stay with us. If there's anything I can do, let me know."

"So, is it?" Clarissa asked, her expression brightening.

"Is it what?" Maureen tucked the business card into her purse.

"Haunted," Alex said. "And we all know the answer to that one, don't we?" He laughed a short little laugh. "Oh boy, is it ever! Right, Ms. Doherty?"

Clarissa giggled. "Don't worry, honey, when our book

comes out every ghost junkie in the world will want to stay here."

Maureen was tempted to repeat the words she'd spoken so many times recently. But she didn't say, "I don't believe in ghosts." She stood, fake-smiled, said, "Nice to meet you," and fast-walked toward the exit.

> *Another message from a stranger*
> *Holds an answer, comes with danger.*

Chapter 13

Maureen skipped the stairway in favor of the elevator and rode all the way up to her "penthouse," as she was beginning to think of the suite. The privacy involved in being the only person on the third floor was attractive. She heard Finn's welcoming "woof" as soon as she left the elevator and hurried down the corridor to unlock the door. Finn did his usual tail-wagging happy excitement performance.

The sound of a woman singing issued from the bedroom. Had she left a radio or the television on? Was Gert still there?

"Hello, Gert? Is that you?"

"Oh, hi, Maureen," came the answering voice.

Definitely not Gert. But Maureen recognized the voice. "Lorna Dubois," she said. It was a statement, not a question.

The woman stood in front of the full-length mirror on the closet door, turning from side to side. "This is more like it," she said

The apparition—or whatever it was—wore a silk print shirtdress. Maureen's silk print shirtdress. "That's my dress."

"Of course it is," the image agreed. "You do have pretty good taste after all."

"It's a Tory Burch," Maureen said, "and I've never even worn it yet myself."

"Tory Burch, huh?" Lorna Dubois did one more twirl before the mirror. "Well, it's no Edith Head, but it's quite nice. Now, what's in the other suitcases? I've already tried on everything I liked in the closet."

I'm not drunk, Maureen thought. *And I'm not hallucinating. I'm actually seeing what I think I'm seeing.*

"You're really here." She spoke to the image wearing her dress—which was now black and white instead of navy and white.

"Yes. Of course I'm here."

"I mean—you're real."

"Not exactly." Lorna hesitated. "I mean, technically I'm still dead."

"But what I mean is—you're actually a ghost and I'm actually seeing you."

"That shows a remarkable grasp of the obvious, Maureen. You act as though this is your first time. I believe we met last night?"

"I know, but I didn't believe in ghosts then." Maureen sat on the edge of the bed. "I guess now I have to rethink that."

"So, you're not mad about me trying on your clothes?"

"No. I'm not, but you're taller than I am, and you have more boob. So how come the dress fits you and me both?"

"Oh, the dress is still in your closet. I'm wearing the *essence* of the dress." The woman sat on the bed beside Maureen. "I just have to *see* this dress, or your bathing suit, or your underwear and *poof!* I'm wearing it. Understand?"

"My underwear?"

"The *essence* of your underwear." Lorna Dubois moved the neckline of the dress to one side, exposing a narrow strap of a Lily of France push-up bra. "See?"

Maureen hesitated, then reached a tentative finger toward the white strap. "It's really pink," she said, "not white." Her finger went right through the image. "Oh my God. Did I hurt you?" She pulled away, sat upright. Finn whined.

"No. Didn't even feel it." Lorna shrugged. "I've hardly ever mastered the 'full materialization' thing. That's when we look solid, not kind of transparent—like me."

"So," Maureen said, looking closely at the black-and-white, kind of transparent-looking woman beside her on the bed, "maybe you're the essence of Lorna Dubois? By the way, is that your real name?"

"I think it's something like that, about the essence," the ghost agreed, "and no. The studio gave me that name, but they let me keep my initials. I used to be Lena Dombrowski. Now, do you mind if I wear the dress tonight? The Babe's going to be down at the L&M Bar—after closing, naturally. I'd like for him to see me in this."

"The Babe?"

"Babe Ruth. The Yankees and the Rays play tonight. When he's in town Babe likes to drop by Haven after the game."

"Babe Ruth likes to—um—visit Haven?"

"Sure. He used to stay right here in Haven House sometimes, back when the Yankees had spring training in St. Petersburg." Lorna reached down and scratched behind Finn's ears. He leaned into her hand and knew he was being scratched in his favorite place—even if she was just an essence. "Yep. The Babe was down here when he hit that famous home run—six hundred and twenty-four feet."

"I did not know that," Maureen admitted. "I'll look it up. I'll bet our guests would like to know about Babe sleeping here. Does he—um—by any chance haunt the inn too?"

"No. At least, I've never run into him around here. Of course I stay mostly right here in the penthouse. Nice and private." She wrinkled her nose. "Less chance of one of those ghost hunters getting a picture of me."

"Like Mr. Wilson?"

"Yes. He was one of the worst. He had a special camera.

I've heard that he actually got a picture of Billy Bedoggoned Bailey playing the piano." Her voice dropped to a whisper. "A full manifestation, I heard."

"Billy Bedoggoned Bailey? Was he a famous piano player?"

"No. Not really famous. He played with some famous bands back in the forties—Harry James, Duke Ellington— but no." She smiled a sad little smile. "Kind of like me. Never famous, but always working." She stood and posed in front of the mirror again. "You've probably heard him. He plays the piano in the dining room."

"The *player* piano?" Maureen squeaked. "He plays that piano?"

"Yep. That's the one. See, they've got it wired up so it plays a loop of songs they recorded from the old piano rolls." She grinned. "When I was a kid we had one. You put the roll in and pedaled with your feet to make it play fast or slow. Billy figured out how to unplug the thing and when he feels like it he just sits down and plays it. The keys go up and down just like they should, but it's him playing. He's been dead a long time, but he still keeps up with the music. Sometimes he throws in an Elvis song or a Broadway show tune just for the hell of it."

Maureen interrupted, "You said that Conrad Wilson somehow got a picture of Billy playing the piano? A full manifestation? I guess that means he saw the piano player just as plain as I'm seeing you?"

"Nope. He didn't actually *see* Billy. That damned camera did. Gert told me that the man went around taking pictures everywhere. Day and night. See, he couldn't tell if he had anything until he put the memory card in his computer. Oh yeah. Pictures of everything—just trying to catch one of us."

"Gert told you? She talks to you? "

"Sure. I love Gert. She's an old-time Vegas showgirl, you know. My kind of people. She's my connection to what's going on downstairs. Penelope used to talk to Gert too."

"How did she know about the camera? Surely he didn't tell her."

"You'd be surprised how much a housekeeper overhears. It's like they're invisible." Lorna looked down at Maureen's feet. "Cute shoes. Anyway, Gert heard him talking on the phone to someone about it. He told them about the camera and said he had absolute proof that Haven had plenty of ghosts—and that he'd send them one sample picture to prove it. Then they could talk about money."

"You think he sent somebody the picture of Billy playing the piano?"

She nodded. "I think so. And if he took a bunch of pictures around Haven, he might have had enough pictures of all of us to ruin Haven forever!"

"Pictures of *all* of you?'

"Yeah. Billy and me and Vice President Charlie Curtis and a few others stay here sometimes. Plenty more of us around town too."

"A vice president?"

"Sure. Nice guy." She laughed. "Even if Wilson got a good shot of him, nobody would know who he was. Shoot. Billy and I were more famous than Charlie. He was veep to Herbert Hoover. He just likes it here. Mostly seasonal. He does Washington, DC, in the summer."

"I see," Maureen lied, because she didn't see at all. "And there are other buildings in Haven that are—um—haunted?"

"Sure. A lot of 'em on the boulevard and quite of few of the regular houses."

"Like, for instance, the bookstore?" Maureen asked. "And the bar?"

"Probably."

"The theater?"

"For sure. I ran into John Carradine there myself once."

"Aster at the bookstore told me that everyone in town hates the ghost hunters," Maureen said. "True?"

"Sure. We do our best to stay out of their way." She shook her head. "But it's a small town and there've been rumors for years that there are ghosts here. It started with the guy in suite twenty-seven. So every once in a while there'll be a flurry of the pests show up. Like Wilson."

Maureen thought about her pleasant new office space, then pulled the business card from her purse. "Ever heard of these two?"

Lorna held out her hand, but Maureen, remembering that the woman wasn't quite solid, laid the card on the bed. The ghost picked it up. " 'Clarissa and Alex Morgan,' " she murmured. "Ghost investigators? No. Gert hasn't said anything about them. Did they just arrive?"

"I think they came the same day I did," Maureen said. "They're writing a book and I'm afraid we're in it."

Chapter 14

After Lorna Dubois disappeared, wearing Maureen's Tory Burch dress, Maureen and Finn began the long-postponed romp on the beach. Maureen took off her shoes and walked along at the edge of the white rippled sand visible beneath clear water. She unhooked Finn's leash, looked up and down the beach, and seeing no other dogs, she began a game of fetch-the-stick.

An almost-deserted beach is a good place to get in touch with your thoughts, Maureen told herself. *Even if your thoughts are some of the weirdest ones you've ever had.* She deliberately forced herself to remember the black-and-white image of Lorna Dubois. It had been comforting to think of her as a hologram, a hallucination, a blot of mustard—but no. Lorna Dubois was real—or as real as a spirit, a wraith, a *ghost*, can be. Maureen was convinced of that. She even believed in Billy Bedoggoned Bailey, even though she hadn't seen him. Maybe the thing in suite twenty-seven was real—or had been real—too, but at least so far there'd been no hint of haunting in her new office. The sound of a distant bell from a sea buoy interrupted her contemplations. She wasn't sorry.

"Whoa. Wait up a minute Finn!" Maureen called. Finn obediently returned and dropped the now-soggy stick at her feet. "We've wandered pretty far from where we started.

We'd better head back." They'd arrived at a long pier. A tall and somewhat weather-beaten sign proclaimed: LONG PIER FISHING CHARTERS.

"I know this place, Finn," she said. "I've been here before. See that sign? I had my picture taken in front of it. I remember. I had a fishing pole in one hand and my fish in the other."

"Woof?"

"We went to a restaurant and they cooked that fish for us. Maybe we'll charter one of these boats someday and I'll catch another fish. Would you like that? We can ask Ted to cook it for us." She turned and tossed the stick in the direction of home.

As Maureen walked the beach, tossing Finn's stick, she thought about the searching questions Officer Hubbard had asked her. *I suppose he'll be grilling Ted the same way. The poor guy won't know any more about it than I do,* she thought. *But I guess the police have to question everybody that way. I hope he's not going to bother the guests.*

It was a disturbing thought. Paying guests were scarce enough, and even without a careful study of the figures Larry Jackson had given her, she knew that the inn was, in its present state, a losing proposition. Being questioned by the intense and downright intimidating Hubbard might very well cause a waiting line at the checkout counter.

But what could she do about it?

She put the stick into a nearby waste barrel and began to jog. "Come on, Finn," she ordered. "We need to get back to business." The golden stalled for a moment, regretting the loss of his stick, then obediently trotted along beside her.

Maureen knew how to promote a slow-selling sportswear item. *If it's a real dog you just mark it down to cost and get rid of it.* "But the Haven House Inn is *not* a dog," she said aloud. At Finn's questioning look she added, "Not that kind of dog." First, she thought about location. "Location, location, location," she said. "That's what the real estate people always say—and we've got that for sure. We're accessible, but far enough off the beaten track to be interesting—and we've got history. Hey, Finn, did you know Babe Ruth slept in our inn?"

"Woof woof," Finn said.

The new brochure was already taking shape in her head. She'd need new pictures. Have to hire a good photographer. "Not a creepy ghost hunter photographer," she promised herself, "but one who does the fancy real estate layouts." But, she realized, there were parts of the aged building that not even a top-notch photographer could make look appealing.

"This will take some money, Finn," she said. "We have five thousand dollars and we may as well invest it in our new home. Okay? We'll still have our unemployment check and we don't have to pay for rent or for my food for a while."

"Woof."

"Good. I knew you'd agree. Look, we're almost home. I'll race you to the Haven Casino Ballroom!" Finn reached the historic waterside building first and waited patiently for Maureen to catch up and to attach leash to collar. The two proceeded onto the boulevard, passing by the L&M Bar with a new respect since learning that a baseball great still visited there. They hurried past the bookshop. There wasn't time for a cup of tea, Irish or not.

She spotted the yellow tape at the far end of the porch well before they'd reached the inn. She hoped it didn't have "Crime Scene" printed on it. *Kiss of death to business*, she told herself, laughed at the unintentional joke she'd made, and wondered how much more of the stuff Hubbard had festooned around the place. *Her* place.

When she and Finn reached the front steps, she noticed that another carved pumpkin had been added, relieved that the lettering on the tape simply spelled out DO NOT CROSS.

Not really exactly welcoming, but a whole lot better than CRIME SCENE. Next, she'd need to check the dining room.

"I'll take you upstairs first, Finn," she said. "Queen Elizabeth doesn't like pets in there."

Molly and Gert were in their usual places, but the men were missing. Some maintenance duties to attend to, Maureen supposed. She stopped to greet the women, thanking Gert for doing such a fine job of putting her clothes away, and slipping a generous tip into her hand. "Thanks, Ms. Doherty." Gert winked at her companion. "I'm buyin' the wine tonight, Mol," she said, "that is, if the bossy cop is through messing around with the bar."

"I'm just about to go in and see what's going on in the dining room," Maureen said. "You two seem to keep an eye on what's happening around here. Do you think the police activity has the guests upset?"

"A few have checked out already, Ms. Doherty," Molly offered. "But maybe they were going to leave today anyway. Don't you worry. This time of year, folks from up north will be lining up to stay here. This is a good place. You'll be glad Ms. Gray gave it to you."

"You sure will," Gert agreed with her friend. "Why was it she left it to you? I forget."

"I don't know. I'm trying to figure that out." She wondered if the Morgans were among the guests who'd checked out. She halfway hoped they had.

Molly spoke in a stage whisper. "You can bet Queen Elizabeth was pissed when she found out the old woman wasn't leaving it to her. Wasn't she, Gert?" She slapped her knee and set the rocking chair into motion. "Stomping around here, swearing a blue streak. It was a riot!"

Maureen was surprised. "Elizabeth expected to inherit the inn? I didn't know that."

Both rocking chairs creaked in unison. "Don't know why. She was an employee, just like us. She got her apartment for free and got good pay too—for running the restaurant and all. You going to keep her on—and us too, like it's always been?"

She hadn't expected the question. "Well, I—um—I don't have any immediate plans to change anything," she stammered.

"That's good. We all sure do like living here," Molly said. "And you seem easy to get along with."

"True enough." Gert gave a broad wink. "Seems like you get along with all sorts—if you get my drift."

Maureen recognized the veiled reference to the semi-transparent third-floor guest but chose not to acknowledge it. "Well, Finn and I have to go. See you both later."

She and Finn passed the dining room, listened at the door for a moment for sounds of activity. The piano played "Sentimental Journey.". Was it a recording or was Billy Bedoggoned Bailey at the keyboard? There was no one at the registration desk. Presumably, anyone who wanted service would ring the bell. Did Elizabeth spend her day listening for the bell and running back and forth between the dining room, the lobby, and her office?

"We're going to have to hire some more help, Finn," Maureen muttered. "This is highly inefficient." They rode the elevator up to the penthouse. She filled Finn's water bowl, turned on the bedroom television to keep him company, and looked around the rooms for any signs of ghostly activity. She opened the desk drawer in the living room. The papers and the brown envelope were just as she'd left them. She'd go over them soon for sure. Meanwhile, nothing appeared to be out of order. But why should it? If Lorna Dubois saw anything she coveted, she'd just grab the essence of it and make it her own.

Maureen locked her door and started down the stairs. It wasn't yet time for dinner, but there were early-bird prices on the menu she'd seen at lunch. Maybe she could get an idea of what the impact of the death had been on the restaurant. She'd ask Elizabeth about the checkouts—and, she hoped, the check-ins.

The piano was still playing when she pushed the louvred doors apart. "The White Cliffs of Dover." *That's a real oldie*, she thought, wondering whether Billy was amusing himself by improvising on the standard loop. Elizabeth was in her spot behind the lectern, red apron pocket full of menus. "Good evening," she began, handing Maureen a menu. She looked up. "Oh, it's you, Ms. Doherty. Sit anywhere you like. Quite a few for early-bird this evening."

She was right. More than half of the tables were occupied, some by more than one couple. "What's going on?" Maureen asked. "Or does this happen every week?"

"I wish," Elizabeth said. "No. They're just curious about the murder—especially because it was a ghost hunter. It was in the afternoon paper, so some folks from St. Pete and Tampa had to come out and see what they can see. There's even a reporter from the Tampa paper over there." She gestured with the menu to a man seated at the bar. "The Channel Nine news crew is outside. I'm just hoping we don't run out of anything. I sent George over to Publix for more salad materials and chicken breasts and a bottle of one-fifty-one rum. The cop took ours."

"Chicken breasts?" Maureen asked.

"No. He took the grenadine, the fruit juice, and the curaçao too, but we had backups for those."

"I hope the police will return the liquor." Maureen thought about the replacement costs.

"I don't think we could use it even if they do," Elizabeth said. "I mean, I'd be afraid to serve it. We don't know what they do to it down at the police station." She lifted her shoulders and smiled. "We'll just pour it down the drain and chalk it up to experience, I guess."

Easy for her to say, Maureen thought. Her five thousand

dollars wouldn't go far with the "pour it down the drain" attitude on display in the inn's dining room. "Elizabeth," Maureen said, in as gentle a tone as she could manage, "maybe the next time the officer needs to examine our inventory he could do it here."

"Hey, Maureen!" a familiar voice called from the bar. "Come over and join us. Gert's buyin'!" Molly swung her barstool around and waved. "Come meet our new friend." Molly and Gwen were seated on either side of the man Elizabeth had identified as a reporter from Tampa.

"Guess I'd better see what they're up to," Maureen excused herself, and started across the room. *If the reporter is looking for information about this place he sure has picked the right drinking buddies*, she thought. The player piano started up just as she reached it. She recognized the Jim Reeves song immediately. It was "Maureen," and she knew it had been written long after the advent of the player piano. "Thanks, Billy," she whispered as she passed, just in case the song selection was something other than coincidence. She was more than a little amazed by her own acceptance of what a day ago she would have ridiculed as superstitious nonsense.

"Here she is," Molly said. "She's the boss here now. I told you she was pretty. Maureen. This is our new friend Jake. He works for a newspaper."

Maureen felt her cheeks coloring. "How do you do, Jake," she said. "I'm Maureen Doherty. Welcome to Haven House Inn." They shook hands. He was definitely good-looking. "Hi, Gert. Hi, Molly. What's going on?"

"Gert's spending her tip money," Molly said. "Right, Gert?"

"Right," Gert said. "We're just sitting here, talking about the ghost hunter getting himself killed. Join us. Name your poison, Maureen."

If anyone beside Maureen noticed the inappropriate choice

of words, considering the current situation, no one said so. Ted was back at work as bartender. She sat facing him, asked for a glass of the house rosé. "Glad to see you, Ted," she said. "I stopped by earlier to tell you how much I enjoyed your soup today. Leo said you were busy."

"Thanks, Ms. Doherty. Busy is right. Cops asked me questions for an hour or more."

Maureen offered a sympathetic nod. "I hear you. Me too."

Maureen was more listener than participant in the conversation at the bar. She'd been at the inn such a short time she had little to contribute, and other than a polite inquiry as to her health, the newspaperman directed all of his questions to Molly and Gert. Officer Hubbard could have taken lessons on interrogation technique from Jake. He placed his phone on the bar, set to record. His questions were focused, but not intimidating, delivered in a conversational, nonconfrontational tone.

"So, Gert," he said. "I can tell you make friends easily. You must have gotten to know Mr. Wilson pretty well during the weeks he was here."

"Not so well, really," she said. "He was a bit standoffish, if you know what I mean. But we had the occasional chat, him and me, when nobody else was around."

That was a surprise to Maureen. It was apparently a surprise to Molly too.

"You never told me that, Gert," Molly said. "What did you talk about?"

"Vegas," she said. "We were both from Vegas. I mean, neither one of us was born there, but we both worked there. Different time of course. He was a little younger than me."

"A little!" Molly snickered. "Like about forty years younger than you!"

Gert raised a penciled brow. "Shut up, Mol. Anyway, I worked onstage, you know." She favored Jake with a flutter of heavily mascaraed eyelashes. "Lots of feathers and not much clothes. But Conrad, he worked on the machines—the slots, you know It takes some skill to keep them operating just right—so they pay off just enough to keep the customers coming back, but still favor the house. A genius with machines, that boy."

"That's interesting, Gert." Jake gave her a big smile. "I'd heard that Mr. Wilson was a writer. Did he talk about what he was working on here?"

"Not with me, he didn't," she said. "I was more interested in talking about Vegas. Gambling odds, that stuff."

"He wrote about ghosts," Jake said. "Did he talk to you about the ghosts that are supposed to haunt this hotel?"

"Listen, honey." Gert tapped her wineglass on the bar for emphasis. "He talked to everybody about that. But like I told him, there's no ghosts in this place. I ought to know. Me and Sam have been here longer than anybody. Never seen one."

Maureen almost gasped out loud. That was a flat-out lie. Gert not only saw ghosts; she had regular conversations with at least one. Maureen looked past Jake at Molly, who, with an absolutely straight face, nodded agreement with Gert's statement.

"That's right," Molly said. "No ghosts here. Nope."

Jake didn't look happy with those answers. He tried another tack. "He was quite a photographer, I understand. Did he ever take your picture?"

"He sure did." Gert patted thinning but still-jet-black hair. "Couple of times. He showed 'em to me too, on his cute little TV."

Jake nodded. "A portable TV. I had one when I was a kid. Used to take it on camping trips."

"Sometimes at night Mr. Wilson used to sit way over in his corner of the porch and watch that TV," Molly said. "He was real considerate, though. Kept the sound turned off so he wouldn't be bothering anybody."

"I understand he always carried a camera. Took lots of

pictures everywhere in the building," Jake said. "Did he show you any of those pictures?"

"No. I'm not interested in that stuff at all. It's just an old building. Nothing special about it that I can see. You, Molly?"

"Just a raggedy old building," Molly agreed. "But it's home." She looked at Maureen. "No offense intended."

"None taken, Molly." Maureen watched the reporter's face in the mirror behind the bar. The ready smile was gone. He clearly wasn't getting the answers he wanted. She was pretty sure if he asked Sam and George about ghosts he'd get the same kind of denial. Those four weren't the easy marks you might assume.

Jake made a sudden spin on his stool and faced her. "Tell me, Ms. Doherty, you've heard the tales about the infamous suite twenty-seven, I suppose?"

"I've heard that they closed it back in the seventies." she replied. "Guests apparently found something—um—disturbing about it."

"I know about that," Molly interrupted. "It was a stupid, made-up story. They said there was a really creepy ghost in there. Used to sit on the bed and watch people. Nobody would rent the suite after a while, so they just used it for storage. Put the things people left behind in there. Ms. Gray—she didn't want to get rid of anybody's belongings. She always thought they might come back for them—even stuff from the forties! Gert was in there once. Tell them, Gert."

"There were old trunks and suitcases and boxes of stuff. Lots of water toys. People buy them while they're here and then leave them. But the old woman, she wouldn't part with any of it. Said it didn't belong to her."

Jake looked happy again. "Did you ever see the ghost when you were in there, Gert?"

"Of course not. I told you. There's no ghosts here."

"Can I go in there, Ms. Doherty?" He faced Maureen again. "Would you let me take a look at suite twenty-seven?"

"It's not a guest suite anymore," she said. "It's my office now."

"It is? Your office? Have *you* noticed anything strange? A drop in temperature? Unexpected noises? Anything unusual? Frightening?"

"Sorry, but no," Maureen answered truthfully.

"Did Mr. Wilson ever go into suite twenty-seven?"

"I doubt it," Maureen said.

"He did." Gert spoke softly. "He did go in there. With his camera. Took a lot of pictures, I heard."

"Who let him in?" Molly asked. Maureen wanted to know the answer too.

"I'm not at liberty to say." Gert tipped her head back, nose in the air.

" 'Not at liberty to say,' " Molly mimicked. "Well, la-de-da. How come you never told me about that?"

"I don't blab everything I know," Gert said.

"Since when?" Molly countered.

"Promised not to tell. Pinky swore." Gert held up one multiringed hand with pinky extended.

Jake nodded understanding. "I'm assuming money changed hands."

"I guess," Gert said, "though I sure didn't get any of it."

"Perhaps if some more money was offered . . . ?" Jake left the thought unfinished.

Maureen held up both hands. "Wait a minute. It's *my* office we're discussing. In *my* inn. In *my* personal space. Nobody gains admission to suite twenty-seven unless I say so. Thanks for the wine, Gert. Nice to meet you, Jake." She stood. "Excuse me. I have to walk my dog."

Chapter 15

Maureen knew that Finn was happy napping, and might not have wanted to go for another walk, but she was in the mood for a nice head-clearing stroll on the boulevard, so she clipped on his leash, hand-fed him a couple of his very favorite treats, and took the stairs down to the first floor. She resisted the temptation to peek into the dining room—to see if the three were still at the bar. There were several guests in the wicker chairs and Elizabeth was busy at the registration desk. The flurry of business was encouraging even though it was probably the result of the recent death and "ghost exploitation," a topic Maureen knew was unpopular with most Haven House residents—both human and otherwise.

The four top-of-the-stairs rockers, two on each side of the broad staircase, were unoccupied. There were guests here and there rocking, but it almost seemed that there were invisible RESERVED signs posted on the four.

Gert's tip had been a generous one, so Maureen thought it likely that the women would remain at the bar for some time. George had been sent to forage for food and liquor. Maybe Sam was busy on a repair or upkeep project. A glance at peeling green paint gave evidence that much of the Haven House Inn was beyond Shabby Chic.

Maureen said a pleasant "Hello," or "Hope you're enjoying your stay with us," to the guests as she passed. Finn, as usual, made friends quickly.

"Going to be a pretty sunset, Ms. Doherty," one of them said. "You and Finn going down to the beach to catch it?"

"That's where we're headed," she said.

The streaks in the western sky already promised a colorful show by the time they'd reached the bookshop. "Uh-oh. There's Aster—all set up in her front yard with table and chairs and a frosty pitcher of something and a plate of cookies. Peter's favorite shortbread, I'll bet."

"Yoo-hoo. Ms. Doherty!" Aster called. "Come watch the sunset with Erle Stanley Gardner and me." She pointed to a large black cat sitting on the wide windowsill in front of the shop's display window. Maureen hesitated. "Don't worry about Finn," Aster insisted. "Erle Stanley likes dogs. Always has."

"I'm not sure," Maureen said. "He hasn't met any cats yet." Finn took a hesitant couple of steps back and sat. Firmly.

"Really? I figured he'd be all palsy-walsy with Bogey and Bacall by now."

"We haven't had the pleasure yet." Maureen moved toward the table. "Ted, the bartender, says they are both fine. He feeds them. But they haven't come inside since Ms. Gray died. I don't even know what they look like."

Aster no longer sported pink rollers and the gray hair lay in uneven waves. The bathrobe had been replaced by flannel pajama pants with pictures of Mickey Mouse on them, topped with a khaki shirt with sergeant's stripes on the sleeve. The rain boots were still unsecured. "Well, I can help you out there. I'll tell you all about those two rascals. Look. If Finn and Erle Stanley don't get along, I'll just put him inside. He's a bookstore cat, you know. Used to being indoors."

The golden and the black cat solved the problem on their own, opting for some extra social distancing—Finn a leash length away from the table and Erle Stanley at the far edge of the windowsill. Maureen accepted the offered chair, lemonade, and cookie.

"Well then," Aster began, "first of all, they're both rescue cats. Bogie is a big boy. Even bigger than Erle Stanley. He's a striped tiger cat. Got one ear looks like it was bitten half off. Oh, he's had a tough life, that one. Bacall now, she's a big cat too, but she's a princess. French Chartreux, they call her. Silvery gray with those copper-colored eyes. Anyway, Penelope wanted a cat, so she went to the animal shelter. Those two were in cages right next to each other and it looked as though they'd become friends. Kind of curling up as close as they could get to each other, you know? So Penelope said she'd take them both. Seems they were both chipped. Bogie had somehow got here all the way from West Virginia and they'd been unable to find his owner. Bacall was local, but her owner had moved to a no-pets place and had to give her up."

"An odd couple." Maureen smiled. "That's nice."

"Yep. Bogie taught her the joys of the outdoors and she showed him how nice it is to have a comfortable bed and regular pedicures and good restaurant food."

"I hope they'll come inside soon. I can hardly wait to meet them," Maureen said. "I'm pretty sure Finn can adjust."

"Sure he can. Here, have another cookie. These were my Peter's favorites. Shortbread, you know. Now tell me all about the murder, honey. Did you see all the murder mysteries I have in the shop? A whole section devoted to 'em. I'm real interested in murder. Is it true the ghost hunter was poisoned?"

"What?" The glass shook in Maureen's hand, splashing a few drops onto the table. "What makes you say that?"

Aster handed her a paper napkin. "Here, darling. Wipe that up. That's what people are saying, that's all. Saying that Conrad Wilson got what was coming to him. Sticking his nose into where it didn't belong. Somebody slipped him a mickey in his drink." She nodded satisfaction and folded her arms. "Good riddance, that's what I say. You don't think he was poisoned?"

Maureen thought of how Officer Hubbard had taken the bottles from the bar. No wonder anybody who knew about that would assume Wilson had been poisoned. But it might mean that Ted was involved. Maureen admitted to herself— she didn't *want* to believe that.

"At this point, I don't know what to think," she said. "The police haven't told me anything."

"Aw, sweetheart, that's too bad. I thought you'd know all about it. By now Penelope would be right on top of it." She raised her glass. "Oh well, you'll learn. Looks like it's going to be a lovely sunset. Since you don't seem to know much about the murder under your own roof, maybe you'd like to pick up a murder mystery book or two? Have you read Carolyn Hart's latest? Lovely mystery and there's a ghost in it too. Which reminds me, you must have learned a thing or two about ghosts by now, haven't you?"

Maureen had, but she wasn't about to share that information. She shook her head and nibbled on a cookie, giving her time to think.

"My office is in suite twenty-seven," she said, as though that answered the question.

Aster bobbed her head enthusiastically, apparently satisfied with the answer "Seems like there was some goin's-on across the street last night." She pointed to the L&M Bar.

"Oh? Noisy crowd? Haven seems so laid-back compared to where I come from."

"I don't mind hearing the young folks having fun. Peter and I enjoyed an evening out once in a while." She looked around and put a hand beside her mouth, whispering. "It was after the bar closed. Once in a great while the jukebox starts up at three, four in the morning—and there's *nobody* inside. I've called the electric company myself a couple of times. They say there's no short circuit or anything else they can find to make the darned thing go off like that."

Maureen could only wonder if the Babe had liked seeing Lorna in the Tory Burch dress.

Chapter 16

Elizabeth had been right about the publicity surrounding Conrad Wilson's death causing a rush of reservations. An increase in staff had become even more necessary. An assortment of neighborhood women and girls had been pressed into housekeeping service under the direction of Gert and Molly. The inn's laundry was busy keeping linens fresh and the kitchen staff had been amplified.

"How can I help?" Maureen asked.

"What do you know how to do?" Elizabeth sighed. "Can you cook? Clean? Run a dishwasher? An ironing mangle?"

Maureen hesitated. What could she do? "Do you need any printed material? Menus? Room rate sheets? Posters? I know how to design those and I have a first-rate large-format printer and access to some excellent artwork. I could even man the registration desk at the same time. You can't very well run back and forth between the dining room and the lobby the way you've been doing."

"I get paid for both jobs, you know," Elizabeth said.

"Of course. I understand," Maureen said.

"Okay. I'll give you a crash course. You know how to run a credit card? Operate a cash register? The reservations are all handled on computer. You good at that?"

Yes, Maureen could handle all of that. She learned where

the room keys were kept and how they were coded. The souvenir keys, displayed on the desk, were two dollars each. She decided she'd work on the menus later in her office. She picked up one of the plastic-coated menus along with a pile of daily specials menus, which were printed on copy paper.

The police tape had been removed from the porch and replaced with a couple of sawhorses and an UNDER REPAIR sign. Maureen wished the UNDER REPAIR sign were true. So many things needed fixing—but not at that moment.

Some of the local papers had supplemented the reports of Wilson's death with the old ghost stories and had attracted guests from nearby cities from Tampa to Orlando. At least four of the new ones claimed to be ghost hunters and brought with them an assortment of strange apparatuses.

The two New Yorkers had returned and requested Wilson's old room. Maureen denied the request because the police hadn't finished with their investigation. Maureen thought of the storage locker where she'd learned that guests' abandoned belongings were stored. If no one showed up to claim Wilson's worldly goods, would they wind up there too? When she had some time, Maureen intended to inventory the contents of the place. But like other plans—that one would be shelved for later.

She soon found that being in the lobby with the increase in business left her in a position to overhear a good many conversations. It was an interesting perspective. Some of the ghost hunters had fans among the other guests. She saw copies of *Got Ghosts?* and *Haunted Times* being autographed. A television producer called and asked permission to film inside the inn. Maureen denied the request. "We want our guests to enjoy the inn's unique old Florida charm. We feel that the television cameras would be obtrusive."

Elizabeth agreed with the decision. "We sure don't need nosy reporters running around in here talking about murder. Anyway, Officer Hubbard hasn't found any evidence of poison anywhere in our immaculate kitchen, so he'll be looking elsewhere to place blame for that man's death."

Maureen remembered the five reasons for death she'd heard from Hubbard: *natural death, accident, homicide, suicide, or judicial execution* The first and last reasons could safely be eliminated, but the middle three were still in play.

"By the way, Ms. Doherty," Elizabeth interrupted *that* unpleasant train of thought. "Do you have any changes in mind for the annual Halloween celebration?'

"Changes? Halloween?" Maureen frowned. "This is the first I've heard about it."

"Really? It's kind of a big deal in Haven." Elizabeth's glance was somehow both polite and condescending. "I was just about to send George over to our St. Petersburg warehouse storage locker to pick up some decorations. Why don't you tag along and maybe you could attend to that part of it anyway?"

"All right," Maureen agreed, thinking of the ten years of creative input she'd had helping to plan decorations for *every* holiday for a six-story-tall, city-block-wide department store. "Anything else I could help with?"

A raised penciled eyebrow. "I've already ordered posters, flyers, and such. You might want to take a peek at the advertising schedule. There'll be the full-page ad in the *Times*, of course—and Penelope liked to use radio. I'm thinking of TV this time too."

Maureen's eyes widened. "TV? Radio? What's our budget for this?"

"Budget? Oh, just a tad more than last year, I should think. Not a lot more."

Maureen thought of the spreadsheet the lawyer had given her. The business was already bleeding money. "Does the whole town of Haven take part in the celebration?" she asked.

"Well, sure. Everybody decorates—has special events. The

boulevard is like a big street fair! Farmers' Market. Jack-o'-lantern carving. Costume contests. Kids' parties. People come from all over."

"I mean, do all of the businesses chip in for the expenses? The advertising?" Maureen wondered.

"Oh no. We've always taken care of that."

Maureen shook her head. "I'd like to see the figures before you commit us to any contracts." Bartlett's of Boston had always kept meticulous figures of every promotion.

Elizabeth did not look pleased. "I suppose so. When I get time, I'll look them up."

"Today," Maureen spoke firmly, wondering what the cost of an off-property warehouse would be. "What time will George leave for the warehouse? I'd like very much to go along and attempt an inventory."

Elizabeth's laugh was short. "Good luck with that! Penelope kept *everything*. You'll see. I'll have George call your cell. Should be within the hour."

Maureen took Finn back up to the suite via the elevator, filled his water dish, and changed into jeans and a Boston Celtics T-shirt. That warehouse sounded as though it might be pretty messy. She picked up the menus and took the stairs down to suite twenty-seven and printed out some simple generic inventory sheets. She'd deal with the menus later.

George parked the late-model Ford pickup with HAVEN HOUSE INN emblazoned in large letters on both sides—in front of the inn as promised. Maureen waited at the curb, briefcase armed with inventory sheets, pens and pencils, cell phone, bottled water, and canvas gloves, wondering as she climbed into the passenger seat how much the truck had cost.

"Glad to have you aboard, Ms. Doherty," George said. "Hardly anybody else around here is brave enough to come with me to the warehouse."

"Brave? Why? Do you drive too fast?"

"Naw. I'm a good driver. See, all that stuff used to be

crammed into suite twenty-seven before they made it into an office. Even Elizabeth won't go near it." He grinned "Afraid of the ghost. All of 'em. They won't admit it, but that's why. Molly's been there with me a couple of times, but she's not crazy about it."

"I don't think I've ever heard the whole story about whatever or whoever the man is that's supposed to be haunting my office," she said.

"No kidding? You really want to hear it?"

"Of course I do. Everybody is so hush-hush about it, I haven't dared to ask how the story got started."

"Strange thing is, as far as we know nobody ever died in there."

"That's a good thing, isn't it?" Maureen realized that Lorna Dubois had died down the street at the playhouse, but *she* haunted the inn, and probably Billy Bedoggoned Bailey hadn't died at the inn either.

"Okay. Here's how I heard it. Seems this guy and girl checked into the inn. It was sometime in the seventies I think. Suite twenty-seven. Mr. and Mrs. John Smith, they said—yeah, I know, wink-wink, nudge-nudge, right? Anyhow, people in the rooms nearby heard a woman crying that night—real sad crying. Then everything got quiet. The woman went down-stairs later that night and drove away. Next morning the housekeeper cleaned the room, made the bed." His voice dropped to a whisper. "But both the man and woman were gone. Left their toothbrushes and everything."

"I suppose Ms. Gray tried to find them—to return the be-longings?"

"I suppose she did. But they'd used a fake name, fake ad-dress. Even the license plate number was fake. They were both just gone," he said. "Just flat out disappeared."

"Creepy," Maureen said. "Did the police investigate?"

"Nothing to investigate," he said. "They'd paid for the suite in advance. No law broken. Ever since, a lot of the guests who slept in that room said they saw him—John Smith—come out of that closet in your office. He stood over them, just staring. Sometimes he sat on the bed, touching them."

"Creepy," she said again, meaning it. "Really creepy. I'm almost sorry I asked."

"Yeah. There are different stories about the ghost. Some people said the guy was crying for his mother. He sat on the bed and whispered, 'Mother, Mother.' "

"That would terrify me," she said. "Really depressing."

"Yep. Most people said the place is depressing. They couldn't take more than one night in there. Some said it was a feeling of evil and that the whole room turned icy cold sometimes."

"That reporter, Jake, from the newspaper said that. About the room getting cold."

"That's not the worst of it," George said. "The suitcases they left—his and hers—are in the storage locker we're going to. Nobody ever claimed them."

"Eeew. That's even more creepy. Is the storage locker haunted too?"

"No. Not that I know of anyway. But just the same, hardly anybody except maybe Sam actually wants to come over here with me."

"Well, if I can work in suite twenty-seven with no problems, I guess I can handle a storage locker." Maureen hoped she sounded more confident than she felt.

"Want to know a secret?" George winked.

"Sure," she said. "I love secrets."

"The only person who actually wanted to come over here with me was the dead guy."

"Conrad Wilson?"

"Yep. Brought that fancy little camera with him too."

They'd pulled up in front of a huge, sterile-looking building surrounded by a chain-link fence. George pressed a key fob and a gate swung open. "We're around back, where the really big lockers are. It's a big one."

Maureen asked again, "Conrad Wilson came here with you?"

"That's right."

"Did you tell the police?"

"Didn't tell anyone. Not even Molly. He gave me a hundred bucks. Told me not to tell anybody. Was I going to say no? Anyway, it was a long time ago. At least a month. Didn't have anything to do with him dyin' like that. You aren't going to tell anybody, are you? I only told you because you don't put much stock in that ghost stuff either. I can tell."

Maureen thought about Gert's story of money changing hands when Wilson wanted to see suite twenty-seven. There was more than one person who had access to the rooms and could use some extra money. "I don't see any reason to mention it," Maureen agreed, and it was true. However, she'd begun—with darned good reasons in black and white—to put at least some stock in "that ghost stuff." Ghosts, real or imagined, were already impacting her bottom line. "After all," she reasoned aloud, "Mr. Wilson was a reporter. Wrote for ghost magazines. He probably went lots of places around here."

"Everywhere," George said. "Took pictures everywhere." He stopped the Ford. "Come on. This is it." She climbed out of the cab and watched as George unlocked a tall, broad door.

"Looks like a two-car garage," she said.

"Bigger," he replied. "Much bigger." The door rolled up, revealing what appeared to be hundreds of large, oblong plastic boxes, stacked one atop the other all the way to the eight-foot-high ceiling of the place. There was a narrow path between the stacks leading deep into the darkened building. "Well?" he asked. "What do you think of it?"

She paused, trying to think of an appropriate word.

"Overwhelming," she said. "It's overwhelming. How do you find anything?" Plans for doing any sort of inventory that day evaporated. Her late benefactor had been a hoarder, no doubt about it, and this hoard was spectacular.

"It's not quite as bad as it looks," he said. "See?" He pointed to a box marked BEACH TOWELS in neat block print. "Ms. Gray marked most of them with black marker."

"But—what are they all *for*?"

"It's all stuff folks left behind after they checked out of the inn." He shrugged. "She figured they might come back for their things someday. Kept everything for years. Every once in a while, someone *did* come back and remember something they'd left and they'd be so happy to get it back—it just made Ms. Gray *so* pleased that she'd saved it for them—and it just kept piling up like that. Some of this junk has been here probably forty, fifty years."

Maureen shaded her eyes and looked up. "How do you get to the top of the pile?"

"Ladder," he said, pointing to an adjustable aluminum stepladder, leaning against the wall just inside the door. "Those Halloween decorations are right in the front row. Christmas ones too. Wait a sec. I'll get them."

George seemed pretty agile for his age, and scampered up the ladder, pulling a box from the top and handing it down to Maureen. "These are the newest ones. Last year's." He stayed on the ladder while Maureen removed the cover and looked inside the box, revealing a jumble of pumpkins, black cats, witches, ghosts—the usual trappings of the holiday.

"These are mostly plastic—modern designs. I was thinking of something more in keeping with the age of the inn—you know, the old-fashioned decorations." Maureen couldn't disguise her disappointment. "But I guess they'll do, unless there are some older ones."

George moved the ladder a little deeper into the locker without climbing down. He just sort of hopped it along the narrow path, bracing himself against the piles of boxes. "Elizabeth always uses the newest ones, and adds a few more new ones every year. Like I told you before, Ms. Gray, she never got rid of anything. I'm willing to bet we've got decorations back to when she first came here."

"Do you know when that was?"

"Back in the fifties is what I heard. I was here in Haven but don't remember much about back then. I was just a kid. But Molly says she heard that Ms. Gray came here just about like you did. Somebody left her the place and a pile of money and she just ran it ever since."

Maureen smiled to herself. *That's not quite like I did*, she thought. *Not much left of that pile of money.*

"Could you find some decorations from back then?" she asked.

"Sure. Might take a minute or two."

"Sorry to cause you extra work," Maureen apologized.

"No problem." George's smile was broad and genuine. "I get paid by the hour—and I guess you're the one who's payin' me."

It was true. Maureen gave a brief salute in his direction. "Guess so. Any way I can help?"

"Sure. Think of a way to get rid of it all. It was easier to get at when it was spread around in suite twenty-seven."

Maureen visualized her spacious new office, the accompanying even larger empty bedroom and bathroom, trying to picture the multitudes of boxes there. George moved the ladder deeper into the place. "What's all the way in back there?" she asked. "More boxes?"

"All the way back?" George waved a hand. "A wall full of suitcases, overnight bags, backpacks, that people left behind."

"Including the ones the Smiths left behind?"

"Guess so. Ms. Gray put stickers with the people's name on them on each one."

"A *wall full* of suitcases? And the inn didn't—or couldn't—return any of them to their owners?"

"Oh sure. Ms. Gray sent letters, made phone calls. But you'd be surprised how many people use fake addresses. Like the John Smiths. Maybe they're traveling with someone they shouldn't be, you know?" George winked. "And some folks just don't care about their stuff, I guess. It doesn't happen so much these days, what with e-mail and cell phones and all. Most of the luggage back there is ten, twenty, thirty, forty, fifty years old."

"Weird," Maureen said. "I wonder what's in them? Did you ever look?"

"Not me." He held up both hands. "Elizabeth might have but not me. Molly and me, we don't ever do anything that might piss off any ghosts—just in case there are any. That's why I'm not afraid to go in suite twenty-seven." He frowned. "You haven't seen anything in there, have you?" Without waiting for an answer, he plopped another plastic box on top of the one marked 1950s HALLOWEEN. "Here's some sixties stuff. Think that'll be enough? You'll probably be buying some new things too. Got your costume yet?"

Maureen had used the same witch costume for years at the annual trick-or-treat promotion at Bartlett's. She'd given it away with the winter clothes back in Saugus. "Not yet," she said.

"Ms. Gray's costume is here. It might fit you. It's really nice. It has a crown and a wand and everything."

Maureen had an immediate and unsettling mental picture of herself as an aging Disney princess. "I'm sure I can whip up something. Let's take the fifties and sixties boxes, and maybe the unopened packages of paper plates and paper napkins out of last year's box. No sense buying new ones."

"Why not take the whole box? You can pick out what you need. And do you want me to grab that costume? It's right up front here in a dry cleaner's bag."

"Okay. If you want to."

"No problem."

The two of them loaded the boxes and dry cleaner's bag into the back of the Ford and headed back to the inn. There wasn't much conversation. Maureen looked out the window at the passing Florida scenery and George concentrated on the afternoon St. Petersburg traffic. She had more to think about than Halloween decorations. Attorney Jackson's frank assessment of this new business had been discouraging. The realization that *she* was now responsible for paying the bills bordered on terrifying. Was Elizabeth paying the bills from the desk in her cheerful little office—happily running through the remainder of Penelope Josephine Gray's onetime fortune? If so, didn't she realize that time was running out on the hay-ride?

Maureen glanced around the Ford's interior, noting the new-car smell. "Does the inn own any other vehicles besides this one?" she asked.

George nodded. "Oh sure. There's another truck—not as new as this one—Sam drives it, and Elizabeth's big, black Lexus of course. And I think the inn bought the old beater that Ted uses for grocery shopping." She'd have to take another look at those spreadsheets. Were there car payments listed there, along with goodness knows how many holiday advertising expenses for the whole town?

George parked at a side entrance just past the far end of the porch. "Where do you want me to put this stuff? Up in your office—I mean suite twenty-seven? Or in your own place?"

"The office will be fine. Shall I go up first and unlock it for you?"

"No problem. I have passkeys to all the rooms. Maintenance, you know."

"Oh. Of course," she said. It did make sense. Sam must have them too. And what about Gert and Molly? Housekeepers certainly needed access to keep things tidy. It all made sense, but the thought was still disturbing. She needed time to get a handle on this place, but time seemed to be the one thing she didn't have.

The side entrance opened into a corridor housing a guest laundry, soda and ice machines, leading to the main lobby and the elevator. At its base was a cat door. So Bogie and Bacall had access to the inn from outdoors. Maureen was pleased about that, and made a mental note to use the side entrance herself occasionally, bypassing the front lobby and—not incidentally—the questioning quartet in the front-porch rockers.

Chapter 17

She heard Finn's welcoming "woof" as soon as she stepped off the elevator and approached the suite. She unlocked the door and was met with excited prancing.

"What's all the excitement about, boy?" She scratched behind his ears. "What's going on?" The golden led her to the narrow window just behind the cat tower where a branch of the oak tree just outside held the answer to her question. There they were, peering in. Bogie and Bacall.

"Looks like they want to come inside, doesn't it?" She searched for the crank that would open the window. "Will you behave if I let them in? It's their house too, you know."

She turned the handle and two panes swung inward. Bogie moved carefully from the tree branch onto the narrow balcony and entered first, crouching on the middle platform of the tower. Aster had been right about him. He was big and tough looking. He fixed green eyes on Finn, giving a warning hiss.

Finn sat, watchful, not moving. Bacall followed, putting one foot daintily in front of the other, she climbed onto the top tier of the carpeted structure. She looked around, then sat upright, tail wrapped around front paws, as regally as any proud lioness might.

"Woof," Finn said.

Bacall uttered a trilling purr. Bogie stood, puffing out his fur, making himself look even bigger, glared at Finn for a long moment, then sat in a pose similar to Bacall's.

Maureen didn't know what to make of it all. "What do you think, Finn?" she whispered, not taking her eyes away from the cat tower and its occupants. "Are they going to accept us?"

Finn seemed to have it figured out. He backed away from the tower, uttering a soft "woof," and sat, tail wagging in his very friendliest fashion. Bacall extended a paw, and batted a small red ball to the edge of her platform, then with her nose knocked it to the floor. Finn took the cue, picked up the ball, returned it to the base of the tower, retreated to his former position, and waited for her next move. Next came a catnip mouse, followed by a well-chewed badminton shuttlecock. Finn carefully returned each one.

"I get it," Maureen said. "You're promising not to mess with them or their stuff."

Bogie apparently got it too. He jumped down to the floor, tail held high, walked slowly and deliberately past Finn and Maureen, and headed into the kitchen. Bacall left her top-tier perch and hopped down to the one Bogie had vacated, lay at the edge, eyes focused on her toys below.

Maureen picked up the red ball. "Here's your ball," she said—placing it beside the gray cat, followed with the other items—"and your mouse and your birdie." Bacall acknowledged the gesture with another of those trilling purrs, descending gracefully from the tower and following Bogie into the kitchen.

"I guess they're hungry," she said. "Crisis apparently averted. Good job, Finn. Maybe you'd better stay here while I feed them. Okay?" She gave the "stay" command. Finn sat and Maureen followed the cats.

Within a few minutes, cats fed, watered, and apparently

happily hunched over their individual bowls, Maureen tiptoed away from the tranquil scene and rejoined Finn in the
living room.

Finn was no longer alone.

"Oh, hi there, Maureen. Old Finn is quite the peacemaker,
isn't he? That could have been ugly, but he handled it like a
pro." Lorna Dubois, gorgeous in Maureen's brand-new,
super-cute Kate Spade flower-print knotted halter bikini top
with matching classic bikini bottom, knelt beside Finn,
scratching behind his ears.

Maureen couldn't help thinking that—even in semi-
opaque black and white—Lorna's movie starlet, twenty-six-
year-old form filled out the swimsuit better than Maureen
ever would, or even would have when *she* was twenty-six.
"Hello, Lorna. You were here for all that?"

"Sure. It freaks the cats out if I pop in suddenly. So I
waited 'til they left. It didn't seem like a good time to rile
them up."

"Going to the beach?" Maureen asked, in as pleasant a
tone as she could muster at the moment.

"Oh, this?" The ghost stood, did a model-type turn. "No.
Just wanted to see how it looked. Pretty good, huh?" Another whirl. "I might want to wear it for Elvis's birthday celebration at Graceland in January. They have an indoor
pool."

"Graceland?"

"Yeah! Everybody who was anybody goes to Graceland at
least once a year. Elvis's birthday is one of the best times to be
there."

"Let me get this straight. You people—um—spirits get to
travel around at will, haunting as you go?"

"Well, not all of us. Every place has its resident popula-
tion—the ones who stay in one place, you know?" Lorna sat
on the floor beside Finn. "Some of them stay in one town—

or maybe one house. Some even stay in one room. Like the guy in suite twenty-seven." She put her arms around the dog's neck. "Would bore the hell out of me."

"Have you seen him? The ghost?"

"I haven't. Never went into those rooms." She adjusted a strap on the bikini top and looked away from Maureen. "I think he's a really bad one. I don't want anything to do with him. All the rest of us in Haven are nice, or interesting, or at least easy to get along with. I don't even like talking about him."

"Okay. Let's talk about Elvis then. Does he stay at Graceland all the time?"

"No. He gets around a lot. I've only seen him once and I go to Graceland at least a couple of times a year. I've heard that he spends a lot of time in California. He still likes to keep an eye on Priscilla."

"How does he look now?"

"Now? He's twenty-five again. He looks like he did when he first got out of the Army. Young and fit and trim and sexy." Lorna's smile was wide.

"That's nice to know. Tell me, do you ever think about moving on from here? Going to 'the light' or 'crossing the rainbow bridge,' or whatever the next destination is?" Maureen changed the subject. "I've always wondered about that."

"Me too," Lorna agreed. "It's true about that light, though. I saw it when I fell into the prompter's box and broke my neck. The thing is, I didn't know what it led to. Still don't. Anyway, I like it here."

Bacall selected that moment to stroll back into the living room, giving Finn a wide berth, acknowledging Maureen with an almost ankle rub before climbing once again onto the top of the tower, where she proceeded to wash her face and paws. Oddly, she seemed to walk straight through Lorna. Maureen couldn't help gasping. "Doesn't she see you?"

"Sure she does. She does that on purpose."

"Why?"

"Who knows? She thinks it's funny. Cats are weird, aren't they, Finn?"

"Woof," Finn agreed.

"Does Bogie do it too?"

"Him? Never. Most of the time he just pretends he can't see me."

"If you'll excuse me, I'm about to pretend I can't see you either. I have work to do in my office."

"Suite twenty-seven?"

"Of course."

"I guess you haven't seen—uh—anything down there?"

"A sighting of the man in the closet? George told me about him." Maureen smiled. "Not a thing. Whoever—whatever was there, if it ever was, probably left years ago."

"They say he sits on the bed." Lorna shuddered. Or shimmered. "That he cries for his mother."

"There's no bed. Nothing in the bedroom at all. Nothing in the closet except some old guest registers."

"If you say so. See you later. Bye, Finn."

Before Finn could woof goodbye, she was gone.

Chapter 18

George had delivered the Halloween decoration in their plastic boxes to suite twenty-seven as promised. They were arranged in a row, side by side, just inside the doorway of the empty room. They'd have to wait a while for her attention, Maureen decided. She closed the door on them and with a sharpened #2 pencil, a calculator, a yellow pad, spreadsheets, payroll records, and a handful of random invoices spread out over the top of the beautiful desk, Maureen contemplated the future of the Haven House Inn, and—not so incidentally—her own.

At first glance it didn't look good. With further inspection, it looked worse. Plainly, the Haven House Inn was close to insolvency and creeping up on bankruptcy. On the plus side, the taxes were up-to-date and there was no mortgage. It appeared that Maureen owned the place free and clear—such as it was.

Elizabeth's payroll figures made some sense. Paychecks, handwritten in the company checkbook by Elizabeth, seemed to balance properly. Total hours worked at the stated wage per hour, minus taxes and Social Security, looked fine. But where was the record of employees' rent paid? Grocery receipts were haphazard, tossed into a file folder. Some were from Tampa and St. Petersburg food wholesalers, but too many were at full retail from neighborhood grocery stores. Guest receipts were more orderly because of credit card records—but totals seemed too small.

After two hours, Maureen put down her pencil. The bottom line showed a projected minus within months. If the place was going to keep from drowning in red ink, something had to be done to stop the leaks. The obvious ones needed to be plugged and new avenues of revenue needed to be found. Like, right now.

Maureen's successful career in retailing led her immediately to the fact that the fastest way to bring in cash is to sell merchandise at a profit. That led to the recent discovery that she owned a literal warehouse full of merchandise that was costing money for storage. Penelope Josephine Gray had thoughtfully lettered all of those plastic containers with their contents. Maureen recalled a few she'd noticed. Beach towels. Bathing suits. Beach toys. Children's clothes. In the next room she already had a treasure trove of decorations that undoubtedly were regarded as "antiques."

Maybe we'll be hosting Haven's largest garage sale, she thought. Penelope Josephine Gray might not approve, but the Haven House Inn's hoard had to go. And quickly. The inventory Maureen had planned for "later" had to happen soon. She'd need some expert help with this. She began a list. "Antiques appraiser. Estate sale planner. Tax-deductible charities."

Her concentration was broken by the buzzing of her phone. Impatiently, she answered, "Yes?"

"Maureen? . . . It's Elizabeth. You need to come down here right away. Officer Hubbard wants to talk to you."

"All right," Maureen said. "I'll be there in a few minutes."

"Now," Elizabeth said, and hung up.

"She doesn't need to sound so pleased about it," Maureen

grumbled, organizing the papers on her desk, putting them into an empty drawer. "What does he want now, anyway?"

Since Elizabeth had made it sound urgent, Maureen opted for the elevator. Glad she'd taken time to shower and change from jeans and T-shirt to a neat pale blue denim jumpsuit, she approached the lobby where Officer Hubbard and Elizabeth stood at the entrance to the dining room. Elizabeth smiled. The policeman did not.

"Good afternoon, Officer Hubbard," Maureen said. "You wanted to see me?"

"Yes, Ms. Doherty. Let me get right to the point. I'd like your permission to take a look at your apartment."

"My apartment?" she echoed. "Whatever for?"

"Routine investigation," he said. "Your permission?"

"What in the world would you be looking for in my apartment?"

He scowled. Not an attractive look for him. "Are you refusing?"

"Of course not." What was going on here? Maureen looked from the policeman to Elizabeth and back. Elizabeth was *not* frowning, but shrugging her shoulders in an *I don't know what's going on either* posture. "Do you want to go up right now?" Maureen asked.

"Yes," he said.

"Okay. Come on. Do you prefer the elevator or the stairs?" They'd already drawn a few stares from guests. She hoped he'd opt for the stairs, where the odds of sharing space with anyone were minimal. She headed for the stairway and he followed. Thankfully, Elizabeth stayed behind.

When they'd reached the third-floor landing, Maureen pulled the room key from her pocket and started toward her suite. Hubbard followed. She heard Finn's soft, welcoming "woof" and wondered if the cats were at home too.

"Nobody else lives on this floor except you?" Hubbard asked.

"Just me," she said, pushing the door open. "Elizabeth calls it the penthouse. Come on in."

The cats were at home. Bogie looked down from the top of the cat tower. Bacall had positioned herself right behind Finn as he gave me his usual hand-nuzzling, tail-wagging welcome. Hubbard hesitated in the doorway. "Ms. Gray's cats are back, I see."

"Yes. They arrived today. Fortunately, they seem to have accepted Finn and me." He stepped inside the room. "Is there anything in particular you want to see?" she asked, keeping her tone even, her words polite.

"You've been here a short time." He walked toward the large window, looked outside. "Is everything here just about the way you found it? As Ms. Gray left it?"

"Yes. I haven't changed anything. Just added a few things I'd brought with me. A couple of lamps, some pictures, books, Finn's dog food, a vase." She pointed to the crystal vase with its now-wilted daisies. "I've unpacked my clothes of course. My office items are downstairs."

"In suite twenty-seven," he said.

"Of course."

"Had Ms. Gray left the rooms here . . . provisioned for you?"

"You mean like with groceries and cat food and paper towels? Someone did a lovely job with all that. I don't know that it was Ms. Gray."

"Uh-huh. Mind if I look around?"

She did mind. "Help yourself," she said. "May I tag along?"

"Sure. It's your penthouse."

She followed him into the kitchen. Bacall and Finn did too. He pulled open the door of the cabinet full of canned goods. "Nice," he said. "All this was here?"

"It was. I haven't used any of it yet. I've been eating in the dining room."

"Sure. Why not? You own it." He closed the cabinet, opened the silverware drawer, and closed it.

Was he being deliberately annoying? "Yes, I do," she said.

"The bathroom in here?" He pointed to the bedroom door.

She didn't answer but followed him into the bedroom. "Wow. Nice room," he said, opening the door to her closet. "This all your stuff?"

"Yes."

He closed the closet and opened the bathroom door. "Pink," he said.

"Yes."

He pulled open the mirrored medicine cabinet. "These all your things?"

"No. I've never looked inside it before." She peered over his shoulder. She tapped the makeup case she'd left on the marble countertop along with her shampoo and deodorant. "I haven't finished unpacking my own bathroom stuff yet." The glass shelves contained the usual items—rubbing alcohol, peroxide, petroleum jelly, aspirin, laxative pills, a couple of brown medicine bottles, a package of cotton swabs, adhesive bandages. "Must have been Ms. Gray's," she said, glad she hadn't put her own various feminine products on display for prying eyes to inspect.

"Uh-huh," he said. He reached into an inside jacket pocket, removed a pair of blue gloves. From another pocket he drew several clear plastic bags. "Uh-huh," he said again as he pulled on the gloves. He reached into the cabinet, moving aside a blue glass eye cup, picking up one of the brown bottles. He studied the label. Maureen recognized the Walgreens drugstore logo but couldn't see the small print from where she stood. Hubbard slipped the bottle into a plastic bag, sealed it, and picked up another. This time, "A-ha" replaced "Uh-huh."

Maureen moved closer and understood the "A-ha" immediately. Beneath the Walgreens logo she read the word "digitalis." She remembered Hubbard's explanation for what had killed Conrad Wilson. "A large dose of a fairly common heart medicine," he'd said—and digitalis surely fit that description. She watched silently as he slipped the bottle into another plastic bag and sealed it.

Chapter 19

It was Maureen's turn for an "A-ha" moment. The brown bottle in *her* medicine cabinet might very well contain the poison that had killed the ghost hunter. She watched the policeman's face as he pocketed the bottle. "Surely you don't think . . . ? You're not somehow connecting me to . . . ?" She felt as though she needed to sit down—and would have if the closest place to do so hadn't been the pink-chenille-covered toilet seat.

His voice was gruff. "I don't think anything—I don't make connections. That's not my job. I collect evidence. Period." He left the bathroom and looked back at her. "That's all for now. Shall I let myself out?"

"No. No. That's all right." She remembered her manners. "I'm coming." She hurried past him, past the watching cats and dog, and opened the door. "Will you keep me informed about what you learn from"—she nodded toward his suit pocket—"from *that*? From Ms. Gray's prescription?"

"Of course. I'll be around." She watched as he strode toward the elevator, then ducked back into her own space. Her safe, serene, quite attractive, well-provisioned, and comfortable space. At least, it had seemed to be all that until a few minutes earlier. The cats had come down from the tower and now sat, watchful, together on the blue couch. Finn lay nearby, tail wagging, and gave a short "woof."

Maureen sat in a beige chair. "Well, you guys," she said, "I don't know exactly *what* to think about all that." She waved toward the still-open bedroom door. "But the man says he's just collecting evidence. The medicine belonged to Penelope. I'm sure her name is on the bottle. It has nothing to do with me, right?"

The animals watched. She answered her own question. "Right. Now I need to get back to my office and figure out how to keep this place afloat. Want to come with me, Finn?"

Without his leash Finn trotted happily along as once again Maureen descended the stairs to the second floor and unlocked the door to suite twenty-seven. The door to the bedroom was open and she could see the plastic boxes of decorations neatly lined up in a row. She'd get to them soon. Halloween was just around the corner. She closed the bedroom door and concentrated on business. For now, generating enough cash to get through the week without running up any more unnecessary charges was more important than pumpkins and black cats. She pulled open the drawer and returned the sheaf of papers to her desktop.

She stared at the figures the lawyer had shared. She thought of the brown envelope full of offers for the Haven House Inn, then discounted that possibility. She double-checked her own figures. She knew she'd need some long-range plans to get the place on a profitable basis, but there wasn't time for long-range planning. What could she do with the place *right now*? She'd already decided to sell as much of the contents of the hoard in the storage locker as possible. That could be done fairly soon. What about all the vehicles she apparently owned—or owed money on? Did the payroll make any sense? What about the dining room? With the quality of the food she'd experienced so far, the tables should be full for breakfast, lunch, and dinner. Why weren't they?

The pile of menus was still on the corner of her desk where she'd tossed them earlier. She reached for the plastic-covered one. "I haven't read to you for a while, have I, Finn? Want to hear about food?" At the word "food" the golden perked up his ears, sat expectantly, watching his mistress's face.

In the bright light from the desk lamp she could tell that the menu had seen better days. The edges were curled up and it appeared to have coffee stains on it. Maybe it hadn't looked so bad in the dimly lit room with its dark bark-cloth draperies, but this was unacceptable. Even the paper menus had clearly been used more than once. She studied the contents of the plastic-covered one. It had breakfast, lunch, dinner, desserts, and beverages listed. It seemed pretty basic. She began to recite aloud, " 'Cereal, muffins, omelettes, bacon, and sausages for breakfast,' " she said. " 'Hamburgers, hot dogs, and a few sandwiches and a house salad for lunch.' Not too exciting so far, huh?"

"Woof," Finn said. Maureen read on: " 'For dinner, we have steaks, grilled or fried, native fish, grilled or fried, chicken, grilled or fried, assorted vegetables, and potatoes, baked or fried.' " She shook her head. "Big whoop. Here're the appetizers. Shrimp cocktail, soup du jour, or Caesar salad. Pretty boring, huh? Even at these low prices. How about desserts? Key lime pie, hot fudge sundae, layer cake. Not too bad. But they could be a lot better."

"Woof," Finn agreed. *How old were these menus anyway?* she wondered. The specials on the paper menus sounded much more appealing and the prices made more sense. She realized that she'd only eaten the specials herself—and they'd all been prepared by bartender Ted.

"I'm going to dip into my five-thousand-dollar stash and spend it on the dining room," she told the dog. "New, light-colored curtains, some beach décor on the walls, and re-vamped menus—and I'm going to start tomorrow."

Decision made, she felt better and sat back in her chair, smiling. A slight sound from the next room brought a frown. A branch scratching on a window? A scurrying mouse? It was an old building after all, but Bogie and Bacall should have long since attended to any rodent problem. Again, the sound. She stood, walked to the bedroom door, put her ear against an upper panel. Nothing.

Finn watched from beside the desk as she turned the glass knob, pushed the door open, and reached for the light switch. A low-watt ceiling fixture in the center of the room provided pale illumination. She made a quick mental note: *Replace all the old bulbs with LED soft light ones; save energy and money.* She stepped into the room, squinting in the dimness, and walked around the row of plastic boxes. The closet door was slightly ajar. She pushed it closed, heard the latch click. Maybe George had opened it for some reason. Maureen was sure she'd closed it earlier.

She stood still for a moment beside the boxes, listening. Finn had still not approached the room. She heard herself breathing, even imagined she heard her own heart beating. It was absolutely quiet at that moment in suite twenty-seven. She looked down at the neat row of plastic boxes, brightened a bit by the light spilling from her office.

There was the slightest dent in the cover of the last box. Almost as if something had pressed on it. Almost as if some-one had sat on it.

Had John Smith mistaken the row of boxes for a bed?

She whirled, almost leaped across the marble doorsill into the office, slamming the bedroom door behind her, trying to shake the bad thought away. Finn jumped at the sound and ducked under the kneehole of the desk.

She sat in the desk chair, reached down, and patted the

dog. *Nonsense*, she told herself. *Take deep breaths. Be logical. George had those boxes piled up in the truck, and again on the luggage carrier. There are any number of ways he might have dented one.* She glanced again toward the closed bedroom, picked up her papers and notepad, turned off the desk lamp, and with Finn trotting ahead of her pulled the door to suite twenty-seven open, stepped out into the corridor, closed it softly, and locked it.

Maureen and Finn rode the elevator up to her suite, looking forward to the company of the cats—maybe even Lorna Dubois. "This place is getting to me," Maureen muttered as she stepped out onto the carpeted hall. "It'll be good for me to get started on the revamping of the dining room—even if Queen Elizabeth doesn't approve of my ideas."

Opening her door, she was happy to see Bogie and Bacall curled up together on the couch. Finn, with a gentle "woof" and with his entire backside wagging, came forward to offer the cats his enthusiastic greeting. The cats sat, apparently declining to participate in such a display of emotion, but not leaving the scene either.

"Okay, guys," she said, "We've got a lot of work to do. We have to decorate this whole place for Halloween without spending any money, then we have to figure out how to get rid of a warehouse full of junk at a profit, and next, we dip into my five thousand bucks to lighten up the dining room décor and at the same time I'll redesign those tatty old menus."

The cats seemed to be listening. She continued. "Don't breathe a word of this to anybody." She leaned toward the animals and whispered, "I think maybe the ghost of suite twenty-seven may have paid me a visit tonight."

"No kidding?" The voice came from a beige chair where Lorna Dubois, wearing Maureen's red satin pajamas, which now appeared to be black and white, popped into view.

"Don't do that!" Maureen, one hand at her throat, commanded.

"Do what?"

"Appear out of nowhere like that. It's enough to give a person a heart attack."

"Sorry," Lorna said. "Penelope used to say the same thing. Only she really had a bad heart. She gave me a little bell to ring whenever I was going to appear. It's around here somewhere. I just tapped it and it rang."

"The push bell in the lobby," Maureen said. "Elizabeth must have grabbed it. I'll get you a new one."

Lorna leaned forward. "So you saw John Smith? What does he look like?"

"I didn't *see* him—or anybody," Maureen insisted. "It was just something creepy happened. It's probably nothing. Forget about it."

"Tell me everything." Lorna clapped her hands together, widened her eyes—probably, Maureen thought, a move she'd done hundreds of times in all those B movies she'd talked about.

"Well, the closet door was open a crack." Maureen sat in the other beige chair. "I'm pretty sure I didn't leave it that way."

"Oh, pooh. That's nothing. One of the cleaning girls could have done it." Lorna waved a dismissive hand. "There must have been more. Come on. Give. I won't tell a soul." She crossed her heart.

"Well, all right." Barely believing that she was actually having a conversation with a ghost—about *another* ghost— Maureen began. She described the wide plastic bins filled with decorations, and how George had arranged them in a tight row in the formerly empty bedroom. "After I closed that closet door, I looked at the boxes. The one at the end of the row looked like it had a kind of *dent* in it." She paused, took a deep breath. "Almost as if someone—something—had sat on it."

Lorna nodded, platinum waves curving gracefully around the perfect oval face. "You're thinking maybe those boxes, in the dark, could have looked sort of like a bed to—um—to someone?"

"Yeah. What do you think? Am I nuts? I mean, what if suite twenty-seven—my office—really *is* haunted?"

"Of course it's haunted, you big silly. People have been reporting seeing John Smith in there for years. Do you think *they're* all nuts?" She put both fists under her chin and pursed rosebud lips—another adorable, practiced, film-starlet move no doubt—and continued. "No. He's really there and he's really scary. The question is, *why* does he haunt that particular room in this particular inn in Haven when nobody knows how he died, where he died, or why he died?"

Chapter 20

Even after the cats had climbed to their tower sleeping quarters, Finn had curled up at the foot of the Heywood-Wakefield bed, and satin-pajama-clad Lorna Dubois had popped out of sight, sleep did not come easily to Maureen Doherty. Thoughts streamed and drifted and sometimes raced through her mind. Those brown medicine bottles—they had, without a doubt, been found in *her* medicine cabinet. That dismal financial report from Attorney Jackson . . . was certainly *her* responsibility. Could she—*should she?*—attempt to save the place or sell it to the highest bidder and go back to Massachusetts? Was her inherited inn, and quite possibly her entire new hometown of Haven, Florida, some sort of ghost portal? Spirit shuttle? Apparition passageway?

There were no ready answers. She slid into a fitful slumber where a grinning Zoltar pounded the keys of a player piano while Ted the bartender piled pancakes into a bowl marked BOGIE. When she awoke, it was still dark outside. Five a.m. Maureen's thinking process remained fuzzy, questions still unanswered, unlikely happenings still unexplained.

She padded to the bathroom, splashed cold water onto her face, peered into the mirror, and addressed her reflected image. "Come on. Wake up! We have things to do."

A nice brisk run on the beach will get my mind right, she

decided. Within minutes she'd dressed in denim cutoffs and the old Red Sox T-shirt, pulled on well-broken-in running shoes and, without waking the sleeping Finn, hurried downstairs and slipped out the side door into the cool, early Florida morning.

A faint pinkish glow in the eastern sky foretold a pretty sunrise. The streetlamps were still on, the boulevard deserted, shrill cries of ravenous seagulls piercing the stillness. The tide was low. Maureen made her way onto the hard-packed sand at the edge of the gulf and headed toward the Long Pier in the distance.

The run had the desired effect. Feet pounding on the sand, lungs bursting with exertion, she paused, leading forward, hands braced against thighs, waiting for her heart rate to slow, her breathing to resume normal rhythm. Then, wide awake, cobwebs cleared away, she turned, facing back toward the casino building, the brightening sky revealing another runner moving in her direction. She'd slowed to a jog, raising one arm in friendly greeting, realizing that she was alone on a darkened beach, not far from where there'd been a murder—still unsolved—and she had no idea who the man running toward her was, or what he might have in mind. She made a mental note to bring Finn along next time. The man came closer. "Hi, Ted!" she called.

"Hi, Ms. Doherty." He gave a salute. "Nice morning." She smiled, waved, nodded her agreement about the weather, and the two passed each other, but not before she'd noted that the bartender looked very good in shorts and T-shirt.

She slowed her pace to a walk as the casino building came into sight. Thoughts had become more orderly. The idea of a ghostly bottom denting a plastic box was the first to be cast aside. The very real problem of the inn's looming financial crisis was not to be so easily dismissed. Her earlier fund-raising concepts had some merit. She was quite sure about that. They needed to be put into order, then put into practice. Getting rid of Penelope's hoard would take some time. Someone, probably an expert, had to separate the junk from the possibly valuable. That would *cost* money at the outset. Cutting costs now was more to the point. That meant a serious sit-down with Elizabeth. The carefree tossing around of what was left of Penelope Josephine Gray's fortune had to stop—and it had to stop immediately.

The streetlamps were still lighted, and neon OPEN signs already glowed in some of the shop windows when Maureen walked toward the inn. *I can do this*, she told herself. *I can march right up to Queen Elizabeth and tell her that things around here have to change. That* I'm *in charge now.*

She ran up the front steps. There were a few folks in the porch rockers already, some with coffee cups. "Morning," she said, hurrying past them, anxious to begin this new day, to move forward with her pledge to save the Haven House Inn.

Inside, she sniffed the good breakfast smells of coffee and bacon issuing from the dining room. She knew Ted was on the beach, so someone else must be cooking. There was no one behind the registration desk. *Just as well Elizabeth isn't here*, she thought. *I need a shower and a change of clothes before I confront her.* She hurried up the stairs to the third floor and was greeted by Finn and the cats as soon as she opened the door. "Is everybody hungry?" she asked.

"Woof," Finn said, and the cats made mewling little starving kitten noises.

"Oh, come on. It's not that bad," she said, moving past them to the kitchen. "Now, how do I keep you all from eating each other's food?"

Maureen filled Bogie's and Bacall's dishes first, put them on a place mat on the floor, and instructed Finn in a stern tone to "Stay." That worked. Now to keep the cats from sampling Finn's favorite Nature's Recipe food. She put a small amount into his bowl. The cats each walked over, took a whiff, and turned away. Crisis momentarily averted.

"Okay, you guys, I'm hungry too," she announced. "Enjoy your breakfasts. I'm going to shower and change and get something to eat. Then I have a really busy day ahead of me. Actually, many busy days ahead of me."

The run and her recent realization of exactly how much needed to be done in order to keep the Haven House Inn alive had resulted in a laser-like focus on the immediate problems she faced. The new clarity brought a welcome, though still-alarming, prospect. She showered, dressed in madras plaid Bermudas and white linen shirt. *Casual, but conservative*, she told herself. *Just businesslike enough for Haven.* Makeup was light, hair neatly brushed away from her face.

"Okay, you guys, wish me luck," Maureen instructed the animals. She tucked the papers and notepad into the fine leather briefcase she'd used back when she was "buyer of the year," left the suite, locked the door, and literally *marched* toward the elevator.

Elizabeth was at her post behind the registration desk. "Good morning, Elizabeth," Maureen said. "I've been going over some figures and we need to talk."

"Yes, well, between breakfast and the desk, I guess you can see I'm busy." Elizabeth's tone was firm. "I have to be two places at once, you know."

Maureen glanced around the reception area. It was empty. "Excuse me," she said, and pushed open the plantation doors to the dining room. The long-table buffet arrangement was in place with a beaming Herbie—in chef's hat—providing service to the short line of diners. Waitress Shelly stood by, along with a young man wielding a coffeepot. "Breakfast seems to be going smoothly. Perhaps Shelly can watch the desk and we can talk in your office."

"Both the dining room and the lobby are my responsibility, you know," Elizabeth said, not moving from behind the desk, narrowing her eyes, watching Maureen.

"I understand." Maureen returned the woman's gaze and

spoke softly. "But I'm sure Shelly can handle it for now. Shall I speak to her, or would you prefer to?"

Elizabeth blinked first. "I'll tell her." The woman turned, pushed the doors open. "Shelly! Come out here and take over the desk for a few minutes. Bring the menus."

Maureen was quite sure this was going to take more than a few minutes but didn't say so.

"We'll be in my office," Elizabeth told the waitress, who looked perfectly at ease with the situation. "If you have any trouble, just knock on the door. I'll come right out and handle it."

"Thank you, Shelly." Maureen followed Elizabeth into the cheerful yellow and white room, placing the briefcase beside a chair, watching the woman seat herself behind the desk.

"Well, what is it?" Elizabeth's self-confident attitude was back. "I need to get back to the dining room in case of a rush."

"I'm sure the breakfast staff can handle it." Maureen picked up the briefcase, opening it on her lap. "You realize, don't you, that Haven House Inn can't survive much longer under the current system of management?"

"Are you insinuating that I'm not doing my job?" Elizabeth, scowling, raised her voice.

"I'm not insinuating anything." Maureen pulled the spreadsheet from the briefcase, placing it on the desk. "I'm pointing out that a system that may have been acceptable in the past isn't working anymore." She pointed to the bottom of the page. "We're very nearly out of money. How did you plan to keep operating?"

"I'd planned on the place being sold," Elizabeth almost snarled. "It's ready to fall down around our ears. What are *you* planning to do about it? I've heard that you're not rich, like the old woman was."

"I'm not rich," Maureen admitted. "I plan to operate it at a profit."

Elizabeth laughed, a short un-funny laugh. "Fat chance of that happening. What are you going to do? Raise the rates on the old dump?"

"Absolutely." Maureen knew she sounded a lot more confident than she felt." I'll raise the rates and I'll give the guests their money's worth—starting with your restaurant. Elizabeth's."

Another burst of bitter laughter. "My restaurant? It wasn't even named for me. Penelope named it after the queen of England back in 1970. I answered a want ad for a manager fifteen years ago. Been here ever since. There used to be a big picture on the wall of Queen Elizabeth at her coronation. I took it down and bought the neon sign. There was always plenty of money. Penelope trusted me to do whatever I wanted to with the place. So I did." Maureen thought of her lucky Bermuda coin. *Queen Elizabeth again?*

"I see. As I said, we'll be making some changes. I asked you yesterday to get the figures together for the Halloween advertising you'd planned. May I see them?"

Elizabeth actually pouted as she pulled a sheet of paper from her desk drawer and slapped it onto the desktop. "Here. This is the best I could do with such short notice."

Maureen couldn't stifle the sharp intake of breath the bottom line produced. "You can't be serious!"

"I've already signed a contract for a full page with the newspaper." Elizabeth's smirk was back.

"All right. We'll honor it." Maureen pushed the paper back across the desk. "But the inn is *not* going to pick up the tab for the whole town's Halloween celebration. We'll call the other businesses today and offer them the opportunity to have their names included in a full-page co-op Halloween advertisement. Then we'll divide the cost among all of the participants."

"Today?"

"Don't worry about it. I'll do half the list."

"What about the radio and TV?"

"I'm sure they all do community service spots. I'll send releases to all the local media. Won't cost a dime. Now about the dining room . . ."

"There's nothing wrong with the way I run the dining room." The woman stood, looking down at Maureen. "Penelope loved the way I ran the dining room. She loved *me*. She should have left the whole damned old place to me."

Maureen spoke slowly. Calmly. "We need to get hold of the expenses. For instance, we're paying retail for too much of the food. Together, you and I can make this work. Sit down please." Elizabeth sat.

Below the edge of the desk Maureen had fingers on both hands crossed.

Chapter 21

One quick phone call to the Haven Chamber of Commerce provided Maureen with a list of addresses, e-mails, and phone numbers for most of the businesses along Beach Boulevard. She'd estimated that a full page with Halloween art could easily feature forty sponsors, including the inn. Since Elizabeth already knew everybody in town, and was friendly with many, the idea of the co-op ad went well. By lunchtime Elizabeth had signed up thirty of them while Maureen managed to sell the remaining ten—including the bookshop, a thrift store, the L&M Bar, and the law office of Jackson, Nathan and Peters. She hoped the Halloween weekend celebration would attract enough diners—and maybe even a few lodgers—to the Haven House Inn to pay for their share of the ad.

"So far, so good," Maureen told Finn as she attached his leash for a somewhat overdue walk. "And Elizabeth might turn out to be not so bad after all." The cats had already left the suite. The animals' food dishes had been picked up and washed, so one of the housekeepers must have dropped in. "I think I'll get a 'Do Not Disturb' sign," she said. "I'm not crazy about people wandering in and out of here all the time."

"Woof," Finn agreed. The golden tugged her toward the

stairs, which he had decided he preferred to the elevator. "I sold one of the co-op ads to a Mr. Crenshaw at the Second Glance thrift store," Maureen said. "Let's stop by there and see if they have one of those push bells for Lorna." They left the building via the side door, avoiding the lobby and the porch. She dropped her voice, even though there was no one nearby. "Can you believe that, Finn? I'm going shopping for a gift for a ghost."

A police car was parked in front of the inn. *Is Hubbard back again?* she wondered. *I hope he'll finish up with this investigation before Halloween weekend. Police running around the place could put a damper on everything.* She glanced up at the far end of the porch. The sawhorses with the UNDER REPAIR sign were still there. So was a uniformed cop. She walked a little faster, not looking back. *If they want to talk to me again, they'll just have to wait.*

Finn made the necessary stops along the way to the Second Glance. Maureen had always liked thrift stores, and it occurred to her that this one might be a likely spot to get rid of some of Penelope Josephine Gray's massive hoard. A sign on the side of the lavender-painted storefront announced that all proceeds went to a local charity that aided abuse victims. A bell over the door jingled when she opened it. "Hello!" she called. "Mr. Crenshaw? I'm Maureen Doherty. We talked earlier today about the Halloween newspaper ad. Are dogs allowed in here?"

A man stepped from between merchandise-crowded aisles. "Hello, Ms. Doherty. I'd rather he waited outside," he said. "We have a store cat. There's an old hitching post around to the side. You can hitch him up there and I'll let you in the back door."

"Okay, I don't think he'll mind." Maureen walked around the lavender building and looped Finn's leash over what certainly appeared to be a straight-out-of-*Gunsmoke* old western hitching post. "Be right back, boy," she promised. Second

Glance did indeed have a selection of push bells. She chose the most elaborate one, with incised carvings on its bronze-colored surface, and Mr. Crenshaw welcomed the idea of accepting whatever good used merchandise Maureen might want to contribute. "It's tax deductible, you know," he said, "and by the way, I'm an accredited appraiser, so it there are any antiques or other items of value I can give you a pretty good estimate of what they're worth."

"Perfect," she said as he wrapped her purchase. "Where's your cat? I've already met Erle Stanley Gardner over at the bookshop, and I've recently acquired two of my own."

"Yes. I'd heard that you inherited Ms. Gray's cats along with the inn." Once again, Maureen wondered if everyone in Haven knew all of her business. "But you asked about Petunia. She's around here somewhere. She sleeps most of the day. The darn ghost keeps her awake most of the night."

"Ghost?"

"Oh sure. Most of the Haven ghosts are pretty quiet, but mine fancies herself an opera singer. Bursts into song around midnight. I stay away from here once it gets dark. Not really fond of opera. The shops on either side of mine aren't open at night either, so she's not really bothering anybody." He looked around, then whispered, "She's not very good."

"I'm confused," Maureen said. "You say 'most of the Haven ghosts.' I guess that means there are—uh—rather a lot of them in the neighborhood?"

"Oh dear, no. It's not as if *everybody* gets to have one. No indeed. None of the newer places have any as far as I know, and even some of the old-timers are ghostless. Poor Mrs. Patterson over at the bookstore does everything she can to attract one, but so far, no dice."

"I see," Maureen said, though of course she didn't. "I'm planning to stop at her shop today. She sems very pleasant."

"She is that. The poor soul tries so hard to attract her late husband to visit her. Bakes his favorite cookies every morning, I understand."

"I've had the cookies. They're really good. She could probably sell them." Maureen accepted her wrapped bell. "Thank you, Mr. Crenshaw, for placing your Halloween ad. Let's hope for a successful weekend."

"I'm sure it will be. It always is. I'll let you out the side door. Your doggy probably misses you."

Maureen and Finn emerged from beside the lavender building and approached the crosswalk leading to the opposite side of Beach Boulevard and the bookshop. The mention of the late Mr. Patterson's favorite cookies reminded her that she'd totally skipped breakfast. A few of those shortbread sweets would be most welcome. A police car rolled to a stop just as she stepped off the curb, a uniformed officer at the wheel. Frank Hubbard leaned out of the open passenger window.

"Are you deliberately avoiding me, Ms. Doherty?"

"Of course not. Is there something wrong at the inn?"

"I don't know. Is there? I presume you're heading back there now?"

"I'm going to stop at the bookshop first," Maureen explained. "It shouldn't take long."

"I'm sure you can do that later," he spoke firmly. "You seem to have developed a habit of slipping out through side doors and ducking behind buildings whenever you see a patrol car. We need to talk."

"Of course. We'll head for home right now. Come on, Finn." She reversed direction. The patrol car made a U-turn and cruised slowly along beside her—all the way back to the inn.

It was disconcerting. Slipping out the side door? Ducking behind buildings? What was the man talking about? Maureen had used the side door to avoid the lobby and the rocking-chair quartet. Ducking behind buildings? Did he mean tying Finn to the hitching post beside the thrift store?

"I think Officer Hubbard has a naturally suspicious nature," she told Finn. "I suppose that's part of his job, but we'll set him straight, won't we?" This time she used the front stairway, her package containing Lorna's bell in one hand, fully aware that those observing her couldn't help noticing that she'd acquired a rolling police escort. Head high, she climbed the steps, moving between the growing accumulation of lighted jack-o'-lanterns. There were only a few people on the porch. Did that mean there'd been more checkouts since morning? Probably. She was going to have to speed up her efforts if she was going to be able to save the place.

She reached the top of the stairs and turned in time to see Frank Hubbard get out of the patrol car. Stepping over the grinning pumpkins, he followed, then moved past her, holding open the green front door to the lobby.

"After you, Ms. Doherty," he said.

Chapter 22

"We need to have a talk, Ms. Doherty," Hubbard said. "Could you put that dog away somewhere?"

"I'll just run up and put him in my apartment," she said. "I'll be right back."

"Don't leave the building," Hubbard said. "I'll wait right here for you." He sat in one of the white wicker chairs. Without acknowledging the order, she and Finn headed for the stairs. She noted once again that there was no one manning the check-in desk.

"He's sure in a snit about something, Finn," she said. "I hope whatever it is doesn't take long." She unclipped the leash and pushed the dog quite unceremoniously into the living room. The cats weren't in evidence. "I'll be back as soon as I can."

She took the elevator back down to the first floor. Hubbard stood when she entered the lobby. "I've already arranged with Elizabeth to use her office," he said. "We'll just need to go into the dining room for a moment to pick up the key. If you'll kindly follow me?" He pushed the louvred doors open. Maureen followed.

Elizabeth, in red apron with menus in hand, hurried toward them. "Oh, it's only you two. I thought for a minute you were late lunch customers." She waved a menu toward the nearly empty room. "We could use a few."

"Couldn't we have our talk at one of the tables, Officer?" Maureen asked. "I was so busy I skipped breakfast today and I'm truly hungry. Won't you join me for lunch?"

"I can't accept any gratuities," Hubbard said, frowning.

Elizabeth tapped his arm with a plastic-covered menu. "Oh, Frank, knock it off. You and all the Haven cops get free coffee and doughnuts here all the time. Sit at a table near the front so it won't look so deserted in here."

Maureen watched Hubbard's expression. *I'm all in favor of supporting law enforcement,* she thought, *but how much free food are we handing out every day to the good citizens of Haven?*

"Well, okay, Liz. But we'll sit over there in the back." Hubbard pointed. "This is official police business."

"Fine." Elizabeth led the way to the table he'd indicated. "Need menus?" She waved one in their direction.

"No thanks." Maureen put her package on the empty chair beside her, facing Hubbard across the round table. "I'm just going to have a chicken salad sandwich and a cup of coffee."

"Ham and cheese for me, with coffee," the officer said. "And potato chips and a pickle."

Elizabeth motioned for waitress Shelly. "She'll take your orders. I have enough to do around here without waiting tables." She fast-walked back to her usual position beside the dining room entrance, where she'd be able to hear the push bell in the lobby.

"I'd like to get something straight, Officer," Maureen began. "I don't know exactly what you meant when you said I was ducking you, but that's simply not true."

"Really?" He sounded doubtful. "Never mind that for now. I have a few questions about the contents of your medicine cabinet."

Shelly appeared at Hubbard's elbow. "You want to order something?" They each repeated their orders, with Maureen adding the pickles and chips to hers. The coffees arrived almost immediately. Maureen slowly added cream to hers and sipped thoughtfully—buying her a few moments to try to process what he'd just said.

He had questions about the contents of her medicine cabinet?

It's not even really my *medicine cabinet,* she thought. *At least, not yet. It's still full of Penelope Josephine Gray's stuff. Things I've never used. Never even touched.*

She didn't volunteer any further comment. He didn't either. They waited for their sandwiches, neither one speaking until the plates had been delivered and the waitress had moved a good distance away from their table. Maureen nibbled on her sandwich. Didn't touch her chips or pickle. Maybe she wasn't as hungry as she'd thought she was. She sipped her coffee.

Frank Hubbard had eaten most of his sandwich before he broke the uncomfortable silence. "I ran a check on those medicine bottles."

"Ms. Gray's medicine bottles," Maureen said.

"Yes. They had her name on them. One contained cough medicine. It had been prescribed several months ago. It was partly full. Her fingerprints are on it." He answered her unasked question, "We have a record of Ms. Gray's fingerprints because the inn has a liquor license. If the license gets transferred to you, we'll need yours too."

"Of course."

"The other bottle contained her heart medicine. Digitalis capsules. The same drug that poisoned Mr. Wilson."

"Yes. I know."

"That was a new prescription. Yet the bottle was half-empty."

"You believe Ms. Gray's medicine was used to kill Mr. Wilson."

"Yes. Actually, we're sure of it. And strangely enough, there were *no* prints at all on that bottle. There should have been some. Ms. Gray's or even the pharmacist's." His eyes were focused on Maureen's face. "But someone had wiped that bottle clean. A good number of those pills wound up in Mr. Wilson's system. Do you have any idea how that could have happened, Ms. Doherty?"

"Are you seriously suggesting that I could have—would have—poisoned a man I'd never even met?"

"I'm not suggesting anything. I told you before. I collect evidence. The contents of a medicine bottle I found in your bathroom were used to kill a man. That is evidence. My job is to ask questions about it. You discovered the body. You admitted to touching the body. When we arrived the body was on the floor at your feet, although the man was sitting in the chair earlier. There are several witnesses to that fact. Do you have any idea how *that*—"

Maureen pushed the remains of her lunch away. "I think I would like to talk to my lawyer before I answer any of your questions, Officer Hubbard."

"Of course." He stood. "We'll talk more later. She watched as he left the room, then reached for her phone.

"Hello? . . . Lawrence Jackson, please. This is Maureen Doherty and I think I have a problem."

Chapter 23

"Yes, Ms. Doherty? . . . Larry Jackson. What seems to be the problem? Somebody trying to hold the inn liable for that man's death?"

"Not exactly." Maureen tried to keep her voice level. "Somebody seems to think it's possible that *I'm* responsible. Me. Personally."

"I don't understand."

"I don't either. I just had a talk with Officer Hubbard. He seems to believe that the poison that killed Mr. Wilson came from the medicine cabinet in *my* bathroom." She attempted to give the attorney a brief version of what had just transpired. "Besides all that," she finished, "he thinks I've been trying to hide from the police. That I've been 'ducking behind buildings,' 'slipping out through side doors.' "

"Um—were you?"

"Of course not. Listen. Are you in your office? Can I see you now?" She saw Shelly approaching. "I can't talk where I am right now."

"Yes. I'll be here for the next half hour or so. Can you come right over?"

"On my way." She put the phone in her purse, picked up her package, and left an appropriate tip on the table.

Elizabeth was still at her menu-dispensing station. "Everything all right, Maureen?" she asked.

"Sure. Fine. Just remembered an appointment. Gotta rush." She held the package toward the woman. "Can I leave this with you? I'll pick it up later. It's nothing important."

"Of course. I'll put it in my office."

"Thanks." She hurried out the front door, dismissed the inquisitive quartet with a brief wave and a have-a-nice-day, and started down the boulevard toward the beach. There was a uniformed policeman at the end of the porch and she made it a point to wave and smile as she passed—just in case anyone might think she was trying to avoid him.

Larry Jackson greeted her at the door of the red-roofed white cottage housing the law firm of Jackson, Nathan and Peters. "You sounded very concerned on the phone." He ushered her into his office. "Please tell me exactly what's going on."

She began again, describing as best she could recall what Hubbard had said about the digitalis bottle—without any fingerprints.

He took notes, nodding once or twice, then interrupted. "Did the officer actually *accuse* you of the crime?"

"No, sir. He didn't. But his questions certainly pointed that way."

"I think you may need to talk with my associate Ms. Nathan. Nora handles our—um—criminal law cases."

"Criminal?" Maureen repeated the word. "*Criminal!* I'm not a criminal!" She felt hot tears welling up. "I'm nobody. I'm a has-been ready-to-wear buyer. How could this be happening?"

Jackson reached for an intercom button. "Nora? . . . Could you come in here for a minute?" His kind brown eyes showed concern. "Now, now, Ms. Doherty. Don't cry. Please?"

Nora Nathan was a tall, slim woman. Steel-gray hair was

fashioned in a no-nonsense French twist. Maureen immediately recognized the two-piece black business skirt-suit—an A-line Anne Klein with single-button jacket. Well made, not too expensive but not cheap, Maureen had had a similar one in blue in last fall's wardrobe. She'd given it away before she'd left Massachusetts

Larry Jackson discreetly exited the room, leaving the two women alone.

Attorney Nathan practically exuded confidence. She sat beside Maureen. "What's going on?"

Once again, Maureen explained her situation, this time dry-eyed, with growing irritation. She was innocent of any involvement in Conrad Wilson's death and she felt a new confidence that she'd come to exactly the right place for help in proving it.

"I know Frank Hubbard," Nora said when Maureen had finished. "We've butted heads before. He's an honest enough cop, but when he gets an idea in his head he's like a bulldog. We can handle it."

"That makes me feel better, but I have to ask—are you awfully expensive?"

"Relatively, but Ms. Gray has our firm on an annual retainer. Other than some possible court costs, you're good with us until the end of the year. I'll get in touch with Hubbard and see what he's got." She cocked her head to one side. "Is there any reason why you might have wanted Mr. Wilson dead?"

"None," Maureen said. "I'd never even seen him before the night he died."

"Do you know of anybody else who might have wanted him dead?"

"Well, there are a lot of people who didn't like him doing his 'ghost hunting' around Haven. He called himself a 'psychic detective.' "

"I read about him in the paper. Quite well known in the ghost business, apparently," Nora said. "How do you feel about ghosts?"

"Until recently, I'd never given the topic much thought," Maureen admitted. "But people in Haven seem to talk about them quite a bit. Strange, isn't it?"

Nora Nathan shrugged well-tailored shoulders. "You get used to it."

Maureen had no ready answer for that. *I wonder if this neat little red-roofed cottage has one*, she thought. She wouldn't have been a bit surprised if it did.

"Will you call me soon, and let me know what I should do next?" she asked. "Mr. Jackson has my number and I guess you know where I live."

"Sure do. You planning to sell the old place anytime soon?"

"No. I'm trying to figure out how to make it profitable."

"No kidding?" Nora stood, and offered her hand. "Good luck with that. We'll be in touch soon. Here's my card." They shook hands and as she left the building Maureen felt better than she had since her morning run on the beach—which seemed as though it had been a very long time ago.

There was still time to drop in on Aster Patterson at the bookstore, to thank her for participating in the Halloween ad. The bell over the door jangled when she entered. "Hello, Aster?" she called. "Hello!"

"Just feeding the fish," came the answer. "Be right with you."

Maureen studied a display of Halloween-themed books on a round table, where a vintage papier-mâché witch candy bucket filled with foil-wrapped candy Kisses provided an appropriately scary centerpiece.

"No hurry. It's Maureen Doherty from the inn. I'm just admiring your Halloween table."

Aster popped her head out from between the aisles, holding a pumpkin mask over her face. "Boo!" she said. "Did I scare you?"

"Maybe a little bit." Maureen smiled. "That's a great old mask."

"Isn't it? It came from my late husband Peter's family. He loved Halloween. He saved some of the old decorations from when he was a kid." She waved the mask. "Come on out to the kitchen. I must have been thinking of you today. I've made some of that Irish Breakfast Tea. It's not just for breakfast, you know. I have cookies too."

Maureen followed the sound of Aster's flapping rain boots, pausing to admire the angelfish, darting here and there in their tank, chasing bits of floating fish food. Once again, Aster's kitchen table held the flower-sprigged china and the expected plate of shortbread cookies. This time, though, each round cookie was frosted in orange and bore a jack-o'-lantern face, "These are almost too cute to eat," Maureen said. "Do you ever sell your cookies? I could use a few dozen of these for the inn."

"I'll think about that," Aster said. "Indeed, I will. You being Irish and all, you probably know the jack-o'-lanterns originated in Ireland—only they used a carved turnip with a hot coal glowing inside." Not waiting for an answer, she poured tea from the flower-sprigged pot, and popped one lump of sugar into Maureen's cup. "There now. This'll make you feel all better."

"What makes you think I'm not feeling well?" Maureen put one hand to her forehead. "Do I look ill?"

"Not at all. Here, darling, have a cookie." Aster pushed the plate toward her. "No, I meant that thing about the police nosing around in your apartment."

"The police? Who said that?"

"Don't remember who said it exactly. I heard it down at the Quic-Shop market when I picked up the food coloring for my frosting. They said the cops were searching for something up in Penelope's room—I mean *your* room." She made a "tsk-tsk" sound. "That would upset anybody."

"Yes, it would." Maureen accepted the cookie. "But to tell the truth, it upsets me more that it's already a topic of conversation at the Quic-Shop. I've never even been in the place."

"Hard to keep a secret in Haven," Aster said. "Like the man said, 'the walls have ears.' "

"Not just ears," Maureen grumbled. "Mouths too. But somebody around here is keeping a big secret. Like, who killed Conrad Wilson? Have you heard any rumors about that?"

"Sure. Plenty. But it's like one of those Agatha Christie mysteries. Everybody in the story's got a reason to want a certain person dead, but you don't know 'til the last page who done it." Aster helped herself to a cookie. "Then you smack yourself on the head and say, 'Why didn't I see that coming?' "

"I hope the last page shows up pretty soon," Maureen said. "My head is already almost smacked clean off. You know everybody around here. Who's *your* top suspect?"

"My top suspect? Of course, I'm no Agatha Christie—even though I've read all of her books more than once—but my top suspect would be someone *not* from around here."

"Not?"

"Not," Aster declared. "At first I thought it might be Sam. Nasty temper that one. But no. The ghost hunter wasn't from here, and it doesn't seem to me that he was here long enough to make anybody local mad enough to kill him."

"That's true," Maureen reasoned. "And it took some time and planning to do it the way it looks like it was done."

"You mean with the poison out of Penelope's prescription?"

"Well, when you put it that way, yes. Did that information come from Quic-Shop too? About the medicine bottle?"

Maureen realized that she'd stopped being surprised at the accuracy of the Haven rumor mill.

"No. I heard that one from my cousin Ernie, the taxi driver. He overheard a fare he'd picked up at the inn talking on their cell phone on the way to Tampa International."

"I wonder if he'd remember who that was," Maureen said. "Would you ask him?"

"Oh, I'm not sure I could do that. Ernie's not one for gossip." Aster shook her head. "Not at all."

"But you just said—"

"Never mind about all that, dear. More tea?" Maureen held up her cup and Aster filled it, plopping in a single sugar cube. A tiny bit of tea splashed onto the tabletop. Maureen reached for a paper napkin and wiped the spill without being asked, pretending not to notice how quickly Aster had clammed up.

Chapter 24

Maureen left the bookshop with one of Sherry Harris's Sarah Winston Garage Sale mysteries, along with three decorated shortbread cookies "for later." She gave a gentle tap on the window where Erle Stanley Gardner lay dozing alongside a selection of recent Stephen King and Dean Koontz novels and a candy bucket in the shape of a particularly horrific bat. The cat acknowledged her greeting by briefly opening one eye.

The boulevard seemed a little busier to Maureen as she walked along the brick sidewalk, stopping here and there to examine a window display or read a poster. Many of the metered parking spaces were filled and most of the people she saw were carrying packages—a good sign that they were buying, not just looking. She quickened her step as she approached the inn. What could she do right now to take advantage of this increase in traffic—however small it might be?

By the time she'd reached the very edge of her property, she'd designed the poster she'd place at the foot of the stairs. It would proclaim TONIGHT'S DINNER SPECIAL. No matter what Elizabeth had planned for the evening meal, it was about to become "special." Once again, Maureen hurried past the porch sitters with merely a few smiles, an all-encompassing wave or two, and she was in the lobby. Again, the reception desk was unmanned. "Elizabeth!" she called quietly, pushing the louvred dining room doors open.

"I'm right here, for heaven's sake. You don't have to shout." The woman stood just inside the doors. "What do you want?"

"Do we have a dinner special planned for tonight?" Maureen was hopeful. "Something really good?"

"Everything on our menu is good," Elizabeth said. "Let me see. Tonight we have pot roast with fall vegetables. Why?"

"I was thinking of making a few posters to post around the neighborhood. A little last-minute advertising. Can we dress it up a little? Make it a little more appealing somehow?"

"You can talk to Ted about it, I guess. He's running between the kitchen and the bar right now, keeping an eye on both."

"Thanks. I will." Maureen headed for the bar where Ted, in chef's white jacket instead of bartender's red vest, shook a hammered-aluminum cocktail shaker, then poured a drink for one lone bar customer.

"Oh, hello, Jake," she said, recognizing the newspaper reporter and sliding into the seat beside him. "Are you still working on that same story?"

"I sure am, Ms. Doherty," he said. "Just can't seem to let it go."

"This guy's in here every day, Ms. Doherty. Bugging my customers with questions." Ted smiled as he spoke. "He's good at his job, though. Like a big old bulldog."

A *bulldog*, Maureen thought. That's what Nora Nathan had said about Officer Hubbard.

"Ted, I need to talk to you about tonight's pot roast," she said.

"Bor-ing," Jake said, drawing the word out. "Let's talk about murder instead."

"Sorry, Jake," Maureen insisted. "It may be boring, but it's business—and a juicy pot roast is better for business than a juicy murder."

"Maybe," Jake said. "Mind if I listen in?"

"I don't mind," she said. "You, Ted?"

"Not a bit. Can I get you a drink, Ms. Doherty?'

"A little early, for me," she said. "Maybe a Shirley Temple?"

"Shirley Temple's dead, isn't she?" Jake interrupted. "Why is a drink named after a dead kid star anyway?"

"Hardly anybody orders them anymore." Ted put ice cubes into a collins glass. "Kids these days mostly get Coke or root beer or Dr Pepper." He poured a bright red stream of grenadine over the ice. "Been around for years. The name just stuck. There's no booze in it, but it looks like a regular cocktail. People used to order them for their kids so they'd feel grown-up, I guess." Ted smiled at Maureen. "And sometimes grown-ups who remember those days order them because they taste good. Matter of fact, Ms. Gray used to like them." He added 7UP and ginger ale, topping the drink off with three cherries on a sword-shaped cocktail pick. "There you go, Ms. Doherty. Now about that pot roast—"

Jake interrupted again. A common trait in his line of work, Maureen supposed. "You used grenadine in that killer drink you made for the dead guy, right?"

"The Celebration Libation. Right. Grenadine for color and sweetness. Same as in the Shirley Temple."

"Is that the same bottle you used on the dead guy's drink?"

Ted lifted the bottle so that the ceiling lights illuminated the crimson contents. "This bottle? No. The cops took that one. We had to get a new one."

"So there was poison in the first bottle? The one you used in his drink?"

"Nope. At least, they said there wasn't. Now, about that pot roast." Ted faced Maureen. "It's in the big slow cooker along with all the vegetables right now. Enough for about a dozen servings. I always make extra because we can freeze whatever's left over and use it for lunch later."

"If we advertise it as a special, what might go with it?"

"Mom's baking powder biscuits? Molly's special apple pie and ice cream for dessert?"

"Why is Molly's apple pie special?" Maureen asked.

"She puts raisins in it along with the apples, and some kind of frosting on the top. Everybody loves it."

"Sounds good. How much does it cost us to put that meal together?"

"Cost?" Ted returned the grenadine bottle to its place on the mirrored shelf behind the bar. "Elizabeth never asks about cost, but I could probably give you a pretty close estimate."

"Would you do that? Thanks. I'm going to make up a few posters and some flyers. See if we can attract some extra dinner business tonight. But maybe twelve servings aren't enough."

Ted was already at work with paper and pencil. "Of course, we paid too much for the meat, and we could have bought the onions and carrots locally, but never mind." He stopped muttering to himself and looked up at Maureen. "There are enough frozen leftovers to make up another dozen. If it starts to look like we need more I can do the same recipe real fast in the pressure cooker. We always keep a couple of Molly's apple pies in the freezer along with plenty of ice cream. So, let's say each serving will run us about six dollars."

"So we can feature it at twelve-ninety-five for the whole deal, and most people will order drinks too. Not bad. Thanks, Ted. If this works at all, I'm thinking we might do it every night. Maybe you can brainstorm some ideas." She sipped the Shirley Temple. "How about you, Jake? Sound good? Want to bring a date for dinner tonight?"

"I might just do that," he said. "Maybe the killer will re-turn to the scene of the crime."

"Could be," she agreed. "Ted, when did you evolve from bartender to chef anyway?"

"It was the other way around," he said. "I was a cook long before I learned to tend bar. My mom had a little seafood restaurant down by the Long Pier. I've been messing around with food since I was about eight."

"No kidding? And the restaurant was near where the char-ter boats tie up? Is it still there?"

"Nope. Long gone. Just condos over that way now."

"Is that where you were headed when I saw you on the beach this morning?"

"Yeah. Good memories."

"Me too. I caught my very first Florida fish off one of those charter boats when I was a kid."

"No way. We used to cook the catches for tourists all the time. Did you have yours cooked? Maybe I fried it for you—when *I* was a kid."

"You know something?" Maureen leaned back in her seat. "That's actually quite possible. We *did* have it fried at a restaurant—and it was delicious."

Jake waved his glass, signaling Ted for a refill. "Nice trip down memory lane, you two, but back to important stuff—like a recent murder in this very room, quite possibly at this very bar, death by poison in a fancy drink."

"The police confiscated all of the ingredients in that drink," Maureen said. "There was no poison in any of it."

Jake caught Maureen's eye in the mirror, and pointed a finger at her image there. "But, Ms. Doherty, there *was*, I understand, some poison found in *your* apartment."

"Where'd you hear that, Jake? Quic-Shop? Not the most reliable of sources." Maureen knew her tone was angry. She didn't care. "I hope you're not planning to put that in print."

Jake's smile was sheepish. "It was at Quic-Shop, How'd you know? Anyway, the editor said it was 'an unsubstantiated rumor.' I plan to bug the police about it, though—unless you want to talk about it now."

Maureen took a last sip of the Shirley Temple. "No comment, Jake. Ted, I'll get to work on the publicity for tonight's special."

"Okay, Ms. Doherty, and I'll start thinking about tomorrow's."

Chapter 25

It didn't take Maureen long to pull together the components of the poster she'd visualized. Bartlett's of Boston had featured a top-floor restaurant and a first-floor food market. She still had computer access to print advertising archives for both venues. Photos of pot roast dinners were readily available. The same was true of apple pie and ice cream. Large type proclaimed: TONIGHT'S DINNER SPECIAL AT THE HAVEN HOUSE INN FROM 6 TO 9 P.M.! Menu description, price, time, address, and phone number for reservations completed the text. She added a few artwork pumpkins and witches and printed out two dozen eleven-by-seventeen copies, then e-mailed one to the Chamber of Commerce with a request that they share it with their membership.

"Post these around town," she instructed George and Sam. "Some of the shop owners might agree to put them in their show windows. Otherwise tack them to telephone poles, message boards, wherever you think they'll get noticed. And," she added, "be sure to put one at the Quic-Shop." She framed a poster for display on an easel in front of the dining room and prepared smaller versions of the menu for each table.

"When you said 'last-minute' you weren't kidding. We've just finished cleaning up after lunch." Elizabeth picked up one of the table menus. "You really think these will pull people in on such short notice?"

"Worth a try," Maureen said. "As far as 'dinner out' goes in Haven, except for the hot dog stand down near the beach, we're the only game in town. Otherwise, people head for St. Pete. I'm thinking we could do a special *every* night. Why not?"

Elizabeth tossed the paper onto the table. "I guess I won't need any extra serving help for tonight anyway. You'll have to talk to Ted about any future specials."

"He's already on it," Maureen said. "I'll check with you on whatever we come up with. I'm going to take Finn out for a quick walk. We'll see how George and Sam are doing with sharing our posters around Haven."

"Sure. Good luck with that," Elizabeth said, "and I'm going to need George back pretty soon to do some shopping for tomorrow's breakfast. We're almost out of bacon and English muffins."

Unbelievable, Maureen thought. *There should be plenty of both in the freezer.*

"Let's schedule a meeting tomorrow morning to set up a better grocery-buying system," she suggested, "so that we don't run out of basics."

"I'll try to fit it in," Elizabeth said. "Wait a minute. I'll get your package. It's right here in the tablecloth cabinet. You said it was nothing important."

"That's right," Maureen agreed, accepting the bag, which had clearly been opened, its tissue paper inner wrapping sticking out from the top. "Thank you."

As soon as she stepped out of the elevator on the third floor, she heard Finn's welcoming "woofs." She hurried toward the door. "Poor dog," she said aloud, "I'm coming. Sorry I stayed away so long."

"Woof woof," came the reply. When Maureen pulled the door open she was greeted by Finn and both cats. Finn, with happy leaps and rug rolls, the cats with purr-full figure eights around her ankles. She put the paper bag on the floor, responding to the remarkable display of affection with pats and rubs and loving words. "Thank you, guys," she said. "I love you too, but I wonder what brought on such a demonstration."

"I told them you might be having a bad day." Lorna's voice preceded her appearance this time. She popped into view barefoot, wearing a sarong, blond bob disguised with a sleek, long-haired black wig, "We wanted to make you feel better about that cop finding the poison in the bathroom."

"It worked," Maureen said. "I do feel better about that. I have a lawyer working on it and I think I'm making some progress in my plans to make this old place pay for itself." She moved closer to Lorna, inspecting the sarong and wig. "This is a different look for you." She realized, as she spoke, that this sounded like a normal conversation between girl-friends. *I'm talking fashion with a dead movie star who haunts the inn that was left to me by a woman I never heard of,* she thought. *Is this my new normal?*

Lorna twirled. "I know. I thought you'd get a kick out of it. *The New Adventures of Tarzan.* Nineteen thirty-five. I played an island girl. We made it in Guatemala." She tapped a Guatemala sticker on the nearby trunk. "It was a twelve-part serial movie. This outfit's in there."

"I like hearing about your movie career," Maureen said. "And look, I bought something for you." She picked up the bag. "Shall I unwrap it for you?"

"Yes, please." Lorna held up her hands. "I don't want to mess up my nails. Actually, I'm not too good at picking things up. I kind of envy those kid ghosts who can throw things around."

"Poltergeists." Maureen smiled. "I'm glad you don't do that. Here. I found a new bell for you." She placed it on the desk.

Lorna did the hand-clapping move she did so well. "It's so pretty. First present I've had in years." She pointed a tentative finger and gently touched the push button at the top of the bell. The resulting *ding* brought a big smile. "Thanks, Maureen. I'll enjoy ringing it." She sat on the floor beside Finn. "Now tell us about your plans for the inn." The gray cat looked from Maureen to Lorna, then walked through Lorna and climbed onto the cat tower. Bogie took a seat on the windowsill, looking out at the oak tree. "I guess the cats aren't interested, but Finn and I are, aren't we, Finn?"

Finn gave an enthusiastic "woof."

"Plans aren't really formed yet." Maureen sat on the blue couch. "I mean they're just scattered thoughts—like I might do this, I might do that. You see, time is short before Ms. Gray's money runs out. I have to figure out how to make the inn pay for itself or I'm afraid I'll have to sell it. And I guess you know what that means."

"No. What exactly does that mean?" Lorna asked.

"My lawyer says it means a 'teardown.' It means the land the inn is on is worth more than the inn itself. He says it might be condos or even a fast-food place. I'd hate to see that happen."

Lorna wrapped her arms around Finn's neck. "They'd tear it down? Where would we go? Me and Billy and all the rest?"

"I don't know," Maureen said. "You seem to travel quite a lot. Could you go to Hollywood or maybe wherever you were born? I don't know how that works."

"It's true some of us travel around, but we each have a 'home place.' This place, this old inn, is my home place as much as the closet in suite twenty-seven is that guy's home place. Do you get it? Like the Babe and the vice president and Joe DiMaggio *visit* here, but they all have home places too." Lorna looked as if she might cry. "I don't want my home place to be a Burger King!"

"Joe DiMaggio comes here?" Maureen said. "You never told me that."

"I didn't? Yeah, he shows up every once in a while. Sometimes Marilyn comes with him."

"Marilyn? Marilyn Monroe?"

"Sure. They were here together back in nineteen sixty-one. All lovey-dovey. I remember. Ms. Gray even had a picture taken with them. It's in her album with all the others."

"All what others? I haven't seen any album."

"The movie stars. The famous people. She loved having her picture taken with them. But let's get back to talking about how you're going to save this place, please." Lorna sat beside Maureen on the blue couch, tossing long black hair over one shoulder. "You really do have to save this place. For me and the others."

"Those pictures might help a lot. Remember I told you my idea about figuring out which room Babe Ruth slept in, so we could call it the 'Babe Ruth Suite'? What if we could put a picture of the Babe with Ms. Gray in there? That would be a great sales tool." Maureen was excited. "Where did she keep the album? I can hardly wait to see it."

Lorna shook her head. "I haven't seen it since Ms. Gray died, now that you mention it. And there hasn't been anybody famous staying here for years. Last one I remember who was sort of famous was Buffalo Bob Smith. He stayed here back in the late nineteen-nineties. He even brought that little puppet with him. Howdy Doody. He was signing autographs at a collectibles show over in St. Petersburg."

"Do you think Elizabeth might know where the album is?"

"Maybe. She isn't too interested in historical stuff, if you know what I mean. She likes new things better."

Like white wicker furniture and neon signs and plastic pumpkins, Maureen thought. "I'll go downstairs and ask her," she said. "Come on, Finn, time for a walk."

The two hurried down the two flights to the first floor. Elizabeth was at the reception desk, the old-fashioned black telephone to one ear. She put a hand over the receiver and whispered, "We've started getting some reservations for tonight already. I sent Sam to the store to get another roast and some vegetables. Molly's out in the kitchen making more apple-raisin pies."

"Great," Maureen said, while thinking, *Sam's probably shopping at the Quic-Shop and paying double-retail. We'll stop that foolishness tomorrow.* She sat in one of the wicker chairs, waiting for Elizabeth to finish the phone call.

"Yes. Thank you," Elizabeth said to the caller. "We'll see you tonight. Six o'clock." She hung up, made a note in the open reservation book, and walked around the desk. "Did you need to see me, Maureen? As you can tell, I'm pretty busy. All this extra work, you know." The woman didn't bother to disguise an annoyed glare aimed at Finn.

"It'll just take a minute, Elizabeth. I understand that Ms. Gray kept a photo album with pictures of famous guests. I'd like to take a look at it. Do you happen to know where it is?"

"Lord, no. When Penelope died we had to drop everything and rush fix up the suite and the office for you. I told Gert to move the old woman's personal stuff to someplace else." Elizabeth closed the reservation book just as the telephone rang again. "I'm busy, Maureen. Ask Gert."

"I will." Maureen pointed to the phone. "Better get that. Probably another reservation for tonight." With a quick tug on Finn's leash, she headed for the front porch. Gert was there, in her usual rocking chair. George was there too, apparently back from his last-minute run for overpriced breakfast food.

"Hey, you two." Maureen sat in the chair usually reserved for Molly, confident that pie making topped porch rocking, financially speaking. "I'm glad you're both here. Thanks,

George, for getting those posters out so quickly. I have another request. Would you get together with Mr. Crenshaw down at the thrift store? He's offered to take a look at Penelope's hoard and to give us an estimate of what it's worth."

"Can do, Ms. Doherty. All the shop owners liked those posters." George scratched the back of Finn's neck. "I guess they figure after people tie on the old feedbag, they'll want to walk off the calories shopping."

"Let's hope so. Gert, I have a question for you."

George patted Gert's knee. "Now Gertie here, she loves answering questions. Even if she doesn't know the answer, she'll make one up for you. Right, Gertie?"

"Shut up, Georgie." Gert stopped rocking and focused bright eyes on Maureen. "What do you want to know, honey?"

"I'm looking for a photo album that belonged to Ms. Gray. It's supposed to have pictures in it of famous people who've stayed here over the years."

Gert bobbed her head up and down a couple of times. "Yep, seems to me I remember seeing a book like that around this old place somewhere." She folded her arms, leaning back in the chair, resumed rocking, watching Maureen's face.

"Do you think you could find it? It's kind of important."

Gert was silent, rocking, watching.

George interrupted, stage-whispering behind one hand, "She needs to know if you're willing to make it worth her while to remember."

"Oh, of course." Maureen reached for her wallet. Gert had seemed happy with the tip she'd been given for the good job she'd done on the apartment. Another twenty dollars added to that amount ought to make her even happier. Maureen folded the bills and pressed them into Gert's promptly outstretched hand.

Gert smiled, tucked the money into her ample bosom. "It's coming back to me now, dearie. There are a couple of those big black albums. Says 'Photos' in gold on the front of each one. Pictures of Ms. Gray with some old-time movie stars, ballplayers. Those the ones you're looking for?"

"Exactly." Maureen couldn't keep the excitement out of her voice. "Those are the ones. Can you find them for me?"

"Wouldn't be a bit surprised if I could," she said. "I put them in that fancy new office of yours. Suite twenty-seven."

Chapter 26

As she and Finn set out for their walk, Maureen was excited about the prospect of using the "famous visitors slept here" feature—complete with framed photos in the room—to promote the Haven House Inn. Gert, one of the very few people who'd dared venture into suite twenty-seven, had apparently added the black photo albums to the pile with similarly colored and shaped books—the guest registers—on the top shelf of the infamous bedroom closet.

With Nora Nathan looking into the medicine bottle problem—fortunately on retainer, courtesy of Maureen's late benefactor—and the first "dinner special" promotion already in the works, she dared to feel that she'd regained a bit of her missing self-confidence.

"We can do this, Finn," she told the golden as they passed by one of her posters, prominently displayed among T-shirts and beach bags, bathing suits and flip-flops, in the window of BeachyKeen Gifts. "Building up the dining room business is just the beginning. No reason we couldn't have a gift shop like this one on the premises—better than this one. I have ten years' experience in retail sales, for Pete's sake."

Finn's "woof" was unmistakably positive. "You're right. There's no end to what we can do with the old place." Maureen broke into a jog. "And there's no reason we'll *ever* need to depend on ghost hunters—or ghosts—to fill our rooms or our rocking chairs. I can hardly wait to get started. As soon as we get back, we're going up to my office and grab those photo albums, okay?"

Not waiting for an answering "woof," she thought about her recent tentative butternut-squash-soup-induced plans to invest her five-thousand-dollar bonus in new light-colored draperies for the dining room. "And we're going to redo the dining room too, okay?"

"Woof woof," Finn agreed. They'd reached the casino and she turned left, toward the Long Pier and the long-ago restaurant where Ted the bartender's mother had taught him to fry fresh-caught fish. "And another thing, Finn," she said. "I think tomorrow's dinner special might be 'fresh-caught native Gulf fish, fried or broiled, with sweet potato fries and Elizabeth's green goddess salad, and jack-o'-lantern frosted shortbread cookies and orange sherbet' for dessert."

She checked her watch. It was too late to contact one of the local restaurant wholesale suppliers to arrange for a delivery. Tomorrow morning for sure. If Ted was still around tonight she'd get with him to figure out quantities. She broke into a jog. "Let's hurry, Finn," she said. "I can hardly wait to get into those photo albums, and while I'm there I can grab some of those old Halloween decorations to use as centerpieces for the dining room tables." She didn't say it out loud, but she was looking forward to a meal-planning session with Ted too. That would have to wait until after the night's dinner hours. By then they might have a rough idea of quantities of ingredients they'd need.

When she and Finn reached the inn, both a little out of breath, she led him toward the side door, avoiding the trip across the porch and through the lobby. She hoped, as they made their way past the ice machine and into the rear corridor, that Officer Hubbard hadn't observed their less obvious choice of entrance. She didn't want to answer any more questions about her motives.

She and Finn used the back staircase up to the second floor and suite twenty-seven. There wasn't any other activity in the area, and as she unlocked the door and stepped inside the room she rubbed her arms, feeling a chill in the air. There was a thermometer on the heating/cooling element below the largest window. She bent to read it. The air conditioner was set at 78 degrees, though the digital readout said 65. Strange. She turned off the AC and removed Finn's leash. Shivering, he headed for the kneehole under her desk, while she walked around the row of plastic boxes and went straight for the bedroom closet. This time the closet door was closed.

She turned the glass knob and the door swung open easily. "So that's why it was ajar before," she muttered, noticing the dry cleaner's bag hanging just inside. "George must have put Penelope Gray 's Halloween costume in here and then left the door open." She cast a sidelong glance at the row of boxes. "Dent-free," she said. "What did I expect?" she scolded herself. "A ghostly butt print?" Impatient now, she stepped inside the closet, reached over her head for the stack of books on the top shelf. She lifted two books from the top of the pile, noted the gold lettering, and put the two guest registers on the floor. These were followed by six more. The pair of photo albums were at the bottom of the pile. Leaving the guest books on the closet floor, and the door open, she carried the albums—almost reverently—to her desk and switched on the gooseneck lamp.

The albums were the old-fashioned kind, similar to those she'd seen at her own grandmother's house in Massachusetts. These were bigger than Nana's had been but had black pages and the photos were held in place with little triangular stick-on corners. Someone, presumably Ms. Gray, had written notes in silver ink under each one. The first page held four deckle-edged black-and-white photos. They each showed three pretty women with beehive hair-dos. Two showed them in beach attire; in another they sat in rockers on the front porch of the inn. The last one showed them posed with a youthful Penelope Gray at one of the round tables in the dining room. The caption at the top of the page read: "The McGuire Sisters." *The McGuire Sisters?* Apparently they were famous enough to be recognized by their last name. Maureen tapped it into the computer. They'd been popular singing stars of the 1950s, according to Wikipedia. That established the general time period for album number one.

Page by page, Maureen leafed through the first album. Some of the faces she knew at once—Frank Sinatra, Lucille Ball. Others only had familiar names—Arthur Godfrey, Milton Berle. Most of the pictures were black and white, but as she neared the end of the pages there were more color shots.

By the time she closed the back cover, she'd already made plans for how the special room identifications would work. She'd have the best photos of the most famous guests blown up and framed. She'd pore over the guest books and figure out when each star of stage, screen, or ballpark had actually stayed at the Haven House Inn. There'd be wooden plaques on the doors to those rooms. "This will attract new guests for sure, Finn," she told the dog, who was now asleep on her right foot.

She wiggled her foot free, trying not to disturb the slumbering pet, carried the album back into the bedroom, and replaced all of the guest books on the top shelf. She also put the first album back onto the shelf but placed the remining one onto her desk. She'd have plenty of time the following day to study it. Now for the decorations. Lifting the cover from the bin marked: 1950, she had to smile at a grinning crescent-moon–shaped papier-mâché candy basket. A green Frankenstein monster bucket of the same material had bright yellow eyes, and a black cat in yowling posture was scary-cute.

"These are going to look so great on all the tables. Let's take them downstairs and show them to Ted and Elizabeth."

So much to do and not much time. There were still police officers lurking around every corner of the inn, trying to figure out who had killed Conrad Wilson. The newspapers and local television hadn't let up on the man's death either—still focusing attention on the writer's murder by poison and on the inn itself—and they all had sidebar information about the reputed ghosts. This wasn't good publicity. And Officer Hubbard's nosing around in her medicine cabinet wasn't a good look either.

"Maybe I can try to help Hubbard figure out who actually *did* kill the man, instead of just complaining about how wrong he is about everything," she said aloud. There was a soft "woof" from under the desk. "Maybe *I* could ask some questions around here. At least I won't get sidetracked by ghost stories. Maybe *I* can get some straight answers—not a lot of tap dancing around the point like Gert and Molly did when Jake tried to get them to talk about the murder. It was a good bet that they knew a lot more than they'd shared with the newspaperman.

"I've been acting as though the murder is none of my business, Finn," she said. "But it darned well is, isn't it? Heck, if I'm consulting a lawyer who specializes in criminal law and a cop is snooping around in my medicine cabinet, I had better treat it as if it's my business!"

Finn left his hiding place but didn't follow when she went back into the bedroom, firmly secured the closet, picked up the plastic bin of decorations, then returned and opened the door to the corridor. "Come on, boy. Let's go. It's still freezing in here. I'll take you home, then go downstairs and talk to Ted about food—and maybe ask a question or two about murder."

Chapter 27

The lobby was empty when Maureen arrived. She tucked the plastic bin under the reception desk and took a quick peek into the dining room. There was no doubt that her last-minute advertising blitz had paid off. Most of the round tables were occupied by at least a few patrons and some of the tables were full. *If a stack of posters and a handful of flyers can do this in a few hours, I can hardly wait to see what some* real *promotion will do for the old place.* From where she stood in the doorway she could see that Leo was behind the bar, and that Herbie and Shelly and two other servers were at work in the room.

"Hi, Ms. Doherty," Leo greeted her. "What'll it be?"

A glass of the house rosé, please, Leo," she said. "Nice to see some activity here, isn't it?"

"Sure is." He poured the wine. "Hope it keeps up. I can use the work. Want some popcorn with that?"

"Absolutely. I haven't eaten much of anything today." She glanced around the room once more. "Are the police still hanging around, asking questions?"

"They were here earlier." He passed the bowl of hot popcorn, drizzled with butter. "Still trying to figure out how the poison got into that guy's drink. They talked to Ted for a long time. Elizabeth was pissed about it. They had to call me in early. Like I said, though, I can use the work."

"They've checked all the liquor bottles," Maureen said. "No digitalis—I mean, no poison turned up in any of them."

"I know. I heard about that," Leo said. "But somebody slipped old Conrad a mickey somehow. No doubt about that. Had to be an inside job." He looked toward the end of the bar where a customer held up a hand. "Oops. Excuse me. Duty calls."

Maureen sipped her wine, turned slightly on the barstool so that she could watch the dining room as well as the length of the bar reflected in the mirror. She recognized the man who'd attracted Leo's attention. Jake, the newspaper reporter. He caught her eye in the mirror, lifted his glass in salute, and—within mere seconds, drink in hand—slid onto the stool beside hers. "Want to share that popcorn, Ms. Doherty? Or may I call you Maureen?"

"You may, Jake," she said, pushing the bowl toward him. "How's your investigation going?"

"Oh, you know. A little bit here. A little bit there. Eventually, it all adds up." He smiled. "You're looking particularly lovely tonight, Maureen."

"Thank you," she said, wondering where the sudden flattery would lead. "Since I'm sharing the popcorn, want to share some of those little bits?" She searched her mind for a good question. "For instance, did they ever find Mr. Wilson's camera?"

"I'm pretty sure the cops have it—that it was on the body. Ted says it was on the bar when he served that Celebration Libation and it was gone when the guy left."

"Do you know for sure who ordered that drink?" She remembered the Morgans' claim that they had bought Wilson a drink.

"Yep. Ted told me it was ordered from a house phone. A couple who were staying here charged it to their room."

So the ghost investigators had told the truth. "The Morgans," she said.

"You already knew that?"

"I'd heard it. But the way rumors fly around here, it's hard to tell what's true and what isn't."

"You mean like, are the ghost stories real?"

"No. Of course that's not what I meant." She reached for the popcorn. "You heard what Gert and Molly said. There are no ghosts here. They ought to know. They've lived here for years."

He edged a little closer to her, the smile more intimate. "Like you said, it's hard to tell what's true and what isn't." He reached into the popcorn bowl, his hand brushing hers. "Have you ever seen *Rear Window*? It's playing right down the street."

Was he going to invite her for a movie date? Or was he referring to the movie's plot? Was what Jimmy Stewart thought he saw from his window true or wasn't it? If this was about to be an invitation, it was interrupted when Ted, in white chef's jacket, appeared behind the bar. "Ms. Doherty? Leo said you were here. Do you need to see me?'

"Yes, I do." She wiped melted butter from her hand with a paper napkin. "Excuse me, Jake. 'Duty calls,' " she quoted Leo, and faced Ted. "Do you have time to work on a menu for tomorrow's dinner special?"

"Looks like tonight's dinner rush is over," he said. "We can use Elizabeth's office." He held up a key. "Sorry to interrupt, Jake."

"That's okay," Jake said. "Talk to you later, Maureen."

"Later, Jake." She picked up her half-full wineglass and followed Ted toward the lobby.

He unlocked the office, then stood aside and motioned for her to enter first. She paused for a moment before taking Elizabeth's usual seat behind the white wicker desk. Ted sat facing her.

"How do you feel today's dinner went, Ted?" she asked. "I know it was terribly short notice, but do you feel that it's something we could do regularly?"

"Regularly, like every day?"

"Well, yeah. Think we can do it?" She hoped the half smile on his face meant "Sure we can" and not "Are you nuts?"

"It won't be easy," he said. "We'll have to have a plan, Ms. Doherty. A system. Today was a good trial run, but to do it every day we need to map it out."

At least they were on the same page. "Using fruits and vegetables that are in season. Taking advantage of wholesale prices. Buying local produce when we can," she said.

Ted's half smile grew bigger. "Especially local fish," he said.

"Exactly what I was thinking about for tomorrow. And please call me Maureen." Her smile matched his. "Do you think Leo could take over the bartending duties? This new plan is going to depend on you. Would you accept the position of executive chef?"

"Pretty fancy title," he said. "Thanks, Maureen. I guess the rumor going around is true then, that you don't plan to sell the place?"

"Some of the rumors in Haven are true," she agreed. "I want to hold on to it if I can. I know it won't be easy. I don't have any money to speak of, but I have ideas—and by the way, my ideas don't involve ghosts."

"Glad to hear that. Some people thought you might want to take the easy way—push the 'haunted hotel' story for all it's worth. Load the place up with ghost hunters and never mind how it might ruin the town."

"I'm thinking we'll start with the daily dinner specials," she said. "Really promote them, build up some loyalty. We'll expand into the lunch menu later."

"Count me in," he said, "for all of it. I guess you've noticed that I like to cook breakfast occasionally. Would I still be able to do that? The neighborhood sems to look forward to my breakfasts."

"I've had your amazing pancakes. Even dreamed about them once," she admitted. "Certainly. You cook breakfast anytime the spirit moves you. I don't want to attempt too much too soon, though. We still have that murder hanging over our heads. Police prowling around don't enhance our image."

"Tell me about it, Maureen." The smile disappeared. "The reason Hubbard is around so much is he thinks I did it."

"You? He thinks you killed Wilson?" She frowned. "I'm pretty sure he thinks I did it."

"Not you! Why would he think that? You just got here. You didn't even know the guy. Hell, Maureen, I mixed the drink that probably killed him."

"The poison, the digitalis, came out of *my* medicine cabinet." She fought back tears, surprised by the intensity of a rising fear. "Hubbard put on gloves. He put the bottle into an evidence bag right in front of me. He's accused me of hiding from the police, ducking police cars. I have a *criminal* attorney on retainer, for heaven's sake."

Ted reached across the desk and touched her arm. "Hey, maybe it's just some kind of cop game he's playing. You know what? Old Sam thinks Hubbard believes *he* did it. Everybody knows how much Sam hates the ghost hunters. He used to talk to Wilson. Got right in his face about what creeps the ghost hunters are. And Sam was on the porch that night, right around the corner from where the guy died."

Maureen sniffled. "Aster down at the bookstore thought at first s it might be Sam," she confided. "I can't even begin to imagine it. Not Sam. Nope. And not you and not me."

"Then who?" Ted asked. "All the questions and the yellow tape—things like that aren't good for business."

"I had a thought about the yellow tape where it says 'Under repair.' Maybe we can get Sam and George to help out by sanding the peeling paint in that corner. Then someone can repaint it. We don't want to try to do too much, too soon. But I have some ideas about the dining room too."

When Elizabeth knocked on the glass window of the office door, annoyance evident on her face as she tapped on her watch, both Maureen and Ted looked up from a scattering of papers on the desk. A nearby wastebasket overflowed with more paper, crumpled into balls. Maureen looked at her own watch. Two hours had passed.

"Wow! Look at the time." Ted jumped up, opened the office door. "Sorry, Elizabeth, if we hogged your office for too long. But you won't believe all we've got planned!"

Elizabeth raised both eyebrows and smirked at the same time. "Huh. Planning is one thing. Getting it done is quite another. I'll take care of staffing and setting up the room for you. Then let's see how you two do with getting all the food in—and out—of the kitchen on time, without disrupting the regular dinner prep." She held out her hand for the office key. "And you'll have to find another place for your meetings. I need my space for all the other jobs I'm expected to do around here."

Ted dropped the key into her outstretched hand. "Here you go, Elizabeth. We'll do our best and we appreciate any help or advice you can give us."

Maureen stood, gathered the papers from the desk, and stuffed them unceremoniously into the briefcase. "We're both happy about how well today's special went over, Elizabeth. Thank you for your help in making it work. I'll be interested to see the day's figures. Hope we showed at least a little profit. By the way, I've put a box of beautiful Halloween centerpieces under the reception desk. I think they'll look great on all the tables. Could you see to that?"

"Oh sure. Why not? I don't have enough to do as it is. Don't forget to empty that wastebasket." Elizabeth pointed to the overflowing white wicker container, pushed her way past Maureen, carefully centered the mahogany and brass engraved desk plate marked MANAGER, and reclaimed her chair.

Chapter 28

"I really like your ideas about the dining room." Ted emptied the wastebasket into the larger receptacle in the lobby, then carefully placed the basket beside the closed office door. He took Maureen's arm, guiding her toward the elevator. "The new uniform sketches are good too. Let's hurry up to your office and rock this thing!"

She loved his enthusiasm. They were alone in the elevator. "About the fresh fish, we're square on what tomorrow night's special will be?"

"Tomorrow's special," he said. "I've already texted the wholesale fish dealer down on the pier. Got a good deal on black grouper. Right off the boat."

"With fries?"

"Sweet potato fries," he said. They were definitely on the same wavelength. "And a salad," he added.

"With that green goddess dressing Elizabeth makes," she finished the thought.

He grinned. "Exactly. But she doesn't make it. Buys it by the gallon from Kraft. Do you have dessert figured out?"

"I do. Aster Patterson's shortbread cookies with Halloween frosting and orange sherbet."

They stepped out onto the second floor. "Perfect," he said. "Suite twenty-seven, right?"

She stopped walking. "That's right. You don't have a problem with that, do you?"

"Not a bit," he said. "I've heard it's really nice."

"It is. Who told you about it?" She hoped he hadn't heard it at Quic-Shop.

"Gert," he said. "Gert told me all about it."

"She gets around," Maureen said. "I wouldn't be surprised to hear that Conrad Wilson had seen it too. Seems like he took pictures of just about every inch of Haven with that little camera of his." They'd arrived in front of suite twenty-seven.

"That camera!" Ted stood aside as Maureen pulled the key from her pocket and unlocked the door. "Hubbard questioned me for a good half hour about it. Wanted to know if I got a good close look at it when it was on the bar that night."

"Did you?"

"Not up close. I mean, it was on the bar. He picked it up every once in a while and snapped a few pictures." Ted sighed. "It was just a regular digital camera. A small one. A Canon, I think. Nothing special about it that I could see."

"Come on in." She approached the desk. "Pull up a chair. What was he taking pictures of?"

"Same as always. Nothing special." Ted sat in one of the maroon-and-gray–striped chairs, pretending to hold a camera out in front of him, pushing an imaginary button as he moved his hands from side to side. "He'd aim it one way, then another. Never seemed to be focusing on anything or anyone in particular. Click. Click. Click. All over the place."

Maureen pulled the sheaf of notes from her briefcase, piling them on top of the desk. "Gert said he was trying to get pictures of ghosts, but he couldn't tell if he had any ghost pictures until he put the memory card into a special TV. He even took pictures in here."

"That's weird."

"I know. Gert believed he actually *did* get at least one picture of a ghost, though."

"Oh that, yeah. I heard something about it. But I mean it's weird that he took pictures in here. Who let him in?"

"I don't know. Gert said she guessed money changed hands."

"I wonder if Hubbard knows about that." He moved his chair closer to the desk. "Well, let's get to work."

Too late, Maureen realized that she hadn't heard that story about ghosts showing up on the memory card from Gert. She'd heard the story secondhand—from a ghost named Lorna Dubois.

"Yes, let's," Maureen said. "And to tell the truth, I didn't hear that part about the memory card from Gert herself. Someone else told me about it."

"Another one of those famous 'Haven rumors,' huh? You can't believe everything you hear around here." He picked up a pen. "I won't bother Hubbard with that one. Anyway, if it's true he's probably already pried it out of Gert herself."

"You're right. It probably got started at the Quic-Shop," she said. "Now what do you think about something on the lighter side, like a nice chicken salad, for day after tomorrow? Maybe stuffed in those big beautiful Ruskin tomato shells, served with devilled eggs and Hawaiian rolls?"

"Not bad," he said. "You're pretty good at this."

It was nearly dinnertime when the two finished making notes, comparing grocery lists, studying online recipes. They'd made telephone and online contact with local restaurant supply houses and meat and produce wholesalers, and had placed an order for six dozen jack-o'-lantern cookies for the following day with a delighted Aster Patterson. "From what I've seen so far," Maureen said, "it looks as if there's been virtually no profit made on the dinner menu for a long time. Some meals were served at a loss."

"It's true," Ted agreed. "Elizabeth said as long as Ms. Gray liked the food, it didn't matter what the cost was."

"Matters to me," Maureen mumbled, looking over the cost estimates for the next week's specials. "If we fill the dining room every day for dinner, the profit will just about cover the costs for food, salaries for the wait- and maintenance staffs, and the tiny ad budget." She waved the papers. "Gotta do better than this. How does Haven feel about garage sales?"

That brough a grin. "My mom loves them. Why? You planning to sell off a few rocking chairs? The white linen tablecloths?"

"Not the rocking chairs. I plan to get them painted, though. But getting rid of the tablecloths? Not a bad idea." She paused. "All that laundering, bleaching, ironing. Pretty labor intensive. Although I really like the look. But we may have to go to paper place mats."

Ted pretended to fall sideways in his chair, clutching his heart. "Paper place mats? Now that would really have given Ms. Gray a heart attack!"

"Yes. You're right. The linens should be one of the last things to go." She thought about Conrad Wilson's body with its tablecloth shroud, then shook the dark memory away. "Actually, I was thinking of a giant garage sale to get rid of all the junk in the storage locker."

"Really? That makes sense. I guess the storage locker is where Wilson's luggage and whatever else he left here at the inn will wind up too. I heard that his agent swears that Wilson owes him money and he wants to claim the camera and the guy's computer."

"No family?"

"Guess not anybody close. Molly says a couple of cousins showed up. All they want is the computer and the camera too. Guess they'll have to fight it out with the agent. Elizabeth says his wallet and watch and rings stay in the safe in her office until somebody claims them. The cops still have the camera, his phone, his laptop, and his tablet. Elizabeth says the tablet is broken, though. I guess his suitcase will go to the storage locker until it all gets settled." He stood. "Well, time for me to go to my bartender job. Will I see you in the dining room later this evening?"

"Maybe," she said. "I've got a lot more figuring to do. I think I'll just microwave some macaroni and cheese for now. I might come down later for a drink, though."

"Shirley Temple?" He grinned.

"Could be something a little stronger this time. I've earned it today."

"Yes, you have—and it sounds to me as though we have a lot more work to do if we're going to get the old place up and running."

Maureen liked the sound of the "we" and said so. "I'm glad you're on board."

"Wouldn't miss it for the world." He stood and shook her hand. "Even if it might be a bumpy ride."

Maureen walked to the door with him. "I'll probably see you later downstairs then," she said.

"Hope so." He rubbed his arms. "It's freezing in here. Is the air conditioning on?"

"I guess so. I think it's on some kind of automatic system. Every once in a while, the temperature just drops. I've been meaning to ask Sam or George to take a look at it."

"Good idea. Where's the thermostat?"

She signaled with a jerk of her thumb over her shoulder. "In there. In the bedroom. Want to take a look and see if you can figure out what's wrong with it?"

"Nope. Not my expertise," he said. "See you later."

After he'd left, Maureen added the new notes they'd made, the contact numbers for wholesalers, and the proposed menus to a new file folder, turned off the computer and the desk lamp, stepped out into the corridor, welcoming the comfortable, preset 78-degree warmth.

Back at the penthouse, the pets seemed pleased to see her, Finn prancing in his "let's go for a walk" mode, Bogie and Bacall together on the windowsill, looking out at the little balcony and the oak tree. She cranked the window open so the cats could use that exit if they chose, and clipped Finn's leash on to his collar. "Okay, everybody," she said. "Some nice fresh air will be good for all of us."

Maureen and Finn took the stairs to the first floor, then took the corridor past the guest laundry, on the way to the side door. It seemed wise to avoid the lobby in case Elizabeth might still be cranky. "No sense looking for trouble," Maureen told the dog.

"Woof," Finn agreed.

"Hello there, Ms. Doherty." The voice was familiar. Clarissa Morgan waved from in front of a large white Maytag dryer. "Hi, Finn."

"Hi, Mrs. Morgan. Enjoying your stay?" Maureen tugged on the leash, urging the friendly golden to skip the usual tail-wagging, hand-licking, love-everybody greeting he enjoyed so much. No such luck. Anyone would have thought Clarissa was a long-lost bestie.

Pulling a pile of clothes from the dryer, dumping them onto a nearby folding table, the woman knelt to receive Finn's enthusiastic salutation.

"So glad I ran into you, Ms. Doherty. May I call you Maureen?" She patted Finn's head with one hand and extended the other for a handshake. "I'm afraid I may have made a bad impression when we spoke last." She pumped Maureen's hand. "I shouldn't have been so critical of poor Mr. Wilson. I allowed an old personal grudge to come to the surface. I'm sorry."

"No need to apologize. Death affects us all differently." Maureen clutched the leash, attempting to direct Finn toward the nearby exit. He did not cooperate but instead sat, facing Clarissa Morgan. "Come along now, Finn. Time for our exercise."

"It was inexcusable." By then Clarissa had a firm grasp on the dog's collar. "We'd had some—um—artistic differences in the past," she said. "When Alex and I learned, by mere coincidence, that Conrad was at the same inn we'd chosen, I thought it would be a good chance to make amends, to let sleeping dogs lie."

"Woof," Finn said.

"Not that kind of dogs, Finn. Clarissa, this is really none of my business. Please don't worry about it."

She loosened her hold on the collar and stood. "I asked for his autograph. Told him how much Alex and I admire his work."

"That's nice. Come along, Finn." Maureen faced the side door.

Clarissa pulled a blue shorty nightie from the pile of warm laundry and dabbed at her eyes with it. "He told me to drop dead. Honest to God, that's what the miserable bastard said. He signed the magazine 'With love, Conrad,' then handed it back to me and said, 'Drop dead, Clarissa.' "

"I'm sorry," Maureen said. "Truly, I am, but," she repeated, "this is really none of my business."

"The thing is." The woman blew her nose on the nightie. "The thing is, I said, 'Same to you Conrad,' and then—that's what he did. He walked away and then he dropped dead. I feel so guilty. It's as if I put some sort of curse on him."

"Now, Clarissa." Maureen put a tentative hand on the woman's heaving shoulder. "That doesn't even make sense. Anyway, I don't believe in curses."

As soon as she'd uttered the words, she thought about how very recently she'd been adamant in stating to anyone who'd listen that she didn't believe in ghosts.

Chapter 29

After a bit more shoulder patting and nightie sniffling, Clarissa Morgan calmed down, folded her fluff-dried belongings, and with profuse apologies for airing her "dirty laundry"—funny, considering the surroundings—finally left Maureen and Finn to their delayed walk.

"That was strange, wasn't it, boy?"

"Woof, woof, woof!" Finn exclaimed.

"Darn right it was. She thinks she cursed him, so he dropped dead. I hope she doesn't go to the police with that theory—although it makes just about as much sense as Ted or Sam or me being responsible for the man dying like he did."

Finn visited a nearby lamppost without further comment. A few of the boulevard merchants still had the day's dinner special posters in their windows, reminding Maureen to get new ones prepared and distributed for the next day's dinnertime offering. "Our day's work isn't finished yet," she told the dog. "I don't look forward to going back to my ice-cold office this evening, but I guess I'll have to."

After their walk, the two used the front stairway. The rockers were nearly full. The success of the promotion was even better than she'd anticipated. The four regulars were already seated in their usual spots. "What's up, Gert?" Maureen whispered to the occupant of the first rocker on the right. "Dinner guests, ghost chasers, or nosy murder types?"

"A few of each, I'd say," Gert offered. "I hung around in the lobby for a while, trying to see if any of them are overnighters."

"What do you think? Have any of them checked in?"

"Yep. The two men over there checked in this morning. Here for the food, I'm pretty sure, and see the one guy sitting alone on the steps beside the big pumpkin?" She leaned toward Maureen, covering her mouth with one hand, whispering, "I think he's Conrad Wilson's agent, or lawyer, or something."

"Why?"

"Asking a lot of questions."

"What kind of questions?"

"Oh, you know. Like who has his camera? Where is his computer? Has any of his family showed up to claim the body?" She shook her head. "Nosy stuff like that."

"What did you tell him?" Maureen took a closer look at the man on the steps.

Gert smiled, then made a zipper motion across her lips. "I know nothing," she said. "I say nothing."

"Good girl," Maureen said. "Has Officer Hubbard talked to him yet?"

"Haven't seen Hubbard since this morning. He was out in the kitchen, and even behind the bar, making a nuisance of himself while we were all trying to get breakfast served and lunch started."

"What's he looking for?" Maureen wondered aloud. "I thought he'd already pretty much examined every inch out there "

"We did too. But no, there he was, spraying that damned fingerprint powder on this and that, here and there." She made a face. "Remember, you said if he had to mess with our booze anymore he should do it here? Did you ever try to wash that crap off of a glass bottle? What a mess."

"Sorry about that. I just didn't want to have to pour good liquor down the drain again. I sure wish he'd get this case solved so we could get things done that need doing around here—things that don't involve cops and ghost hunters and nosy questions," Maureen said. "Keep your ears and eyes open, Gert. Maybe we can hear something, see something, learn something, that will help Hubbard—and hopefully get rid of him!"

Sam, who'd been rocking quietly with his eyes closed, spoke up. "I saw something."

Molly interrupted, "I heard something. Down at the Quic-Shop."

George leaned in her direction. "Huh. Quic-Shop. 'Believe nothing that you hear, and only half of what you see' in that place." The crowd on the porch had started to thin out. One or two at a time, the rocking-chair sitters began to head for the dining room. Before long, only Maureen, the quartet, the newly registered pair, and the man on the steps remained.

"What'd you hear, Mol?" Gert wanted to know. "Who's it about?"

"The dead man. Conrad Wilson. They say nobody's claimed the body yet. The town might have to bury him. Guess they'll have to sell his stuff to pay for it."

"That's not true!" The voice came from the steps below. The man sitting next to one of the pumpkins stood and climbed the stairs to the top. "I'm his agent." He handed a card to George. "If his family doesn't claim him, I'll see that he gets a decent burial."

"See, Molly? Told ya." George glanced at the card in his hand. "Thank you, Mr. Zamora."

Maureen lost no time in stepping forward to greet the

man, to welcome him to Haven House. This might very well be a "learn something" moment.

"Good afternoon, Mr. Zamora," she said. "I'm Maureen Doherty, the owner here. Welcome to our inn. If there's anything I can do to make your stay more comfortable at this difficult time, please don't hesitate to ask." Finn sat, tail wagging, watching the man's face expectantly.

Zamora gave Finn a perfunctory pat on the head, and pulled another card from a silver card case and handed it to Maureen. "I'm Conrad Wilson's literary agent—and long-time friend. I'm here to try to figure out why a good-natured, talented, up-and-coming author like Conrad died in this boring, godforsaken, end-of-the-road hellhole of a town."

Maureen accepted the card and took a step back. *So much for making his stay more comfortable*, she thought. She tried a straightforward approach. "Yes, well, all of us here are interested in finding out exactly that same thing. Had he contacted you at all during the month he'd been here? He kept to himself pretty much, mostly taking pictures all over town. It was said that he was working on a book. Is that correct?"

"Damn right. Not just a book. A blockbuster. A best seller. I've already sold the rights to it." He tapped the breast pocket of a silk Tommy Bahama shirt. "Had a contract in my pocket for him to sign."

"Was it a book about—um—spirits?" Maureen pressed the subject, dropping her voice, aware that others—like everyone on the porch, including the two men—were all listening.

"Spirits? Freakin' ghosts! He promised me pictures of 'em. Dozens of 'em." Zamora didn't bother to speak quietly. "Maybe even hundreds of pictures, he told me. "The whole place is crawling with ghosts," he said. "He even sent me a picture of one. Wanna see it?" He pulled a photo from the same breast pocket. "See? Anyone you know?" He waved it in front of Maureen's face, then spun around, holding it so that anyone nearby could get a fast look at it.

Maureen had recognized the player piano in the Haven Inn's dining room at once. She didn't recognize the profile shot of a smiling man sitting on the piano bench, wearing a striped shirt and straw hat, hands on the keyboard, a bottle of beer close at hand, but she figured it was probably a very good likeness of Billy Bedoggoned Bailey, who, according to Lorna Dubois, had been dead for quite a long time.

"Photoshopped," Sam snorted. "Any kid can do it."

"Not like this." Zamora handed the picture to Maureen. "I've had the best techs in New York City examine it. It's the real thing." He turned around again, this time slowly. "I'm thinking that somewhere in this dead-end town—maybe even in this run-down hotel—there are dozens, maybe hundreds, of pictures like this, and I'm willing to pay a lot of money to anyone who can show me how to find them."

"Count me in," Molly said.

"Me too," Gert declared.

"How much money?" George asked.

"How does a thousand dollars sound?" Zamora reached for the photo in Maureen's hand and snatched it back, tucking it back into his pocket. "A thousand bucks in good hard old-fashioned American cash."

"I'm pretty sure it's a fake, "Sam insisted, "but I'll give finding them a try. First of all, do the cops still have his little camera?"

"I'm pretty sure they do," Maureen said.

"That's probably where all the pictures are stored then," George said. "Or else on his computer. You can bet the cops have that all figured out."

"I don't think so," Gert said. "I don't think they have *any-thing* about this figured out, the way they keep prowling around, bothering everybody all the time."

"I'm afraid you might be right about that, Gert," Maureen said. "Hey, Sam, didn't you say you 'saw something'? What did you see?"

"I did see something," Sam answered. "But maybe what I saw is worth a thousand bucks. Guess I'll keep it to myself for now."

Chapter 30

Maureen wished a "good evening" to the group on the porch, just after the sun had set, and the quartet, along with the agent, decided to go inside for dinner. Maureen was determined to have the microwaved supper she'd promised herself and to run off the posters for the following evening's blackened grouper dinner special. Before she left, she introduced herself to the two men who'd checked in earlier. Trent and Pierre turned out to be interior designers, stopping over for a night before a big home show in Tampa. They declared the "ambiance" of Haven House "utterly charming," found Finn "absolutely adorable and very smart," and said they'd be back again later in the season for a much longer stay.

"That's what we like to hear," she said. "I'll see you in the morning." Finn trotted just ahead of her and they climbed the stairs to their third-floor home. The cats had come inside and were already perched in their tower. Maureen cranked the window closed, wondering how Bogie had squeezed through the space allowed, emptied a can of macaroni and cheese into a saucepan, trying not the think about the pot roast dinner downstairs.

"We don't have time for a leisurely dinner, Finn. We have to go downstairs and work." The golden lay down and covered his eyes with his paws. "You don't want to come down-stairs with me?"

"Woof," he said.

"I'll give you lasties on my macaroni. There's still plenty of cheese left in it." She put the nearly empty bowl on the floor and Finn, unable to resist the cheese, as she'd known he would be, stood up and lapped the bowl clean. "You're so easy, she said. "Come on. Let's go. Let's just get it over with." Not bothering with the leash since they'd be staying within the building, together they descended the stairs and let themselves into suite twenty-seven, where Maureen was pleased to note that the temperature this time seemed normal. Finn headed straight for the kneehole under the desk, while Maureen began the layout for posters and flyers advertising the next day's dinner menu. She easily found online photos of the popular southern pan-fried fish treatment, added advertising copy, heavy on descriptions like "flaky," "Cajun spiced," and "fresh from local boats." As she photoshopped sweet potato fries and a green salad from her Bartlett's of Boston restaurant file into the shot, she recalled Sam's insistence that Conrad Wilson's picture of Billy at the player piano was a fake.

"I guess Wilson *could* have faked the picture." She ad-dressed the dog, who'd positioned himself so that his eyes and nose stuck out from his hidey-hole. "Putting an old-time barroom piano player in front of a piano can't be much more difficult than sticking some fries beside a fish fillet." Finn gave a soft "woof" of agreement.

"But that would mean that Conrad Wilson himself was a fake. That he never did capture any pictures of ghosts with his camera. That the Wilson cousins and the Morgans and the book agent are all barking up the wrong tree."

"Woof?" Finn asked.

"Not that kind of barking." She fed the poster-sized layout

into the printer and waited while the colorful sheets processed. "Not bad," she said, holding one up at arm's length. "Is the print big enough?" Finn didn't reply. She pulled a small plastic container of pushpins from the top drawer of the desk, carried the poster to the closed bedroom door, securing it with pins at all four corners, then viewed it from across the room. "Good enough," she proclaimed, and began printing out the same information on one hundred letter-sized flyers.

"Did it just get cold in here?" Maureen rubbed her arms, much the way Ted had when they'd held the planning session in this room. "All of a sudden I'm freezing."

Finn whined, pulling his head back under the kneehole, hiding eyes and nose from view. Maureen looked back at the poster on the bedroom door. "I swear, Finn, as soon as I touched that door, the temperature in here began to drop. "How can that be?"

She didn't wait for, or expect, an answer. Jake had asked about changes in the temperature when they'd been talking about ghosts. She hadn't wanted to consider it then, and she still didn't. Hurriedly gathering up the posters and flyers, she pulled the door to the corridor open and left the office. The golden was way ahead of her. She hit the UP button on the elevator, where again, the dog hurried inside, seemingly anxious to get away from suite twenty-seven. She unlocked the penthouse door, let Finn inside, put one of the posters and a few flyers on the coffee table, and, promising the animals she'd be back soon, returned to the elevator. It stopped on the second floor, where Maureen was pleased to share the gracious brass-and-wood and etched-glass confines with the inn's newest guests, Trent and Pierre.

"Going down to dinner?" she asked.

"We've already enjoyed dinner. We're going back for a nice Irish coffee," Trent said. "The pot roast was marvelous."

She handed him a flyer from the top of the pile. "Good. Here's tomorrow's special. Maybe you'll be tempted to spend another night with us."

"Maybe we will," Pierre said. "Will you join us now for an Irish coffee, Ms. Doherty?"

"Maybe later," she said, lifting the stack of papers higher. "First I have to get these into the right hands." The men headed into the dining room while Maureen opened the green door and stepped out onto the porch. The evening was pleasant, with a scent of night-blooming jasmine in the air. The tinkle of the player piano drifted from tall windows. Maureen was pleased to see that Sam and George were each in their usual chairs. So were Molly and Gert.

"Good evening, all," she said. "Here are the advertisements for tomorrow's dinner. Can you gents get them spread around town by tomorrow morning? You'll be on the clock of course."

"Sure. We'll all do it," Molly said. "Many hands make light the work. Come on, it's a nice night for stroll around town, and we'll get these in the right places tonight when there's plenty of foot traffic."

Maureen realized that Molly's suggestion meant that all four of them would be "on the clock" and this would add to the already-stretched-thin advertising budget, but she didn't object. Molly was right about the evening foot traffic.

"Everybody loved it," Gert said. "I'll bet we'll get repeat visitors tomorrow." Maureen was sure that Gert was probably right about that, and decided on the spot that she'd take the decorators up on that Irish coffee if they offered again. Stopping in the lobby long enough to remove the pot roast poster from the easel, she replaced it with the blackened grouper advertisement. Carrying a few of the remaining flyers, she pushed open the louvred doors to the dining room. Shelly offered her a menu, which she declined. Elizabeth was nowhere in sight. Maureen was delighted to see, though, that the vintage Halloween decorations had already been placed on each table and that little battery-powered tea lights twinkled in each one. The effect was even better than Maureen had anticipated. She'd be sure to thank the woman for the special effort.

Pierre and Trent had apparently made friends with the Flannagans, and now the four shared a table. There were only a few customers seated at the bar, and Maureen chose a seat at the far end, hoping there'd be time to talk with Ted. As they'd agreed earlier, there was still a lot of planning to do.

Ted's smile said that he was happy to see her. "You came back. Good. Can I buy you a drink?"

"I've been thinking all evening about a nice hot Irish coffee. Can do?"

"One of my specialties. Had a little run on them tonight. That table over there." He gestured toward the Flannagans and friends.

"I know." She watched as he preheated a handled mug with hot water. "That's where I got the idea." Almost in one smooth motion, he poured steaming hot coffee, stirred in brown sugar, added a healthy slug of Irish whiskey, and topped it with a swirl of whipped cream.

"Here you go," he said. *"Sláinte."*

"Sláinte agatsa!" she replied, lifting the mug, pleased that he'd used the ancient Irish toast she'd so often heard from her own grandfather. "Watching you mix this is as much fun as drinking it. You make it look like some kind of sleight-of-hand magic trick."

"No magic," he said. "Like anything else. Just takes years of practice. Did you get all your work done?"

She tapped the pile of flyers, offering him one. "I did. I brought a few for you to hand out. Like it?"

"I do. Good work."

"I haven't seen Officer Hubbard lately. Did he finally go away?" She glanced around the room. "Or is he still lurking around?"

"He's out of my kitchen, finally," Ted said. "Last time I saw him he was having a conversation with the ghost hunter lady. Mrs. Morgan."

"I ran into her earlier in the guest laundry. She was quite weepy. Maybe he upset her."

"Could be. I saw her crying the night Wilson died, after Elizabeth waylaid her and her husband after they got Wilson's autograph."

"Elizabeth did that?" Maureen was surprised. "Must have happened after I went outside."

"Oh yeah. She lit right into the two of them. Elizabeth doesn't like anyone bothering the guests. They'd almost made it to the door when she got right up in their faces. Looked from here like a little shoving match was going on. Mrs. Morgan was swinging that big gold bag and Elizabeth was swatting back at her with a rolled-up menu and Mr. Morgan was trying to get between them." He chucked softly. "Most everyone else was looking at the sparkler in Wilson's drink, but from where I stood it was like watching a Three Stooges routine. Elizabeth finally laid off when Mrs. Morgan started crying. Oh, excuse me. Gotta work." Ted moved away, putting coasters on the bar, drawing two draft beers for a pair of new customers with the same kind of graceful, fluid motion he'd used in preparing Maureen's coffee.

The barstools began to fill up after that, and there was little time for more conversation between the two. Maureen had finished her Irish coffee when Trent appeared at her side. "Won't you come over and join us, Ms. Doherty? Pierre and I have just about fallen in love with this place and we'd love to talk to you about some decorating ideas we have—if you won't be offended."

"I wouldn't be offended one bit, Trent," she said. "I'd love to hear your suggestions. But I'm afraid that right now, my budget for improvements is zip. Nada."

"There's always tomorrow to look forward to," he said. "Come have coffee with us anyway, won't you?"

"I'd love to," she said, and followed Trent to the table. Free decorating advice from a couple of professionals? Why not?

Ethel and Dick Flannagan had left for home, so Maureen had Trent and Pierre to herself, and looked forward to hearing about any ideas for the Haven House Inn they might offer—even if it might be months, years, before she could put them into practice.

The two had already ordered another Irish coffee for her and Shelly delivered it just as soon as she sat down. "Thank you both so much," she said.

"Our pleasure." The men spoke in unison.

"First of all," Pierre began, "we have to admit that we have a teensy favor to ask."

"Okay." Maureen spoke hesitantly. "What can I do for you?"

Trent reached into his pocket. "It has to do with this," he said, and placed a key on the table. Maureen recognized the brown plastic fob, exactly like the one on her own key. At first, she thought it was one of the souvenirs Elizabeth sold at the reception desk. But this one was different. It was heavier, a darker brown, a little more worn looking, than the new ones. She reached for it. Touched it. "This is old," she said. "It's one of the keys they used here years ago. Where in the world did you get it?"

"It's the reason we came here," Pierre said. "At first we were going to stay at the airport Hilton as usual, but then Trent's mother died." He looked at his friend.

"I'm so sorry," Maureen murmured, turning the key over. Taking a closer look. The lettering said HAVEN HOUSE INN. The address and phone number followed. What held her attention was the suite number the key bore. "Suite twenty-seven." She gave Trent a questioning look.

"This was in my mom's things," he said. "When we planned this trip, I looked up the inn online, not expecting it to be here after so many years. We knew right away we'd stay here."

"Of course," Maureen said. "A little sentimental journey side trip."

"More than that," Pierre said.

Chapter 31

"We told you we were going to ask for a teensy favor," Trent said, "and we are, but first I think I need to tell you exactly why we came to stay here in the first place."

"Yes," Maureen said. "Go ahead."

"This key." He held it up, holding it by the fob so that the key itself turned slightly, reflecting the tea-light candle in the papier-mâché pumpkin centerpiece

"This little key," Trent said again, "was important to my mother. Mom never married. She was, as they say these days, 'an unwed mother.' She never denied it. I don't believe she was ever ashamed of the fact. All she ever told me about my parentage was that I was conceived in love in a beautiful little town in Florida. That my father was a soldier. That his first name was Trent. That he had died in Vietnam before I was born." Trent paused, wiped his eyes.

Pierre took up the story. "Martha died several months ago," he said. "She'd been ill for almost a year. She knew her time was nearly over. We were both with her the night before she went. She gave this key to Trent, told him this was all she had of his father. She said she had seen the light—that she would be going to the light soon—and that she knew the love of her life would be waiting for her there."

Maureen reached for Trent's hand. "That's a beautiful story, Trent, and I'm glad you're here. Tell me what the favor is. If it's something I can do for you, I'll certainly do it."

Trent spoke again. "When we checked in, of course we asked for suite twenty-seven. The woman at the desk, Elizabeth, said that those rooms had been converted to office space and were not available to the public. We asked if we could just peek inside. She refused. Quite firmly."

"When we learned that you're the owner now," Pierre said, "we thought we'd ask you. So here it is. Could you please let us look at the suite where Trent was conceived in love?"

"Absolutely." Maureen spoke without hesitation. She spoke from her heart. She also spoke without thinking. There were reasons for making suite twenty-seven off-limits to the public for decades. There was something profoundly frightening, depressing, about those rooms. Was John Smith really in there, horrifying guests year after year? What if Trent, with all good intentions, found that his late mother had handed him the key to something evil? Even Finn disliked going into those rooms and Maureen herself had experienced the sudden drops in temperature that Jake had mentioned— that some say indicated the presence of a ghost.

The smiles on the two men's faces indicated relief. Even joy. What could she do? She'd promised to admit them to suite twenty-seven. Perhaps just a peek was all they'd need. They'd see her attractive office space and be content with that.

"Could we do it now?" Trent asked softly. "I think I'm ready."

With a sincere hope that *she* was ready, Maureen said, "Of course. Let's go."

The elevator ride to the second floor was a quiet one. When it stopped, Maureen stepped into the corridor, taking the key to suite twenty-seven from her purse. At the same time, Trent pulled the almost-duplicate key from his pocket. "Would you mind, Maureen, if I tried mine? I know of course that it'd hardly likely to work after all this time, but may I?"

"Sure. Go ahead." Would Trent's key work? *Stranger things have happened around here*, she thought. *It would be kind of cool if it worked.*

It worked.

The men looked at each other, smiling. "How about that?" Trent said. "Amazing. After almost fifty years."

"I was pretty sure it would fit." Pierre patted his friend on the shoulder. "Martha would be so pleased."

"I know. Shall we go inside?" Trent pulled the door open. Maureen followed the two into her office.

"Oh, this is really nice!" Trent exclaimed. "Look at the big windows. You can see the lights on the boulevard from here. And that desk!" He ran his hand over the polished mahogany surface. "You have exquisite taste in office furnishings, Maureen."

"Thank you," she said. "But I can't take credit for this. My predecessor—who left Haven House to me—was responsible for all of this. Her name was Penelope Josephine Gray."

"She knew furniture," Pierre put in. He pointed to the closed door with the pinned-up poster of blackened grouper affixed to it. "Is that the bedroom?"

"I'm afraid you're in for a bit of a disappointment there," Maureen apologized. "There's no furniture at all. Just an empty room."

"No problem. I'll just use my imagination."

"Okay, here we go." She opened the door, with a silent prayer that there'd be no blast of cold air, no whispers of, "Mother," no enveloping cloud of depression, no "essence" of the late John Smith.

It didn't look *too* bad, she thought. It was, as she'd said, empty except for the plastic bins of Halloween decorations.

But the newly carpeted floor, the freshly painted white walls, the neutral draperies were at least neat and clean looking.

Trent walked to the center of the room, then turned slowly. "Not exactly the love nest I'd imagined," he said, "but yes, I can visualize the way it might have been." He closed his eyes. "A big bed, a bureau, maybe a big chair. A television." He opened his eyes. Color? Or black and white?"

"Color I think," Pierre said. "And maybe one of those folding luggage racks over there where the plastic boxes are, and your mother would have hung their clothes in this closet." He grasped the glass knob, pulling the door open. "Martha was always so neat. A place for everything and everything in its place."

"You're right," Trent said, his eyes open again. "She was. Thank you so much for humoring me, Maureen. This has been a dream come true. Really. I can see it just as it might have been. Romantic and very fifties."

"I'm glad you can see it that way." Maureen felt the temperature beginning to drop.

"It's my job," Trent said. "Being able to look at a blank space and see how it would look with the right furnishings."

"A great talent. Shall we go along now?" She waved a hand toward the office.

"Sure." The men followed her across the marble threshold. The chill in the air was becoming noticeable. She shut the bedroom door, hurried across the room, opened the door to the corridor. "After you," she said, ushering the men out of the office and into the long hall. She pressed the lock down, stepped out of the room, and pulled the door shut behind her, trying hard to convince herself that the whispered word, "Mother?" she'd heard as she left suite twenty-seven was a trick of her imagination. "Wait for me!" she called, hurrying to keep up with the men on the way to the elevator.

"We're going to have a little porch sit before we turn in," Trent said. "I can't thank you enough for your kindness, and in return, I've taken the liberty of making up a few sketches of some areas of Haven House that could use a little—well— a little updating. If you're available tomorrow morning, per- haps we could go over them together."

"I can hardly wait," she said. "What time will be best for you two?"

"How about eight tomorrow morning, downstairs in the dining room?" Pierre suggested.

"Perfect. I guess I'll leave you here then, and take the stairs up to my apartment. Good night. Looking forward to seeing you in the morning."

I should sleep like a baby—or a cat—tonight, Maureen told herself as she climbed the stairs to the penthouse. *I'm ex- hausted. It's been a busy—even terrifying—day for sure, but I got a lot done.* At the head of the stairs the light was dim— reminding her that she hadn't yet ordered those LED bulbs. She looked down the short hall to her apartment and fast- walked the rest of the way home.

Chapter 32

Maureen did sleep like that proverbial baby—with no ghostly visitations, no phone calls, no meows or woofs, at least none that interrupted her dreamless slumber. At seven a.m. waking was a different matter—with two cats clamoring to be fed, one golden retriever pacing back and forth to the front door, indicating a need to go outside. A ding of the push bell announced the imminent arrival of Lorna Dubois.

"Okay, okay, everybody. I'm up. See?" Cats first. She filled the named containers with Meow Mix and put fresh water into the common bowl. She'd slept a little later than usual. No time for a run on the beach this morning. A quick trip to the bathroom, a promise to Finn that they'd go for a walk ASAP, a shout-out to the not-yet-visible Lorna to wait a minute. Maureen shed pj's, showered hastily, and, towel wrapped, opened her closet.

"You ought to wear that Stella McCartney thing again. It looked good on you," Lorna advised from the edge of Maureen's recently vacated bed. Finn had stopped pacing and sat quietly at Lorna's nearly transparent feet—fashionably clad in Maureen's favorite white Birkenstocks.

"Thanks. I think I will. What brings you here so early?" Maureen took the navy-and-white outfit from its hanger. "I was going to wear those shoes. Is it okay if we both wear them at the same time?"

"As long as we don't show up at the same party," Lorna quipped. "Listen, I just popped in to tell you that Elizabeth was up here when you were out last night. Is that okay?"

"I'm not sure. I know she has keys to everything and she *is* the building manager." Maureen selected bra and panties from her underwear drawer. "I guess she could have been checking on the plumbing or the air conditioner or something. I know the AC downstairs in my office has been acting up lately."

"In suite twenty-seven?" Lorna snickered. "That has nothing to do with the AC. Don't you know about some ghost turning the room cold? It's just John Smith hanging around down there."

"How come you don't make the room cold?"

"Not sure. Penelope used to say I did sometimes, but not very often. You should ask Elizabeth about coming in here, though." Lorna began to fade away. "I'll let you get dressed in private."

"Thanks. I appreciate that."

"I knew it was John Smith," Maureen mumbled. "I just don't want to admit it."

"I heard that," came Lorna's disembodied voice.

"Go away," Maureen commanded. After donning the Mc-Cartney outfit, she brushed still-damp hair into place, slipped into the Birkenstocks, and attached Finn's leash. "Okay. Let's make it quick." She was partway down the stairs to the lobby when her phone buzzed. Nora Nathan's name flashed on caller ID.

"Hello, Maureen? . . . Nora Nathan here. Hope I'm not calling too early. I've had a little talk with Officer Hubbard. Can we meet in your office later today to go over a few things?"

"Of course. Anything wrong?" Maureen asked.

"We'll talk later. How's around two this afternoon?"

"That will be fine," Maureen said. "Until two o'clock then.

"Oh boy. Something else to worry about," she told the golden. "Oh well. One problem at a time. First let's take our walk and see if our four friends did a good job of poster placement. We're going to need every cent we can generate with our dinner specials. Next, we'll try to dump as much as we can of Penelope's hoard. Then we'll figure out how to deal with the police. How does that sound?"

Finn gave a less-than-enthusiastic "woof." They crossed the porch, noting that the quartet was missing—probably lining up for an early breakfast, Maureen decided. Finn wove his way down the front steps between smiling and frowning pumpkins, then hurried along the brick sidewalk, choosing to cross to the opposite side of the boulevard for a change.

Maureen stood for a moment, looking across toward the inn. *The building needs paint, and all of the windows could use a good washing*, she thought. *But even as she stands, she looks better than a fast-food joint or another steel-and-glass condo would.* She quickened her step, passing the Quic-Shop with barely a glance except to note her poster was visible, but partly obstructed by a BOGO Halloween candy display. Between lamppost and fire hydrant stops, Maureen and Finn checked each store window up and down the boulevard. The quartet had done their job. There was even a poster tacked up on the bulletin board at the onetime playhouse where Lorna had seen the light and decided to stay in Haven.

Maureen turned around at the cottage housing the offices of Jackson, Nathan and Peters—pleased to see the poster propped up in a front window—crossed the street, and started back toward Haven House, with thoughts about the impending appointment with Nora Nathan. It was good that Nora had talked with Officer Hubbard—since she'd dealt with him before. Maybe Nora could talk some sense into the man!

Finn stopped at the window of the bookshop. The poster was there and so was Erle Stanley Gardner, snoozing in a little patch of sunshine. Finn woofed a hello to the cat, which Erle Stanley acknowledged with a wide yawn. The "woof" was enough to alert Aster to Maureen's presence. The door opened and bathrobe-clad Aster, with tightly wound pink rollers in white hair, greeted Maureen.

"Good morning, dearie. You aren't here to pick up your cookies yet, are you? They're not ready."

"Just walking Finn, Aster. George or Sam will come by later to pick up the cookies. You call the inn when you're ready."

"I will," Aster said, "but send George, please. I'm still not crazy about that Sam."

Maureen was in no mood to hear Aster's on-again-off-again theory about Sam as Conrad Wilson's possible killer. "That'll be fine," she said. "Everyone's looking forward to your cookies." She tugged on Finn's leash. "Thanks for posting our dinner special. See you later."

"Are you sure you don't want to stop for a cup of tea and a little chat?"

"Maybe later," Maureen said, realizing that maybe Aster had become the Florida version of Mrs. Hennessey. "I have an appointment with a couple of decorators this morning." It sounded good, she thought, even if it wouldn't amount to anything in the near future.

"Good for you. Come on back anytime, honey!' "

With a wave, Maureen broke into a jog, which clearly made Finn happy. The two were back at the inn within minutes, breathless, and just in time to see a patrol car roll to a stop in front of the building.

"This time I'd really like to duck into an alley," she whispered to Finn. "I hope whoever it is, isn't here to see me."

She waved and smiled in the direction of the car to avoid any appearance of dodging the cops, and headed for the side door.

With Finn fed and comfortably settled on the blue couch, Maureen brushed her hair, applied a quick lick of lip gloss, and took the elevator down to the lobby. A uniformed police officer, carrying a large to-go coffee cup with a powdered sugar doughnut balanced on top of it, wished her a good morning and left through the front door. It looked as though the free coffee and doughnuts program for Haven's law enforcement was still in place and, Maureen thought, maybe that wasn't such a bad thing after all. Besides, that doughnut looked delicious and she was in need of some quick energy.

She took a seat at one of the empty round tables where coffee cups and silverware were already laid out on the white linen tablecloth. Herbie hurried over with a coffeepot. "Regular, Ms. Doherty?"

"Yes, thanks, Herbie," she said. "I'm expecting some company at around eight. I think I'll just have a powdered sugar doughnut this morning."

"Want that toasted?"

"Sure. Why not? Is Elizabeth around?" Maureen was curious about Lorna's report of Elizabeth entering the penthouse.

"She's in the kitchen, I think," Herbie said. "I'll tell her you're here."

Herbie returned with the toasted doughnut, Elizabeth close behind him. "What do you want, Maureen?" The woman's voice was polite enough, but the expression showed annoyance.

"I heard that you were in my apartment yesterday. Is everything all right? Any repairs needed that I should know about?" Maureen's tone was polite also.

The woman didn't answer right away, glared at Herbie's retreating back, then shook her head. "Nothing's broken. You left a window wide open—for those cats, I suppose. It looked like there might be rain coming." She shrugged. "I went up and adjusted it so the drapes and furniture wouldn't get ruined."

"I see. Thank you."

"Who told you I was there?" Elizabeth's eyes narrowed.

"I don't care to say." Maureen took a bite of the warm doughnut. "Ummm. This is delicious. Thanks for attending to the window, Elizabeth. I'll be more careful about it in the future."

"Good," Elizabeth said. "Anything else?"

"I just wanted to tell you that I like the little tea lights you put in the papier-mâché buckets. Nice touch."

"I thought it might update the tatty old things." She wrinkled her nose. "I'll bet they're older than I am."

"Could be." Maureen sipped her coffee.

"Is that all?" Elizabeth asked. "I'm busy."

"That's all." She watched the woman walk away. How had Elizabeth known the window was open? She'd have to have been standing at the very back of the building, straining to look up through the tree branches. *Is she deliberately spying on me?* Maureen wondered. *Is she interested in something more than protecting my drapes and furniture from a passing shower?*

Maureen checked her watch. Nearly time for Trent and Pierre to arrive. It would be a relief to consider something positive—like making the Haven House Inn more attractive—instead of dwelling on chipped paint, faded carpets, mismatched furniture, and employees who thought money grew on trees, to say nothing of finding a dead man on the porch, and a cop who thought he was Inspector Clouseau.

Maureen's new friends arrived in the dining room at exactly eight, a beaming Trent carrying a large art portfolio, which he placed on the round table in front of her. Trent's idea of "a few sketches" turned out to be a series of full-color, artistic renderings of half-a-dozen areas of the inn. She recognized immediately the much-improved images of the front of the building, a guest suite, the inn's lobby, the dining room, the front porch, and even a small gift shop covering the far end of the porch where Wilson had died.

"Oh, Trent. These are amazing," she said. "You must have spent hours on this. Your ideas are exactly right for the way I picture Haven House."

"These days we have software to help us out. See?" He put a tablet on the table beside the portfolio. "See? We start with the room's dimensions and build from there. I can select colors, furniture, draperies, the whole deal."

"I can't thank you enough," she said. "And when you come back next time, with a little luck I'll hope to have put some of your ideas into practice."

"Maybe we'll come back next June for Trent's fiftieth birthday," Pierre suggested.

"Please do! That would be great."

Gert, in red-vested uniform, appeared at the table with the coffeepot. "Excuse me, Ms. Doherty," she said. "Herbie had to go and take care of a room service delivery. I'll be taking care of your breakfast orders. Coffee all around?" She filled the cups, wrote down orders for eggs Benedict for the two men, and tried unsuccessfully to convince Maureen that another doughnut would be a good source of whole wheat.

"Thanks, Gert," Maureen said. "You certainly get around. I didn't know you worked in the dining room too."

"Maid of all work, that's me." Gert looked over Trent's shoulder. "I see you've got one of those portable TVs too. What's that? A picture of this place?"

Maureen smiled. A tablet probably *did* look like a small television to a generation that wasn't raised with internet access. When Gert had reported that Conrad Wilson had shown her the picture he'd taken of her on "his cute little TV," she must have meant a tablet then too. "It's a picture of what this place can look like if we can get enough money together." Maureen peered closely at Trent's drawing of the renovated lobby, sans white wicker. "Nice, isn't it?" Maureen ate the last of her doughnut, savoring the partly melted sugar.

"Real nice. You can start with my rooms if you want to." Gert chuckled. "Won't hold my breath."

The three spent the better part of an hour discussing means of preserving the vintage charm of Haven House while at the same time offering guests the relaxing feel of an upscale beachfront resort. "I know you can do it, Maureen," Trent said. "See what you've already done right here at this table. You've given us perfectly cooked eggs Benedict, excellent coffee presented on a real linen tablecloth with what appears to be an authentic antique centerpiece."

"Total upscale vintage," Pierre agreed. "You wouldn't want to sell any of these papier-mâché candy buckets, would you?"

"I think I'll keep the ones we're using here in the dining room, but there are dozens more where these came from. Some masks and some of those honeycomb folded tissue paper pumpkins too, and all kinds of old-time Halloween stuff."

"Really? Can we look at them today?" He looked closely at the black cat bucket. "If they're all this good they'd bring fifty to a hundred dollars apiece from our customers who like to throw big, themed dinner parties."

"Sure. Actually, they're all upstairs in the same room where Trent was conceived in love."

"No kidding." Trent was plainly excited. "Let's look at them now. Maybe we can make a deal."

You bet we can, Maureen thought. Penelope Josephine Gray's hoard was beginning to pay off already.

Chapter 33

It didn't take long for Trent and Pierre to buy the contents of all three of the plastic containers—even the new ones Elizabeth had purchased turned out to be (no surprise) top-quality items. The men agreed to keep in touch, asking for first refusal in the event that any more fabulous vintage decorative items should show up. They promised to be back soon for another stay, very happily leaving Maureen with not only the wonderful art portfolio of designer sketches but also a check for nearly three thousand dollars.

Leo was thrilled to have full-time work bartending; deliveries from the food wholesalers were on time; Aster had called to say her cookies were ready to be picked up; Ted seemed to have everything in the kitchen under control. So far, it had been an excellent morning.

Just before two o'clock, Maureen moved to a wicker chair in the lobby to await Nora Nathan's arrival. Nora entered the inn wearing a crisp khaki linen shirtdress with navy accessories, carrying a black leather briefcase. *Sharp, business-like*, Maureen thought. *I need a whole new Florida-business wardrobe.* She stood to meet her attorney. Her *criminal* attorney.

They rode the elevator up to the second floor. "I have a few answers for you," Nora said, "and a few questions as well. This case is beginning to be quite interesting—not nearly as simple as I thought it was going to be."

Does that mean it's going to cost more money? Maureen wondered, but didn't dare to ask. Instead, she said, "So you've talked to Officer Hubbard? He's in and out of here as much as some of the help."

They stepped out onto the second floor. "Love that elevator," Nora said. "You just don't see craftsmanship like that anymore. Yes, Frank is thorough in his work." She smiled. "A police craftsman, you might say."

Maureen unlocked suite twenty-seven. Unlike Larry Jackson and even Frank Hubbard, Nora did not pause in the doorway or hesitate to enter the room. "Lovely office." She walked to the window. "You even have a view. Nice." She paused beside the bookcase, then reached for one of the gold-framed photos. "This your daughter?" she asked.

"My daughter?" Maureen was puzzled. "I don't have a daughter. I have no children." She crossed the room to where Nora stood. "Those photos all belonged to Penelope. I haven't had time yet to look them over."

Nora handed her the picture in its neat, small frame. "She looks just like you."

The smiling child stood in front of a sign proclaiming LONG PIER FISHING CHARTERS. She held a pole in one hand, a fair-sized fish in the other.

"It *is* me," Maureen whispered. "But how can that be?" She returned the picture to the top of the bookcase and sat in one of the nearby striped chairs. "The pictures, the carved manatee, the Florida books—those were just part of the décor. They were all here when I arrived. I'd assumed they belonged to Penelope. So how . . . ?"

She couldn't finish the sentence. Nora finished it for her. "So how did a picture of you as a child become a decorative accessory at Haven House Inn?"

"I don't know. That's definitely me, though," Maureen

said. "I was just talking to someone the other day about that same photo. My folks have an identical one in an album along with pictures of me with Mickey Mouse and having lunch at Cinderella's castle."

"Do you remember who it was that you talked to about it?" Nora's voice was gentle, persuasive.

"Sure. It was Ted. The bartender."

"If I remember correctly, you told Larry that you have no idea why Penelope Gray left this property to you. Is that right?"

"That's right," Maureen agreed. "Neither I nor my parents can think of any connection between our family and Ms. Gray, except that we spent a day in Haven after we went to Walt Disney World. We were celebrating my eighth-grade graduation."

Nora took pen and notebook from the black briefcase. "Did you by any chance stay here? At this inn?"

"Nope. We didn't."

"Is it possible that you were adopted? That you may be related to Ms. Gray in—um—that way?"

Maureen smiled. "You mean that I could be Ms. Gray's long-lost child? Believe me, that thought occurred to me, but it's extremely unlikely."

"Such things do happen, you know." Nora scrawled something in her notebook. "Have you asked your parents?"

"I'm positive that's not what happened in this case." Maureen moved from the striped chair to the one behind her desk. "Just before I was born, my dad got his first video camera. The occasion of my coming into the world was recorded in living, somewhat gory color, for all to see." She held up both hands. "You have no idea how excruciatingly embarrassing watching your own birth is to a kid. And the poor groaning woman in the stirrups was definitely my mom—not Penelope Josephine Gray."

"That's pretty strong evidence." Nora smiled. "I wonder why Ms. Gray had your picture." She tapped the notebook with the end of the pen. "How did you happen to discuss it with the bartender anyway?"

"His mom had a restaurant near that sign," Maureen recalled. "He wondered if he was the one who cooked that fish for me that day."

"Interesting," she said. "But the circumstances of your birth aren't what we're here to discuss, are they, although Larry and I still have concerns that someday someone may come forward and make some claim on the estate. That's why I asked." Once again, the pen was poised over the page. "However, as I mentioned, I've talked with Frank Hubbard about his investigation into the death of Conrad Wilson. Oddly enough, the bartender you mention is also part of the investigation. This Ted was the one who mixed and served the allegedly poisoned drink to Mr. Wilson. Is that your understanding as well?"

"Yes. Although I didn't actually *see* Ted mix the drink."

"Frank—Officer Hubbard—says that the digitalis which killed the man came from your medicine cabinet. That you witnessed his removing the pills from *your* bathroom. Correct?" Nora emphasized the word "your."

"Those were Ms. Gray's pills," Maureen insisted, "and as far as I'm concerned, that's still her medicine cabinet. I haven't put my things into it. I don't even want to touch it, now."

"I understand." Nora's voice was soothing. Calm. "I'm only asking these questions because I need to correlate your account with what the officer told me. Now about your relationship with the bartender. Had you met him before your arrival here in Haven?"

"No. Of course not. I didn't know *anyone* from Haven."

"You admit to having been in Haven some years ago."

"Yes. For a day when I was a child. We chartered a fishing boat and I caught a fish. That's all." Maureen pushed her chair back. "You sound as though you don't believe me."

"Of course I believe you," Nora said. "I need to be sure that your recollections line up with what we already know about Mr. Wilson's death. The man did die on your property, from a poison which may have come from your bathroom, administered by a man with whom you have some sort of relationship."

"I don't have a 'relationship' with Ted. Or anybody else in Haven!" Maureen felt anger rising. Tried to keep her voice steady.

"Yet you've had a conversation with him about a picture taken in Haven. A picture including a fish he says he may have cooked for you when you were both teenagers. Where did this conversation take place? At the bar? In this office?"

"At the bar," Maureen said. "In public. That's hardly a relationship. I barely know the man."

"Apparently you and this Ted are collaborating on some sort of restaurant promotion. The officer says you spent several hours together in Elizabeth's office. That you have promoted him to an 'executive chef' position without consulting the current restaurant manager."

The "current restaurant manager" being Elizabeth, Maureen thought, *worried that she might be losing one of the many jobs she's charging me for.*

"That is a business decision. I believe I can hire and fire anyone I want to. And are you *my* lawyer or not?" This time, anger sounded through the words and Maureen was aware of it.

"Of course I'm your lawyer, Maureen. I'm asking you the questions that Officer Hubbard will ask. We need to be sure your answers will not be self-incriminating."

"Nonsense. How can I incriminate myself when I've done nothing criminal?" Maureen felt a slight change in the room's temperature and lowered her voice. "And I'm sure Ted hasn't either."

"I believe you," Nora said again. "We're trying to see this from Hubbard's position. Don't forget—you found the body. You admit to having touched the body—actually changing the position of the body."

"I didn't change his position," Maureen insisted. "He slid out of the chair by himself."

"Hubbard is wondering if, while removing the camera from his pocket, you caused the body to slide from the chair."

"The camera! I never touched the camera. I didn't see any camera." Maureen felt the beginning of hot tears behind her eyes, threatening to spill over. "It seems as if Hubbard has his mind made up that I killed that poor man. What can I do?"

"If he decides to charge you, and that's a big 'if,' " Nora said, "first we'll address 'probable cause.' There appears to be no good reason for you to kill the man. There is no apparent benefit to you from his death."

"Whoever did it must have a reason," Maureen said. "I suppose it has something to do with the camera—the camera that they say takes pictures of ghosts."

" 'They say' doesn't hold up in court. Who are 'they'?" Nora's pen was poised again.

"His agent says he had pictures of actual ghosts," Maureen recalled. "At least one was taken in the inn's dining room. Gert, one of the housekeepers, talked about the camera too. She says he even took her picture with it and showed it to her on a 'little TV.' " Maureen watched as Nora printed "little TV" in the notebook.

"Interesting," Nora said. "I didn't see any 'little TV' listed among his effects. Do you know anything about a television set? Perhaps a portable one?"

Maureen shrugged. "I think it's possible that Gert mistook a tablet for a TV."

"Odd," Nora said. "Is Gert one of the staff that lives here? I understand that some of them do."

"Actually, several of them do." She held up her hand, counting off on her fingers. "Elizabeth, of course. Gert, George, Sam, and Molly do too. And Ted. That's all as far as I know."

"Hubbard's talked with all of them. Special attention to Ted and Sam, as far as I can see, and you, of course," she said. "He's interviewed all of the guests who were here at the time too. Did any of them stand out particularly to you?"

"Just the Morgans. They're fellow ghost hunters. They bought the Celebration Libation drink that killed Mr. Wilson."

"I have their names," Nora said. "They're staying here now, I understand."

"Yes. Mrs. Morgan—Clarissa—told me that she and Wilson exchanged words that night when she asked for his autograph."

"I didn't know about that. I don't think Hubbard does either." Nora wrote a few lines in her notebook, then looked up. "What did she tell you?"

Maureen repeated, as closely as she could recall, the conversation the two women had had in the laundry room. "She's still upset about it. She cried. Says she feels guilty because of that 'drop dead' remark."

"Hmm. Hubbard says a witness told him that the same couple had some sort of confrontation with Elizabeth that night too." Nora put the pen down." Did you see that?"

"No. Ted told me about it."

Another "Hmm," from the attorney. "So we're back to Ted again." Nora rubbed her arms. "Is it chilly in here or is it me?"

"Yeah. Sometimes the AC in here goes a little haywire. It's a pretty old system. We could finish downstairs if you like."

"Sure. I could use a cup of coffee. And Maureen, don't worry too much about Hubbard. Without some kind of probable cause, he doesn't really have much of anything. The Morgan couple, though. They're interesting. Maybe there's something there."

"Maybe," Maureen said. "I believe Clarissa Morgan is truly sorry about *something* she's said or done. But murder?"

Maureen and Nora got their coffee in to-go cups and joined a few others on the porch, rocking quietly, enjoying the balmy weather, watching the passing activity along the boulevard. The quartet was notably missing—undoubtedly busy with their housekeeping, errand-running duties, Maureen thought. Maybe Molly was baking more pies.

"You know, Maureen," Nora said, "this place does have a certain amount of charm. I can see why you might be tempted to try to save it."

"Can you? I'm glad to hear you say that because I'm deadly serious about it." Maureen immediately regretted her use of the word "deadly," considering their recent conversation, and their proximity to the very spot where Wilson had died. She hurried to lighten her tone. "I'm such an optimist that I even have a portfolio of sketches of how Haven House might look someday."

"Good for you." Nora finished her coffee and picked up her briefcase. "I need to get back to the office, and Maureen, I hope I haven't made you anxious about Hubbard's investigation, because *I'm* totally optimistic about the outcome of this case. We'll stay in touch."

"You have no idea how relieved that makes me feel," Maureen said. "I hope all this mess can be settled soon so I can concentrate on saving my inn."

The two women stood and shook hands. "You keep your eyes and ears open around here, Maureen," Nora instructed, "and don't hesitate to call me anytime—day or night—and be careful."

The lunchtime customers had dwindled to a very few when Maureen went back into the lobby. She tossed the empty coffee cups into a wicker wastebasket and opened the door to the dining room. Only one or two tables were occupied. The barstools were empty. Leo polished wineglasses, carefully returning each one to the overhead wine rack. Would it be all right if she went into the kitchen? Would she be in the way? Would Elizabeth think she was intruding?'

Why should I care what Elizabeth thinks? she asked herself. *This is* my *dining room and it's* my *kitchen. I can go anywhere I please.* She rounded the corner of the buffet table and opened the door leading to the kitchen. She stood, silent, just inside the doorway, watching what appeared to be well-ordered activity. Molly rolled piecrust on a floured board while Gert stood nearby slicing green apples. A pretty teenage girl Maureen recognized as one of the "regulars" who assisted the housekeepers chopped bunches of fresh parsley and a young man placed Hawaiian rolls into baskets lined with Halloween napkins. Another girl grated cheese into a stainless-steel bowl. Ted, in short white chef's jacket, moved among them, pausing occasionally, speaking softly to one or another of the workers.

The only jarring note was the uniformed police officer standing, arms folded, just inside a door leading to the outdoors. What was he looking for? What did he expect to see among the freshly peeled carrots and plump red tomatoes and the just-filled salt and pepper shakers? What did Maureen herself expect to see?

She'd expected to see Elizabeth, for instance, but the woman wasn't there. "Keep your eyes and ears open," Nora Nathan had instructed.

Maureen caught Ted's eye, smiled when he motioned for her to come over to where he stood beside the grill. She nodded, and staying close to the outside edges of the long room, she approached him. "What do you think?" he asked. "Do we look like a high-tech assembly line or what?"

"I'm amazed. How did you manage to get this place so organized—so absolutely synchronized—virtually overnight?"

"I used what my mama taught me," he said. "She knew how to run a kitchen. 'A tight ship,' she always said. 'A good crew. The right tools. A place for everything and everything in its place.' " He looked around the room, pride evident in his expression. "I put in a little overtime last night—rearranging things, sharpening knives, throwing away wilted lettuce. Between George and me, we scrubbed everything down. We were ready for some early-morning deliveries from the wholesalers. Sweet, huh?"

"Sweet for sure," she said. "Where's Elizabeth?"

"I guess Elizabeth isn't happy with the changes. Took one look at all the activity going on here this morning and stomped out."

"And what's with law enforcement over there?" Maureen tilted her head in the direction of the outer door where the cop was unmistakably watching the two.

"Guess I'm still a prime suspect," Ted said.

"Me too," she answered. "With me it's mostly patrol cars, and an occasional personal visit from the man himself."

"Hubbard?"

"Yep." She purposely returned the officer's stare. To her satisfaction, he looked away first. Once again, she faced Ted. "Look, I didn't do it and you didn't do it. It might be up to us to figure out who did so we can get rid of our police escorts. When can we talk?"

"Do you know how to peel potatoes?"

"Sure. Why?"

"I'm missing a worker at one station." Big smile. "I'll pick up an apron and a bag of potatoes and meet you over there by the double sink. We'll talk." He handed her a scrub brush and a paring knife. "Here you go."

Chapter 34

Ted presented Maureen with a hairnet and a long white bib apron. While she slipped the net over her hair, he showed her how to loop the long apron ties around her back and to tie them in front. He stood back.

"There now. You look like a professional."

"Far from it," she said. "I know how to peel potatoes, but I'm afraid I'm pretty slow at it."

"No problem," he said. "I'll have to keep walking around, checking everybody's progress. If I spend too much time with you, our snoopy friend over there will notice. We'll talk whenever I stop at your station. Okay?"

"Good idea," she said. "For starters, do we agree that the killer has to be somebody who was here at least a few hours before Wilson died?"

"Agreed," he said. "Preferably somebody who had a reason to want him out of the way."

"Agreed," she echoed, picking up a potato and the scrub brush. "Who's your first choice?"

"I don't have one. How do you think whoever it is got the poison into the drink?"

"I don't know," she said. "Someone besides you who has access to the bar?"

"Everyone who works here and a few who don't. Looks like we have a lot of work to do. See you on my next trip around the room." He moved away from the sink. "Be careful. Don't cut yourself."

Maureen scrubbed the first potato, then carefully picked up the knife, straining to remember her mother's instructions for potato peeling. *First you scrub it*, she recalled. *That's done. Next dig out any eyes.* There were no eyes or dark spots on Maureen's chosen potato. *Then, slice off a piece of one end so you can stand it up at an angle on the cutting board*, instructed Maureen's memory of Nancy Doherty. *Peel in a downward motion.*

It worked. Maureen put peeled potato number one into a pan of cool water and moved on to the next. By the time Ted returned, there were three potatoes in the pan, she'd had a few minutes to think about murder, and she hadn't cut herself.

"Not bad," he said. "You're doing a good job. I think the likely subjects—besides you and me and maybe Sam—are Elizabeth, all of the kitchen and housekeeping crews, Leo, delivery people, maybe the guests who were here that day."

"Okay. I've tried matching them up. Finding things some of them had in common." Maureen began scrubbing another potato. "Like, the Morgans and Wilson were both ghost hunters. Sam and his three buddies don't like the ghost hunters and, by the way, they each have keys to every room in the place."

"Sam and George have keys to the liquor backup cabinet because they do some of the shopping," Ted added. "Any ideas on where Elizabeth fits in? She doesn't seem to be really fond of any of us, ghost hunters, ghost lovers, or don't give a damn."

"Elizabeth is a bit of a puzzle, isn't she? I can't figure her out at all. Some of your crew really liked Conrad Wilson, though," Maureen said. "Leo and Herbie both told me that he was a good tipper, and Wilson and Gert had something in common because they'd each worked in Las Vegas."

"That's interesting. I knew about Gert. She brags about her showgirl past to anyone who'll listen. What did Wilson do there?"

"Took care of the slots. Made sure they didn't pay off too often. Gert says he was a whiz with machines." She cut a little piece from the potato, stood it on end, and began to pare.

"Nice technique," Ted said. "I'd better move along. The cop is giving me the evil eye. Think about how the poison got into my bar."

Maureen though about it, and realized immediately that with so many people having access to the bar—and just about anyplace else in the dining and kitchen area—it would be hard to narrow down the field of suspects. Since the digitalis was in pill form and had come from Ms. Gray's medicine cabinet, someone would have had to first swipe the pills and then crush them one by one and put them into a bottle. That kind of planning took some time.

Which people had access to the medicine cabinet? Maureen asked herself. *Elizabeth, Sam, George, Molly, and Gert, just for starters.* How many of the part-time housekeepers had keys to the penthouse too? And did anyone else have old keys to the rooms—as Trent had?

When Ted returned there were a few more potatoes in the pan and more than a few questions still unanswered.

"How is it that when the police examined all the bottles you used making Wilson's drink, they found no trace of digitalis in any of them?" she asked. "How can that be?"

"Somehow, somebody switched bottles after I mixed the drink," he said. "The trick is going to be figuring out who—and how."

"Okay. About the bottle switching. I'm pretty sure Gert and Molly and the boys were on the porch along with some of the neighbors and a few inn guests when Wilson left the bar and sat in his regular chair, away from the others," she reasoned. "Anyway, you would have noticed if any of them were touching any bottles."

"The Morgans were outside too," he said. "I don't know where Elizabeth was."

"When I went for help, after I found the body," Maureen said, "she was in the dining room, just inside the door. It looked to me as though she was watching the desk and the dining room at the same time."

"That sounds about right," Ted agreed. "Elizabeth's a great one for multitasking. Just before the cops came she came over to see how I was doing. She even offered to take over at the bar, but I told her I was okay."

She bartends too? Why not? Maureen thought. *She's billing me separately for each task.* She kept the thought to herself.

"The police shut everything down as soon as they arrived," she said. "They sent everybody home or to their rooms. That left time and space for *somebody* to move bottles around."

"Nope." Ted shook his head. "There was a cop stationed behind the bar right away, and I stood there myself until they shooed me away."

"This isn't going to be easy." Maureen frowned. "It has to be an inside job, but it looks as if all of the insiders have alibis."

"Except you and me. Gotta go. Keep thinking." Ted moved away to check on the cheese-grating process and Maureen selected another potato. This one had eyes. She dug into it, carefully removing the blemishes before beginning the downward strokes that would reveal the smooth white surface.

"Dig out the bad parts. The mistakes. That's what we need to do," she muttered. Had the killer made any mistakes so far? The medicine bottle without any fingerprints. That could be a mistake. And what about the time lapse between Conrad Wilson's leaving the bar and the time Maureen had found him? Had the police established who was where? Could one or more of the front-porch quartet have approached the man in the rocking chair and given him a fatal drink? They were all close enough to him and Maureen already knew that they stood by one another. She thought of how Gert and Molly each swore to the reporter that there were no ghosts in the inn, and how Gert had pleaded, "I'm not at liberty to say," when questioned about Wilson's visit to suite twenty-seven. Was the old Vegas showgirl hiding behind more than feathers?

What about the guys—George and Sam? They'd each expressed dislike—maybe downright hatred—of ghost hunters in general. She dropped the potato into the pan with a splash. *Maybe Aster was right. Nobody in Haven likes them. We need to figure out a more specific motive than dislike. How about . . . who can profit from his death? That leaves me out. Ted and Elizabeth too. The Morgans could, but only if they had the camera that takes pictures of ghosts and the computer to view them on—if any of that is even true—and the cops have those.*

"Sorry, Ted," she said when he made his next round of the kitchen. "No answers, just more questions." She shared her scattered thoughts.

"Okay," he said. "Maybe this isn't the right time or place to figure it out. How about someplace quiet, without cops or food prep in the way?"

"It'll have to be after tonight's dinner special is over," she reasoned. "You need to concentrate on that for now." She scraped the potato peelings into the sink and activated the garbage disposal. Ted leaned a little closer to her, to be heard over the sound of the machinery.

"How about a late-night walk on the beach?"

It was agreed. Ted would call her when the dinner cleanup was finished. She and Finn would meet him in front of the old casino at the end of the boulevard. Meanwhile she'd print out posters and flyers for the rest of the week's dinner specials.

Back in the penthouse Maureen tossed the blue-and-white McCartney outfit into the wicker hamper and stepped into the shower. From the next room came the gentle *ding* announcing Lorna's imminent arrival. "I'm in the shower!" Maureen called. "Be out in a minute!"

"That's okay. I'm in here. Boy, this room is awfully pink, isn't it?"

"You're in here?" Maureen peeked from behind the pink-flamingo-embellished shower curtain. "I didn't hear the door open."

"Silly goose." Lorna looked at herself in the mirror. "I can walk right through doors. Walls too. Fringe benefit of being dead."

"Great. Can you hand me a towel?" Maureen stuck out her hand.

"Sure. They're all pink too. Are you going to do some redecorating pretty soon?" The towel sort of floated toward Maureen. She reached for it, wondering at the same time if she didn't grab it, it would fall to floor or just keep on floating.

"Thank you. I'm thinking about it." She wrapped the towel around herself and opened the door to the bedroom, where Finn waited. "Actually, I'm thinking about decorating the whole place." Lorna followed, using the door in the proper manner.

"I thought we were broke." The ghost was now in front of the full-length mirror, admiring herself in a hot-pink cocktail dress. "Did we come into some money all of a sudden?"

"Where do you get that 'we'?" Maureen asked. "And I thought you didn't like pink."

"I like it when it's done right," she said, turning to admire her back view. "Edith Head did this one for Audrey. *Breakfast at Tiffany's*. Nineteen sixty-one."

"Wow! Whose closet have you been shopping in?" Maureen opened her underwear drawer and quickly slipped into bra and panties.

"Big closet." Lorna spread her arms wide. "Paramount Pictures Costume Archives. I drop by there whenever I get a chance."

"Big-time fringe benefit," Maureen agreed. "There must be lots of great clothes in Hollywood."

"I'll say. I think the wardrobe department at MGM must be the most haunted place in America. *Everybody* shops there. I don't know why the ghost hunters haven't figured it out."

"Speaking of ghost hunters, do you have any good ideas about who killed Conrad Wilson?"

"Maybe. What are you going to put on now?"

"Oh, nothing special. Just jeans and maybe a lightweight sweat shirt. I've got some work to do in my office; then Finn and I are going for a walk on the beach."

"Bor-ing," Lorna declared. "Don't you ever have a date?" Finn had perked up his ears at the mention of his name.

"Well . . ." Maureen spoke hesitantly. "I guess you might say the walk on the beach is *sort of* a date."

"No kidding. Who? The hot lawyer? The cute bartender? The nosy cop?"

"So you do get around the inn, huh? You're not as afraid of having your picture taken as you say you are," Maureen accused. "And it's the cute bartender. We're trying to figure out who killed Wilson because the nosy cop seems to think it's him or me."

"I don't worry about the pictures that much anymore since Wilson is dead," Lorna said. "That camera of his creeped me out. You saw the picture he took of Billy."

"I wanted to ask you about that. Are you sure that's Billy in the picture?"

"Absolutely."

"Not just an old publicity shot?"

"Not with a bottle of Sam Adams Boston Lager just left of the keyboard," Lorna said. "That wasn't around in Billy's day."

"Good point. But pictures or not, we need to find out who got the poison into Wilson—how they did it, and why."

"The why is easy," Lorna said. "Whoever it is wants to get their hands on that magic camera."

"Nosy cop has the camera, so that's not happening." Maureen pulled on her jeans.

"Oh. Too bad." Lorna shimmered for a second, then came back into focus. "Could someone have put the poison into his drink when everyone was looking at something else?"

"A diversion tactic? Like the sparkler in the drink on the bar or Elizabeth and Alexa Morgan's little shoving match at the other end of the room?" Maureen liked the idea. "Good one, Lorna. Did you ever play a detective?"

More shimmering. "I worked as a stand-in for Glenda Farrell in most of the 'Torchy Blane' movies."

"Did you solve any murders?"

"Naturally. I solved all of them. I mean Glenda did. Torchy was a newspaper reporter. She was always in trouble with the cops. Just like you are."

Maureen put her sweat shirt on, moved in front of Lorna, and studied her own reflection in the mirror. "How'd she do it? Solve the murders?"

"She found clues. Talked to people. I remember one where a guy was found dead in a hotel. Sort of like this place. Nobody could figure it out. See, there were several people involved. Torchy got one of them to rat on the others." Lorna clapped her hands together. "The weak link. All you and the cute bartender have to do is find the weak link. Gotta go. See you later." She began to fade.

"Where are you going?"

"Tiffany's. Fifth Avenue. I need something sparkly to wear with this. Bye." Finn woofed goodbye and she was gone.

"Want to come down to my office with me, Finn?" Maureen asked. "I have to work for a while." She waved a copy of the proposed week's dinner menus.

Finn ducked behind a chair.

"Oh, come on. We'll go for a nice walk on the beach afterward. Ted's coming with us."

"Woof?"

"Yeah. He's a good guy." The golden, with a tentative wag of the tail, followed her out the door, down the stairs, and—with some prodding—into suite twenty-seven. While the printer whirred out colorful copies, large and small, collated, sorted, and dated, Maureen stacked the window posters and flyers for the following day on top of the desk. "I'll take these downstairs first and get the quartet ready to deliver them—and at this rate of speed, I'll be finished before nine, in plenty of time to grab a bite at tonight's dinner special." Finn knew the word "dinner" and poked his nose out from the knee-hole. "Sorry. No dogs allowed in the dining room. Elizabeth's rule. No dogs or autograph hunters. I'll fix you a treat before we go for our walk. Okay?" With a grudging "woof," the dog retreated to his spot beneath the desk.

At a few minutes before nine Maureen delivered Finn to the penthouse, offered the promised doggy treat, as well as a pair of kitty num-nums for Bogey and Bacall, and with freshly printed materials under one arm headed down the stairs. A hum of conversation and the muted clinking of china and glassware greeted her as soon as she reached the lobby—the welcome sounds of a full dining room.

We've got this, she told herself. *And it's just the beginning.*

Chapter 35

Maureen finished the last frosty taste of orange sherbet and the final crumb of a jack-o'-lantern cookie. Savoring a fresh cup of after-dinner coffee, she relaxed in the straight-backed chair with its pressed-wood faux carvings and studied her surroundings. There was a feeling of satisfaction in having prepared the flyers and posters, turning them over to the quartet for delivery. Next, should she order new draperies immediately, or have all the mismatched chairs refinished first? Get rid of Penelope's horde by holding Haven's largest garage sale on the upcoming Halloween weekend, or wait until after the holiday?

"A penny for your thoughts." Jake joined her at the round table with its flickering tea-lighted witch-faced candy bucket. He'd brought his own coffee.

"Oh, hello, Jake. Just doing a little mental redecorating of the place," she said. "New drapes or new chairs? Recarpet or sand floors?"

"Decorating? You looked so focused I figured you must be figuring out who killed the ghost hunter."

She smiled. "Who killed the ghost hunter? Sounds like a headline."

"I hope it will be—and pretty soon. Mind if I run a few things by you? For verification?"

"Go for it." The player piano broke into a bouncy rendition of "Music, Music, Music." Was it a new recording of an old tune or was it a live performance by a dead artist? She tapped her foot to the beat. "I'll help if I can."

Jake put his phone on the table. "On the record. Okay?"

"Sure."

"Is it true that you've hired an attorney because the inn may be at fault somehow in Mr. Wilson's death?"

Already regretting her quick positive response to Jake's question, she thought carefully before she answered, "The inn has a law firm on retainer for all legal matters."

"Even for a murder on the premises?"

"No one has suggested that Haven House is responsible for Mr. Wilson's death in any way."

"The police say it's an 'ongoing investigation.' "

"Yes," she said.

"Have they questioned you personally?"

"Of course."

"What were you able to tell them?"

"That's confidential. You said you have something you want me to verify." Maureen felt her anger rising. "What is it?"

"Is it true that the pills that killed Wilson came from your medicine cabinet?"

"Some digitalis pills have been found on the property. They are not mine."

"Not prescribed for you?" He sounded disappointed.

"Excuse me. Ms. Doherty?" Waitress Shelly approached the table. "Elizabeth needs to see you in her office. She says it's important."

"Thanks, Shelly." Maureen stood, trying not to show how welcome the interruption was. "Sorry, Jake. We'll talk some other time."

Leaving an extra-generous tip for Shelly—partly for the excellent food and careful service, but mostly for the timely intrusion—Maureen hurried from the dining room and into the lobby. Elizabeth's door was closed, but the glass pane revealed that she was inside. Maureen knocked—timidly at first, and then a little louder. The woman looked up from the wicker desk, beckoning for Maureen to come in. "It's not locked. Come on. Come on. Don't just stand there. Sit down and tell me what the hell is going on around here."

Maureen did as she was told, pushed the door open and sat. "You mean the dinner specials? That seems to be going really well, don't you think so?"

"Oh, that. Sure. No. I mean what's all this I'm hearing about you throwing a giant garage sale over at the storage locker?" Elizabeth pushed a stack of papers aside. "Why wasn't I consulted about it? Are you planning to just get rid of Penelope's collection?"

"Well, if you put it that way, yes. I am," Maureen said. "We're paying out good money every month to store other people's castoffs in a high-security, air-conditioned locker. We can't afford it. Some of Penelope's hoard is worth a few dollars. No decision has been made about actually holding a sale. I've put in a call to Mr. Crenshaw at the thrift store to arrange an appraisal. Who told you about the garage sale?"

"I don't know. Everybody is talking about it. They say you already sold some old Halloween stuff and now you're going to sell the rest of Penelope's collection." Elizabeth's eyes narrowed. "You planning to share that money?"

"When we do it, if we do it, I'm planning to start by updating the dining room," she said. "If we begin to show a little profit, maybe later we'll be able to start working on the guest rooms."

"Huh. Throwing good money after bad, that's what I say." Elizabeth balled up her fist and pounded the desk, scattering papers—some onto the floor. Maureen bent to pick up the few that had landed on her side of the desk. Elizabeth reached across, snatching the pages from Maureen's outstretched hand.

"Whenever *I* see a little extra money coming in around here, I hand out some nice bonuses to the help."

Maureen took a deep breath and fought the urge to comment that the first and biggest bonus would undoubtedly be paid to Elizabeth herself. "That's a generous thought," she said, "but putting some capital back into the business seems like the wisest course right now. The dinner specials are a good start. What do you think about having Sam and George do a little work on the outside of the building? Some sanding and a coat of paint would do wonders."

"Well, let's see first how your little yard sale goes. You'll probably get about enough money from Penelope's dusty old stuff to buy a gallon of paint at Walmart." She stood up. "I need to get back to work in the kitchen. I'll have to make sure the bartender—excuse me, the executive chef—knows enough to get everything cleaned up and put away before the breakfast crew shows up." She'd moved across the room and opened the office door before Maureen had a chance to leave her white wicker chair.

A lone sheet of paper peeked out from under the desk. Maureen picked it up as she left the office, crossing into the lobby. She handed it to Elizabeth, but not before she'd read the heading. "Estimate for repair of an eight-inch HD display tablet. Inoperative device. No charge."

Did Elizabeth actually have *the* tablet—the "cute little TV"—that Conrad Wilson had used to display the pictures he'd taken of Gert? He'd taken those pictures with the camera he always carried with him—the one that Lorna believed could photograph ghosts—and Ted had told her that the tablet was "broken."

Maureen thought about confronting the woman, but the door had closed behind her before she could form the right words. *Just as well*, she realized *No sense in making her more disagreeable than she already is. But* somebody *should look into it. Maybe I should tell Officer Hubbard.* That idea was quickly discounted. *I'll call Nora.* Maureen climbed the stairs to her office, where, she assumed, she'd have some measure of privacy for her phone call to the attorney.

"As far as I know, all of Wilson's electronics are still safely locked up in the Haven PD's evidence room," Nora reported. "Of course, it's possible that Elizabeth's own tablet is broken, but that seems like too much of a coincidence. Want me to check this out?"

"I think it's worth checking," Maureen said. "Even if Officer Hubbard has Wilson's tablet in his custody, maybe Elizabeth is doing some advance planning. The cops will return everything to the inn eventually, won't they? Wilson had been there for a month and hadn't paid his bill yet. I just checked the figures. It's sizable. He used room service a lot."

"Everything has to be safely stored for thirty days. After that, the inn can put a lien on the things he left there to pay the bill. It doesn't seem as though a few secondhand electronics would begin to cover it," she said, "even at the Haven House Inn low rates."

"From what I hear, there'll be several high bidders on the camera and the computer—and very likely the tablet," Maureen explained. "I'm thinking Elizabeth will cut herself in on the profits. She's a big believer in employee bonuses for good work."

"Nothing illegal about that," Nora said. "Keep in touch. This is getting more interesting every day, ghost camera and all."

Maureen had been so busy she'd nearly forgotten about the ghosts—particularly the one who might be lurking in the room next door. In fact, she'd begun to think about that long-ago bedroom as the place where her new friend designer Trent had been "conceived in love." She smiled at the thought, hoping that the men would return to the inn as they'd promised.

"If Trent will turn fifty in June, and his mother's pregnancy was the typical nine months, his parents were here fifty years ago sometime in September." The idea came like a lightning bolt. "I have the guest books in the closet. I can look up Mr. and Mrs. John Smith. I'm sure we can identify their luggage, thanks to Penelope's stickers. Maybe, just maybe, there'll be a clue there to help Trent find his long-lost daddy!"

She rushed across the office, opened the door to the bedroom, turned the glass knob on the closet door, and began pulling down the black-covered guest books, one by one. She sat on the floor, the tall, thick books spread out on the soft carpet. The hunt didn't take as long as she'd thought it might. Mr. and Mrs. John Smith had checked into the Haven House Inn on September 23, forty-nine years ago.

"Bingo," she said aloud.

"Martha," said a disembodied whisper.

"What?" Maureen looked around the empty room.

"Martha," the voice repeated.

Another lightning bolt. The ghost in suite twenty-seven hadn't been calling for his mother all those years. He was calling for a woman named Martha.

Maureen barely had time to digest that revelation when her phone pinged. Text from Ted: "Ready for beach walk? Waiting at the casino."

"On my way," she answered hurriedly, returned the guest books to the top shelf, and left the bedroom, firmly closing the door. After a quick straightening up of the office, she turned out the lights and locked suite twenty-seven.

Finn seemed to have remembered the promised walk and waited just inside the penthouse door. Bogie and Bacall weren't visible. "They may have gone off on some kind of cat-business of their own. They'll be fine," she said, and waited for a moment before leaving, thinking perhaps Lorna might put in an appearance. After all, who else could she talk to about her recent, surprising contact with John Smith?

There was no ding of the push bell and no shimmering manifestation, so with leash in place and flashlight in hand, Maureen and the golden used the stairs and, avoiding the lobby
and porch, left via the now-familiar laundry room route.

By the time she'd passed the thrift store, she recognized
Ted, his tall form silhouetted against the wall of the historic
dance hall, and walked a little faster.

"Hey, Maureen. Hi, Finn!" Ted called as they approached.
"Nice night for a walk. Look at that big, almost-Halloween
moon." He was right. The nearly perfect golden circle reflected on the water and illuminated the sand.

"It's beautiful," she answered. "How do you feel dinner
went tonight? Everything was delicious and it looked to me
like a good crowd."

"Looks like we've hit on a good formula," he said. "Want
me to hold the flashlight?"

"Sure." She handed it to him. "After dinner Elizabeth
wanted to talk to me. Kind of like getting summoned to the
principal's office."

"I know the feeling," he said. "What did she want?"

"She heard somewhere about my plan to sell everything in
the storage locker—to get rid of Penelope's hoard and get a
little more money into our operating account. Wanted to
know what was going on."

"What did you tell her?" They crossed the beach and
began their walk on the hard-packed sand next to the tide
line.

"The truth. That locker is costing us money. The stuff in it
can earn us some."

"What does she think about it?"

"Not a believer, but she didn't actually object to it."

"Good," he said. "At least, she won't be fighting against
the idea."

"Looks that way," Maureen said. "I talked to my lawyer
this evening too."

"Oh? Anything I need to worry about?"

"I don't think so. She straightened me out on a few legal things about the chain of custody of Wilson's things—especially his electronics."

"Thirty days and it comes back to the inn?" he asked.

"Right. You've been doing some checking too."

"I wanted to know how much time we've got to solve this mess, before Hubbard drags one of us off to jail."

"No joke," she said. "Got any new ideas?"

"Maybe a couple. This has to be a group effort, I think. One person couldn't do it all alone: the bottle switching, getting the poison from your medicine cabinet—"

"Penelope's medicine cabinet," she corrected.

"Gotcha." He smiled. "Want to let Finn off his leash? It's okay this time of night. He looks like he'd like a good run."

"If you say it's okay." She unfastened the leash and Finn happily dashed away, Ted following his movement with the flashlight. "So should we think of particular groupings of people who might be working together?"

"That's the way I see it," he said. "The obvious ones are Sam and George, Molly and Gert. If any of them did it, the others will cover for them 'til hell freezes over. No doubt."

"You're right about that. How about Clarissa and Alex? Do you think they're a grouping all by themselves?"

"I think so." Ted tossed a stick for Finn. "But the problem there is they wouldn't know where everything is. Like the pills in Penelope's medicine cabinet."

"Good one. Let's add someone from the local talent to the Morgan group. Who do you like for that role?" Maureen wondered.

"Sam, maybe? Some say he hated the ghost hunter."

"What about Gert? She's pretty nosy but keeps her mouth shut about her friends."

"Good point," Ted agreed. "And she has keys to everything. Elizabeth sems to trust her. How about Molly?"

Maureen shook her head. "Don't think so. She's a sweet-heart, but she talks too much to be a conspirator."

"The problem with Molly and Gert and the others is that none of them were at the bar that night." Finn returned the stick and Ted tossed it ahead once more. "And the bottle with the digitalis in it was switched with a new bottle be-tween the time Wilson left the bar and the cops came."

"Right. All four of the old-timers were peacefully rocking in their chairs when I found Wilson dead," Maureen said. "Where does that leave us?"

"The Morgans were definitely at the bar, within easy reach of all the bottles, Wilson's camera, and Wilson's drink," Ted said. "Can we agree that they are involved?"

"Agreed. Who else was that close?"

"Hey, what about this? Elizabeth wasn't at the bar, but she *was* in close contact with the Morgans!" Ted stopped walk-ing. "Both of them."

"The gold bag, rolled-menu incident." She stopped walk-ing. Finn sat, puzzled, watching both of them. "What was the smallest bottle involved in making the Celebration Liba-tion?"

"Grenadine," he said. "Rose's grenadine syrup. We use twelve-ounce bottles. No bigger than a can of soda."

"And if someone mashed half a bottle of pills and dis-solved them in grenadine, what would happen?" Maureen tried some mental calculations involving ounces and mil-ligrams and came up with a big zero. "Can you figure it out?"

"The grenadine bottle I used that night was about half-full, so there was . . . say, six ounces of syrup—and I guess it would depend on how much medicine was in each pill, huh?"

"I guess. Anyway, that much sugary syrup would cover up any nasty taste from the pills, I'll bet."

"I used a healthy slug of grenadine in that drink." He grimaced. "You need it with the blue curaçao to get that purple color. We can safely assume that whatever the proportions were, there was enough poison in the drink to kill the poor guy."

"Right." They began walking again. "So how did they make the switch?" she asked.

"Clarissa was waving that gold bag around," he said. "If one of the Morgans grabbed the grenadine it wouldn't have been hard to pass a bottle from the bag to Elizabeth, but where would Elizabeth stash it?"

"The pocket. The pocket in the red apron where she keeps menus, and—"

He finished the thought, finished her sentence: "—and all Elizabeth had to do was slip a new bottle of grenadine behind the bar before the cops showed up." They exchanged a victorious high five. Finn gave a happy "woof" and fell into step between them.

They were silent for a few yards. Ted broke the silence. "Motive? Why would Elizabeth get involved in something so messy? I know she liked throwing the old woman's money around, but this . . ."

"You're right. If they wanted the camera, why didn't they simply grab it? It was right there on the bar."

"What if they didn't need the camera—just the memory card? What about that?" Ted sounded excited again. "Wilson surely would have noticed that his camera was missing, even if he was starting to get groggy. When they were getting the autograph, Clarissa put that big bag on the bar, separating Wilson from his camera—*and* her husband Alex."

"Alex is a photographer. He knows his way around cameras," Maureen said. "If he has fast hands, he could have yanked that card out, put in another one—probably with a few random pictures taken around Haven on it—and closed the camera back up in seconds. Then all they'd have to do is pop the memory card into a computer and voilà! Ghosts on parade."

"Okay." He stopped walking again. "Then why did they come back to the inn? Something must have gone wrong."

"What could go wrong? Seems like the perfect crime so far." She stopped beside him.

"If they did what we think they did—if they're killers—you'd think they'd stay as far away from Haven as they could get." They began walking again. He took her hand. It seemed a natural thing to do. "But there they are. Back in Haven again. Why?"

You'll know the where but not the why.

Chapter 36

"I don't know what we should do next," Maureen said as the two approached the Long Pier. "Tell Hubbard what we suspect or keep looking for more answers?"

"More answers," Ted said. "We have motive and opportunity pretty well nailed down, but we must be missing something or else they wouldn't all still be hanging around." They turned at the fishing charters sign and headed back toward the casino. "Maybe one of them will slip up—show us something we can use."

"Look for the weakest link," Maureen murmured.

"What?"

"The weakest link. The suspect most likely to crack," she said. "I heard it—read it someplace. I think that would be Clarissa. She's already cried a couple of times. She even feels guilty for his death. Maybe somehow we can make her feel just a little *more* guilty."

"Good idea," he said. "Any thoughts on how?"

"Work up some more sympathy for the deceased, I guess. How he'd worked for years and was just about to get his big break. His own book of ghost photos."

"Yeah. The big break she and her husband planned to steal." Ted sounded angry.

"Clarissa told me every ghost junkie in the world would

want to come to the inn when *their* book came out." She squeezed Ted's hand. "Same book."

"You know, there's a good chance there *are* no ghost pictures, no matter what the agent says."

She nodded. "Photoshopped. Like Sam said. And Wilson will have died for no reason at all."

"Maybe now *he'll* haunt the Haven House Inn," Ted suggested. "How about that?"

"No thanks," she said, thinking that the inn already had more than enough ghosts as it was. "Let's hope he rests in peace. Want to run the rest of the way?"

"Let's do it. Come on, Finn." The three ran back to the casino, the dog bounding joyously ahead.

When they arrived at the casino, Maureen reattached Finn's leash. Ted handed her the flashlight and the two approached the boulevard. "Look at that." Maureen pointed to the T-shirt store on the corner. "There's the poster for tomorrow night's special dinner. Our delivery team has already done their job. I'll bet you'll have another full house."

"I'll bet the inn will too," Ted said. "After all, it's almost Halloween weekend, and Haven is usually a prime destination for guests in search of ghosts."

"I guess that makes sense since people seem to believe we're haunted," she said, "even though most everyone I've talked to since I arrived here in Haven has 'pooh-poohed' the idea, although lots of them believed enough to stock up on Halloween merchandise."

"Like Halloween pumpkin cookies?"

"Guilty," she said. "But everyone seemed to like them." They'd reached the inn, and Maureen and Finn headed for the side door entrance.

"Want to stop by the dining room for an Irish coffee and another cookie?" Ted asked.

"Thanks," she said, "but I've got some homework I need to get into. I'm serious about starting the redecorating project as soon as we can afford it." She was also anxious to talk with Lorna about the word she'd heard spoken in suite twenty-seven.

Somehow, Maureen realized with a shock, she'd gone from an often-stated "I don't believe in ghosts" to turning down a late date with a definitely attractive man so that she could have a confidential chat with her own resident apparition. "Can I take a rain check on that Irish coffee?" she asked, hoping he wouldn't take her refusal as a snub.

"Absolutely," he said. "See you tomorrow. We'll talk some more." He gave Finn a good-night pat on the head, and climbed the stairs to the porch.

There was no one in the guest laundry when Maureen passed by. She'd almost been hoping she'd see Clarissa Morgan there so that she could begin testing her "weakest link" theory. She was pleased with the way she and Ted had brainstormed about Wilson's murder, and felt confident that they were on the right track. "We have a way to go before we have all the answers," she told Finn. "But I think we're pretty darned close."

Bogey and Bacall seemed glad to see them—greeting Maureen with a couple of ankle rubs and Finn with a nose bump from Bogie and a less personal tail wave from Bacall. "I'll get you guys some treats," she said. With more than a passing glance at the push bell on the desk, she headed to the kitchen. *I wonder*, she thought, *what would happen if I ring the bell? Does it work in reverse? If I push it, will Lorna appear here whenever I want her to?*

With treats and num-nums dumped rather unceremoniously into the proper bowls and placed onto the proper place mats, Maureen returned to the living room. With just a fraction of a second's hesitation, she very gently, with one finger, tapped the bell.

There was a whooshing sound.

"Wow!" Maureen gasped.

"What?" A windblown and slightly frazzled Lorna seemed to drop from the ceiling.

"I'm so sorry, Lorna." Maureen reached toward the image. "Are you all right? I didn't know what would happen if I pushed it."

Lorna sat on the couch, patted her hair, straightened her skirt, and adjusted a diamond necklace that practically screamed *Harry Winston!*

"Not your fault," Lorna said. "The new bell must be more powerful than the old one. That was a wild ride. The old bell gave me about ten minutes' notice. This one is different. What a rush!"

"I wasn't sure it would work at all," Maureen said.

"I guess I forgot to tell you about it," Lorna said. "Or maybe I just hoped you wouldn't figure it out. Penelope used to push it anytime she felt lonesome and wanted somebody to talk to. You won't do that, will you?"

Maureen crossed her heart. "I promise. From now on I'll only ding you if it's important."

"Good. Now that I'm here, what do you want?" The animals had returned to the living room at the sound of Lorna's whooshing entrance. Bogie and Finn sat at Maureen's feet, while Bacall walked through Lorna, then curled up on the couch beside her.

"A strange thing happened tonight," Maureen began. "Actually, several strange things happened tonight, but the one I dinged you for is about John Smith. I think I had a little encounter with him in suite twenty-seven."

"No kidding. Was it awful?"

"Not awful. Just strange. I need to hear your opinion, and I might need your help with something. I guess I told you about Trent and Pierre, the guys who are helping me with designs for Haven House."

"What about them?"

Maureen repeated as closely as she could remember Trent's

story about his mother and John Smith. "Her name was Martha—and his name was Trent—and Lorna, when I left the bedroom tonight, I heard John Smith whisper her name just as plainly as I'm hearing you now. 'Martha,' he said. 'Martha.' Not 'Mother,' like people have said all these years. He's been calling for Martha—and now we know who she is, and that John Smith—Trent—has a son, named after him."

"A good story," Lorna said. "But what has this got to do with me?"

"Martha told Trent and Pierre that she was 'going to the light.' That she would see her true love there. We have to send John Smith—I mean Trent something-or-other—to the light. We have to get them reunited. And get my office un-haunted."

"Where do you get that 'we'?" Lorna began to fade.

"Don't you skip out on me now. There's nothing to be afraid of in suite twenty-seven. John Smith is just a poor lonely soul. Nothing evil about him at all. He's just been waiting all these years for Martha to come back to the Haven House Inn."

"What do you want me to do about it?" Lorna pouted. It was a well-rehearsed movie starlet pretty pout.

"You can tell him how to go to the light—how to get to see Martha again. You can do it ghost-to-ghost," Maureen said. "I have no idea how to go about it. And if he'll talk to you, we can get to hear the rest of the story. Where did he and Martha go that night? And did he really die in Vietnam? Maybe he'll tell you his last name. Come on, Lorna. It would be such a kindness to him—and to Trent too."

"Oh, I don't know, Maureen. I'm scared. I always heard bad things about that suite."

"Finn and I will go with you. You can probably do it through the closet door. Maybe we won't have to see him. Please, do it, Lorna."

"Look at Finn," she said. "He doesn't want to do it either." Finn had once again assumed his lying-down-flat-with-paws-over-the-eyes posture.

"I know. But he's a brave good boy. He'll do it. I'll bet John Smith will talk to you. I'll bet he's seen your movies. He'll be thrilled to talk to a real movie star."

"You think so?"

"I do. And if you get too scared, you can just disappear, can't you?"

"That's true," Lorna agreed. "It's one of those perks of being dead."

"Then you'll do it?" Maureen pleaded. "Pretty please?"

"Oh, all right," Lorna grumbled. "But give me a minute to change. I'm a little overdressed for talking a ghost out of his closet."

"You do look gorgeous, though," Maureen said. "The necklace sets the outfit off perfectly."

Lorna dematerialized instantly, her disembodied "Thanks" hovering in the air. Within less than a minute she popped back into sight, this time in all-over, formfitting black leather.

"Wow. Nice. Where'd that come from?"

"What? This old thing?" Lorna took a turn in front of the mirror. "I popped downstairs and grabbed it out of Clarissa's closet. She has some high-end stuff."

"I've noticed," Maureen agreed. "The girl has expensive tastes. Come on, Finn, let's go downstairs. Lorna is coming with us." Finn gave a soft, reluctant "woof" and, tail between his legs, followed Maureen to the door.

"I'll meet you down there," Lorna said, and disappeared.

Maureen, with Finn close behind her, hurried downstairs, unlocked the door to suite twenty-seven, and went inside. Lorna had kept her word and now sat in a striped chair. She looked up from the copy of *Got Ghosts?* open in her lap. "What took you so long?"

"Very funny," Maureen said. "Are you ready? Let's go in and get this over with. The poor soul has been haunting that room for far too long."

"Okay." Lorna stood. "I think I heard him moving around in there a minute ago. Do you think he knows we're here?"

"I don't know. But you need to tell him how to go to the light. Tell him that Martha is there now, waiting for him. If you can, find out what his whole name is. Tell him he has a son. Ask if he died in Vietnam." She turned the knob and opened the bedroom door. "Mostly, send him to the light." She stepped into the room. Lorna followed. Finn cowered in the doorway at first, then scampered back to his under-the-desk sanctuary.

"I'll try." Lorna stood in front of the closet. "John Smith? Trent? Are you here?"

Maureen watched as the glass knob turned and the door opened slowly. A shape—just a shadow really—moved toward Lorna. "Trent?" Lorna said. "I have a message for you from Martha."

The shadow shimmered, much the way Lorna did sometimes. It made a sound—not exactly words. Maureen strained to listen—to understand. The shadow-thing said, "Martha," several times, but the rest of whatever he was telling Lorna sounded more like a series of musical notes than words. Lorna answered in the same lilting language with only the occasional understandable syllable. Maureen heard "Army," and "cars," and "love." She realized that Finn had abandoned his hidey-hole and was standing beside her, ears alert, clearly listening to the melodic conversation coming from the closet area.

Maureen checked her watch. She'd been aware of time passing but hadn't realized how much. They'd been in suite twenty-seven for over an hour when the shadow made a sudden lurching move toward Lorna, then seemed to envelop her in its darkness. Maureen ran toward the dark mass. "Lorna! Are you all right? Oh my God. Lorna." Then the shadow-thing was gone and Lorna stood there alone. Finn ran too and stood in his protective stance between Lorna and the now-closed closet door. "Are you all right?" Maureen called again.

"Yes. I'm fine. Got a pencil or something to write with? I don't want to forget any of this. Listen. Take this down." Maureen grabbed pen and paper from the desk. "Shoot," she said.

"The ghost isn't John Smith," Lorna began. "He's Army Sergeant Trent Sullivan. He died in December nineteen seventy-two near Kon Tum Province. His remains were returned to America in twenty fifteen and he was buried with full military honors in Arlington National Cemetery." Lorna paused. "Did you get all that, Maureen? He wants his son to know where he is."

"Got it," Maureen said. "Is he going to the light? Is he going to join Martha?"

"He's gone," she said. "Oh, Maureen, he was so happy that he hugged me. And know what? He'd seen a couple of my movies!"

"Did you find out what happened here that night? Where they went?"

"They were young. Martha was working her way through the University of Tampa. Trent had aged out of foster care and had enlisted right out of high school. He was due to report for duty the following day. This was their only chance to be together before he left for the war. Back in the seventies a lot of people still didn't approve of young kids sleeping together, so they checked in here where they figured no one would notice. They arrived in separate cars, but used Trent's license number She had a dorm check-in time so she left first. Then he did. They never saw each other again. He was dead within three months. What a terrible, sad story." Tears sparkled in her eyes. "But now they're finally together. So there's a happy ending."

Maureen felt tears spring to her own eyes, making the bridge of her nose hurt. She'd get in touch with Trent immediately, of course. But wait. What if Trent didn't believe her? What if he didn't believe in ghosts? "What if he thinks I'm nuts?" she worried. "I wish I could talk to Ted about it, but what if *he* thinks I'm nuts?"

She'd already noticed that suite twenty-seven was warmer, now that John Smith was gone. Finn had noticed the difference too, and had begun investigating, happily sniffing around the edges of both rooms.

"Can we please go back upstairs now?" Lorna asked. "I'd like to change into something more comfortable. Your clothes are a lot more my style than Clarissa's."

After Lorna had left—wearing Maureen's rose-colored "world's softest pajamas"—and Finn had curled up beside her on the blue couch, Maureen finally had time to think, to sort out the day's, and night's, happenings.

"First of all," she said aloud—even though Finn didn't appear to be listening—"I think we've got the answer to Conrad Wilson's death, at least *some* of the answer. Elizabeth and both of the Morgans are involved. We only need a little more information, a few more facts, and Ted and I will have enough to give to Hubbard. Hopefully, enough to get him to stop hounding us."

Finn opened his eyes. "Not that kind of hound. Look, I'm pretty sure Clarissa is the weak link we need. She knows how the bottles got switched and I'm sure she and Alex have the memory card from Wilson's camera. I'm betting they couldn't get it to work and they're waiting around here to get a chance to use his equipment. The problem is, the cops won't return any of his electronics for almost a month." Finn yawned, stretched, and put his head on her lap. "Then there's the broken tablet. Elizabeth must have thought it could be repaired—unless her own tablet was broken, and Nora says that's too much of a coincidence."

Finn yawned again. "Stop yawning," she said. "You're making me sleepy."

Maureen yawned. "Time for bed, I guess. We'll figure all this out tomorrow. Ted and I will talk some more, and I'm definitely going to think of a way to tell Trent what I've learned about Martha and his father. Maybe there's some way to tell him without involving ghosts."

Chapter 37

Dressed for the busy day ahead in madras Bermudas and a white silk shirt, with her coffee brewing, the animals fed, Maureen looked around her neat and pretty kitchen. "Maybe it would be all right if I invited Ted up here tonight for an Irish coffee. It would give us a chance to talk in private about the murder." She had to admit to herself that solving Wilson's murder wasn't the only reason the idea had crossed her mind. Some alone time with the handsome chef would be welcome no matter what the topic of conversation happened to be.

"I wonder if Penelope left me any Irish whiskey." She opened the cabinet where she'd seen the liquor supply earlier. Standing on tiptoe, she looked over her inventory. There was a partially filled bottle in the front row. Shorter than the others, it stood out because of the grenadine's bright red color.

Automatically, she reached for it, then snatched her hand back. Could this be the switched bottle? The poisoned bottle? She slammed the cabinet door shut. What was she supposed to do now? Call the police? Call Nora? Call Mom and Dad and say, "Get me out of here"? None of those options seemed right. With a slightly shaking hand, she poured a cup of coffee and sat at the kitchen table. This was a problem she'd hadn't anticipated. First the digitalis pills had been found in her bathroom medicine chest. Now, if anyone cared to look, the poisoned sweet syrup could probably be found in her kitchen cabinet.

What happens to a person who's found in possession of a murder weapon?

She had darned well better tell somebody about it—and do it fast. Whoever put it there knew it was there. Whoever put it there could tell somebody. Whoever put it there could cause Maureen Doherty a whole lot of trouble.

If she and Ted had figured out the chain of possession correctly, using the cover of Clarissa's giant gold bag Elizabeth and Clarissa had switched bottles in front of everyone in the dining room by staging that little scuffle. Elizabeth had put the poisoned bottle into the gold bag, and taken a fresh bottle out—slipping it, rolled up in a menu, into her apron pocket. Meanwhile, Alex had switched Wilson's memory card for one with a few innocent tourist-type shots of Haven on it. So the cops would be left with a clean grenadine bottle, a ghost-free memory card, and no suspects except the bartender who'd mixed the lethal drink and the new owner of the Haven House Inn who'd had the apparent last contact with the deceased.

We can't prove any of it, but I'd better call Officer Hubbard anyway. She reached for her phone. *No. There are probably no fingerprints on that bottle either. He might just take it as a confession of my guilt,* she told herself. *I'd better call Nora instead.* She scrolled through her contact numbers. *Nora Nathan.* Her finger reached for the name, then drew back. *No. I know she'll go with me to the police station, but then what?* Calling Mom and Dad was, of course, out of the question.

She called Ted.

"I'll be right up," he said.

Finn's "woof" announced Ted's arrival even before his urgent knock on the door. "Come on in." She pulled the door open. "I don't know what to do." It seemed the most natural thing in the world for him to put a comforting arm around her shoulders.

She leaned against him for a moment, then straightened her back and moved away. "It's out in the kitchen," she said. "I'll show you."

"You didn't touch it, did you?"

"Nope. Just slammed the door on it, sat down, and freaked out. Then I called you." He followed her into the kitchen. She pointed to the cabinet. "It's in there. See?" She opened the door. He moved closer, peering at the bottle.

"Yep. It's the right brand. Just about the right amount of syrup in it too." He took a step back. "And guess whose fingerprints are probably all over it?" He held up both hands. "Mine."

"What do you think we should do?" She sat at the table, motioning for Ted to take the seat opposite. "Want some coffee?" He nodded. She popped a fresh pod into the machine. "We've got to tell somebody. Somebody has to get that bottle out of here and into the right hands."

"Which one of them do you think put it into your kitchen?"

"Elizabeth," she said promptly. "She admitted she'd been up here. Said it was to close a window because it looked like rain."

She handed Ted the full mug of coffee and pushed the sugar bowl and creamer toward him. "Thanks," he said. "Maybe you should call your lawyer—just in case." She nodded agreement and pulled Nora's number up again. This time she tapped the name. She put the phone on speaker mode so Ted could listen.

Nora answered immediately. "Maureen. I was just about

to call you. What's going on over there? I just found out that Frank Hubbard has applied for a search warrant. Wants to search your apartment. Is there anything you haven't told me that I need to know?"

"There wasn't, until this morning—less than an hour ago," Maureen said. She told the attorney about the grenadine bottle in the cabinet. "And Nora, there is something else. It's kind of a theory. We . . . I . . . don't have proof, but I guess I'd better tell you about it anyway Wilson's killer *could* have done it." She launched into a condensed, but orderly, verbal report on what she and Ted had put together.

"I'm glad you told me this. It may be important. But for right now, Hubbard must have had a tip from someone, Maureen—someone with good information—in order to get a search warrant. It's likely that he knows about the grenadine bottle. They don't just hand those warrants out. Maybe I'd better head down there to be on hand in case there's any problem."

"Would you? I'd appreciate that," Maureen said. "I'm worried. Should I be?"

"Yes. You should. I told you. Frank Hubbard is a bulldog." Finn whined.

"Hush. Not that kind of bulldog," Maureen whispered.

"What?" Nora asked. "Is someone else there?"

"Talking to my dog," she said. "I'll see you as soon as you get here."

"I have a few things to tie up here; then I'll be right along," the attorney promised.

Ted stood, carrying his coffee mug to the sink. "I'd better get downstairs before Elizabeth notices that I'm not there. Maybe you should make yourself scarce too, before Hubbard gets here."

"Good idea. I don't want to have to talk to him before Nora arrives." She walked to the door with Ted. "Better take the stairs," she suggested. "Go out the laundry room door and come back in through the kitchen. She'll think you've been there all along."

Ted smiled. "You have a devious mind," he said. "I kind of like that."

After Ted had left, she gave some serious thought to his idea that she should avoid Hubbard. "There's no place to hide. I'd try to go to Nora's office instead of just waiting here, but there seem to be police cars everywhere I look lately." As she closed the door and faced into the long living room, she remembered Aster's admonition. *Like the man said, the walls have ears.*

Eyes too, Maureen thought. *Everywhere. If only I could make myself disappear, like Lorna does.* She looked at Lorna's trunk, with all its stickers and decals, reminders of the faraway places Lorna had been while she was alive. Her fingers traced one of the colorful labels. "Guatemala," she said. "Guatemala and Tarzan and a sarong and a long, black wig."

It didn't take long at all. The trunk opened easily. The wig, carefully tissue wrapped, was nestled beside the colorful sarong. With a pair of Key West Kinos on bare feet and her biggest round-lensed Jackie O sunglasses, and wallet and cell phone stashed in an out-of-season straw shoulder bag, Maureen left the inn via the side door just in time to see Frank Hubbard's patrol car park pull up in front of the building. She flashed him a pleasant smile and, with hips swaying, proceeded down the boulevard in the opposite direction.

If it wasn't such a serious business, this would be fun, she thought, as her newly acquired persona drew attention, stares, and some obvious male approval—but not the slightest flicker of recognition even though she passed at least half-a-dozen people she knew. Even Aster Patterson, on her patio watering potted marigolds, was completely fooled. At the law office, Maureen wished the receptionist a good morning and, smiling, asked for Nora Nathan.

"Do you have an appointment?" The woman gave her a searching up-and-down look.

"Not exactly," Maureen said, "but I'm sure she'll see me." She leaned across the counter, removed the sunglasses, and whispered, "I'm Maureen Doherty."

Eyes wide, the receptionist gasped. "Ms. Doherty? It *is* you! What a fabulous Halloween costume! Wait until Nora sees you. She'll be amazed. Please put the glasses back on and have a seat like a regular client." She muffled a giggle and spoke into a desk mic. "Ms. Nathan? Someone here to see you."

Maureen sat in a waiting room chair as demurely as one can while wearing a sarong, ankles crossed, hands folded in her lap. The door to Nora's office swung open. The attorney spoke first. "Hello. I'm Nora Nathan."

Maureen stood, Halloween prank over, deadly serious. "It's me. Maureen. I'm ducking the bulldog cop and I'm scared."

"You sure fooled me," Nora said. "Come on into my office and tell me what's going on."

Maureen followed. "I told you on the phone about what Ted and I suspect about Elizabeth and the Morgans. Did it sound crazy to you? I know it's just an idea. We have no proof of any of it. Is there any chance that Frank Hubbard will believe us? Or will he just believe his 'evidence'?"

"I told you before," Nora began. "Frank Hubbard is a good cop. Tenacious, but honest and fair. He'll consider everything. What you've told me, although it's strictly circumstantial, makes sense. You and Ted have thought it out carefully. He'll listen. But meanwhile, we need to tell him you're here. Deliberately avoiding the police doesn't look good, you know, especially since he already suspects that you've been doing exactly that all along—ducking behind buildings, slipping out side doors—remember?"

"But I wasn't. I mean I wasn't then," Maureen protested.

"You are now. Come on. We'll go in my car." Nora gave her an appraising look. "Nothing we can do about the romper or whatever that thing is, but maybe you could ditch the wig."

Chapter 38

On the way to the inn, Nora phoned Officer Hubbard and politely informed him that she and her client were on the way. Maureen, with the wig carefully rolled up and stuffed into the straw bag, couldn't hear his reply, and Nora didn't offer to repeat it. They parked in the rear lot, beside Maureen's Subaru, and the two women entered from the front of the building. Weaving their way between the pumpkins, they climbed the steps and crossed the porch to the lobby.

Frank Hubbard stood beside the front desk, arms folded, foot tapping, not bothering to disguise his impatience. "Maureen Doherty?" His voice was gruff.

"Yes, sir," she said.

He pushed a paper into her hand. "Consider yourself served. Now let's go upstairs and get this over with. Elizabeth is already up there waiting for us with the key."

At Maureen's questioning look, he explained, "She's the building super, so she can open the penthouse, but the warrant is in your name as the owner."

"I'll take a look at that, please." Nora reached for the paper, concentrating on the printed words while the three rode up to the third floor in silence.

Finn's excited barking could be heard as soon as they exited the elevator. *Poor dog must be anxious, knowing that*

Elizabeth's right outside the door, Maureen thought. *The cats must be curious and nervous too. He's right. Let's just get this over with.*

Elizabeth unlocked the door. Finn growled. "That dog doesn't like me," she said, retreating into the hall.

"It's okay, boy." Maureen patted the golden. "It's okay. Come on in, everybody. He doesn't bite." Both cats watched the proceedings solemnly from the cat tower.

Hubbard headed straight for the kitchen. Maureen followed with Finn and Nora behind her. Elizabeth stayed in the doorway. "Which one is the liquor cabinet?" Hubbard asked. Maureen pointed. He pulled a pair of blue gloves from his pocket, slowly slipped them on, and opened the cabinet door. A plastic bag appeared from another pocket. The grenadine bottle was still there. He lifted the bottle gingerly.

"This yours, Ms. Doherty?"

"No. I haven't removed anything from that cabinet. It's just as Penelope left it as far as I know."

He slid the bottle into the waiting bag. "Witness, Ms. Nathan?" he asked.

"So witnessed," Nora answered.

"All right then, Liz," he said. "You can go on about your business. Thanks for opening the door for us—and for making sure no one else got in."

"No problem," she said, backing away from the no-longer-menacing golden. "I'll be in my office if you need me." The door to the penthouse remained open.

"I expect you understand my interest in this particular bottle, Ms. Doherty." Hubbard patted the pocket containing the now-filled evidence bag.

"Yes, sir," she said. "I imagine that you believe it contains poison. Digitalis, probably."

"Correct. And since now I've not only found a bottle containing pills which may have killed Mr. Wilson, but also the remainder of the liquid which almost undoubtedly went into the lethal drink, both in your apartment, either you appear to be a killer, or . . ."—he paused and stared at the cat tower—"or someone wants to make it *look* as if you're a killer."

"Yes, sir," she said again. "Someone surely does."

"I plan to take this bottle to the police station for finger-printing," he said, patting his pocket again. "Since this one will not be returned to the bar, I presume you have no objection to our doing the fingerprinting off your premises."

"None at all," she said. "I'm sure you won't find *my* prints on it." She thought then of Ted's statement that he knew his prints should be all over it. "Maybe, though, there may be no prints at all."

"As was the case with the medicine bottle," he finished the thought. "Your attorney says you have some ideas about the circumstances leading up to Mr. Wilson's death."

"I do." She repeated what she'd told Nora about the Morgans and Elizabeth, the switching of the bottles, and the memory cards. She didn't mention Ted.

Hubbard's expression didn't change. "Is that all?"

"Yes."

"Is my client free to go about *her* business then, Frank?" Nora asked. "Do you have any questions for her?"

"Not at this time," he said. "You aren't planning on leaving town, are you, Ms. Doherty?"

"No, sir. I have an inn to run."

Besides that, she thought, *I have no place else to go.*

The officer left the penthouse and Maureen closed the door behind him. "How do you think that went?" she asked the attorney. "Do you think he believes me?"

"I think he does," Nora said. "Mostly, I think he has to. You have no discernible motive."

"The Morgans and Elizabeth do," she answered. "Still, I hate to think that people I know, people who sleep under my roof, can be cold-blooded killers. Do you mind if I grab a sweater to cover up this South Seas rig?"

"Greed does strange things to some." Nora watched while Maureen shrugged into a long gray cardigan sweater. "If Conrad Wilson had what he claimed he had—actual photographs of actual ghosts—the value of those images may be enormous. If Alex Morgan has the memory card where the photos are stored, and if the Haven police have the device that will display them, all the killers have to do is wait until the two are in the same place and they'll be rich—and so far, there's no *real* evidence against anybody."

"Except Ted and me."

"Yes, well, that. But neither of you has motive."

The ride down in the elevator was, again, quiet. Before the door slid open on the first floor Maureen spoke. "Three bottles of grenadine," she said. "Three bottles all switched around."

"How do you mean?" Nora asked.

"There must have been an original bottle—plain old grenadine syrup. Then someone—someone who knew a Celebration Libation would be ordered—put a bunch of crunched-up pills into that bottle."

"Right," Nora agreed.

"Then, after the bartender had used the poisoned bottle, it had to be switched for a fresh bottle quickly, so no one else would get poisoned—and that's the bottle the police took as evidence, along with the rum and the others after the body was found."

"True, then the police gave all those bottles back to the bar after they'd been tested and came up clean," Nora said. "Where is the third bottle?"

"Elizabeth had to send Sam out to get replacements for *all* of the liquor bottles while the police had the original ones. When they were returned she poured everything down the drain—said she didn't dare to serve them because she didn't know what the police had done with them."

"Makes sense."

"So by then, someone had possession of the poisoned bottle. The clean bottle had been put into the bar stock; then it went to the police; then it got tossed out with the others. So then what was the bartender using if he needed grenadine?"

"There had to be a third bottle."

"Yes. We know that Ms. Gray liked Shirley Temples. I think the third bottle came from the liquor cabinet in my kitchen—and the killer switched the poison bottle for the third bottle. The one that's on the bar now." Maureen faced Nora. "Gert told me that Hubbard fingerprinted a bottle in the kitchen. I wonder whose prints were on that one." The elevator opened, and the women crossed the lobby. "I'll walk with you to your car," Maureen said.

Once outside, Nora spoke softly. "You know, Maureen, maybe you should tell Hubbard your idea about the third bottle. I won't say anything about what you've told me—lawyer-client privilege—but it seems to me it would be helpful if you talked to him. And Maureen, I can't help worrying that you may have already put yourself in danger."

"Me?" The two left the porch and started around the building to the parking lot.

"Certainly. *Someone* is planting evidence in your rooms. And chances are, *someone* may know that you like Shirley Temples. What if you'd decided to use that contaminated bottle of grenadine yourself?"

"It might look as if I'd committed suicide." Maureen stopped walking. "It might look as if I'd killed Wilson and then killed myself."

Nora pulled her phone from her purse. "Shall I call him back?"

"Okay."

Frank Hubbard answered immediately. This time Nora's phone was in speaker mode. "Yes, Ms. Nathan. Does your client have something else to tell me?"

"She does. Can you come back to the inn, or do you want to speak to her on the phone?"

"I'm still on the premises. In the kitchen. I'm picking up another piece of evidence," he said. "The recent on-site fingerprinting turned up some prints that shouldn't be here."

"Shall we join you in the kitchen?"

"If you wish."

The women retraced their steps, moving aside as the black Lexus backed out of the space marked MANAGER. Elizabeth didn't return Maureen's wave. *She's probably on a run to Quic-Shop for some overpriced groceries*, Maureen thought, stepping over a small smiling pumpkin on the bottom step. Looking up, she noted that the quartet were in their usual places. They'd been joined by reporter Jake. Alex Morgan was on the far side of the porch with Mr. Zamora. Several of the rockers were occupied by new guests. Maureen stopped to welcome each one, while Nora waited just outside the green door—which burst open so fast that Nora barely had time to jump out of the way.

"Help! We've been robbed!" A distraught Clarissa Morgan, barefoot, hair uncombed, clutching the front of a white terry-cloth robe, stumbled onto the porch. "Somebody call the police." She ran toward her husband. "I was taking a nice bath. I heard the door slam. Our luggage was opened and our clothes are thrown around all over. And, Alex, the room safe is wide open—empty. What are we going to do?"

Nora spoke into her phone. "Frank? You'd better come out onto the porch. Something's going on."

Within seconds, Hubbard and a pair of uniformed cops, one with gun drawn, appeared in the open doorway. Alex Morgan, holding a sobbing Clarissa, began to swear. Loudly, profanely, uttering an astonishing unbroken string of expletives and blasphemies. Hubbard flashed his badge close to Morgan's face. "Take it easy, sir. Ladies present. What's going on?"

The man, lowering his tone, echoed his wife's words. "We've been robbed." He looked around. "Where's Elizabeth?"

"Calm down, sir," Frank Hubbard commanded, motioning to the officer to holster his gun. "Elizabeth is in her office, making some copies for me." The faint, rhythmic throb of a copier sounded from inside.

"Uh, no, she isn't," Maureen interrupted. "We just saw her leaving the parking lot in her Lexus."

Frank Hubbard lost no time in assembling four people in Elizabeth's office. Nora and Maureen, Alex and Clarissa. Zamora and Jake had followed—Zamora claiming to be Alex Morgan's new agent and Jake brandishing press credentials—but both had been denied entry. One of the officers stayed on the porch with the remaining guests. The second one was dispatched to secure the Morgans' suite and to await backup. Elizabeth's copier continued to whirr out sheet after empty sheet.

"Liz isn't answering her phone." Jamming his own phone into his breast pocket, Hubbard shut off the machine "Mrs. Morgan, you go first. Tell me exactly what happened."

Alex Morgan pulled his wife close. "She told you. Someone broke into our rooms and stole . . . something."

"Mrs. Morgan," Hubbard repeated.

Clarissa sniffled loudly, buried her head on her husband's shoulder, and mumbled something unintelligible.

"She's too upset," Alex Morgan protested.

"Mrs. Morgan. Tell me exactly what happened." The officer's words were louder, spoken more firmly this time.

The weakest link, Maureen thought. *And he's going to make her talk.*

"The room safe is open, Alex," she moaned. "They got it."

"Hush, darling," her husband told her. "Somebody get her a glass of water. Can't you see she's upset?"

No one spoke. No one moved. Clarissa's sniffling grew

louder. A voice came from the lobby. "Don't worry. I'll get the water." It was Jake, who obviously had his ear to the door, and who—true to his word—pulled open the office door within minutes and hand-delivered a cold bottle of spring water to the weeping woman.

"Thank you," she whispered.

"Go on with your story, Mrs. Morgan," Hubbard ordered. "You say you were taking a bath and you heard a door slam."

"Yes. I was frightened. I peeked out of the bathroom and no one was there. Then I saw our clothes thrown around. Somebody had dumped both of our suitcases out." Her voice began to rise. "I grabbed this robe." She pulled it close around her. "I looked in the closet where the guest safe is," she wailed. "It was wide open."

"Come on, sweetheart." Alex tightened his arm around his wife. "You need to take a nap. We can talk to the officer later." He led her toward the door.

"What was in the safe?" Hubbard asked.

"That's personal." Alex reached for the doorknob. Jake stood in the way.

"Personal," Clarissa muttered, eyes downcast. "Anyway, it was cursed. I'm glad it's gone."

"Cursed?" Hubbard frowned, looked confused. "Sit down, Mr. Morgan. Mrs. Morgan, what was in the safe?"

"Wilson's curse," Clarissa said. "Now it's on her."

"Wilson's curse? What are you talking about, ma'am?"

"Excuse me, Officer Hubbard," Maureen said. "Mrs. Morgan believes she cursed Conrad Wilson the night he died. Isn't that right, Clarissa?"

"Yes. I cursed him and he dropped dead. He wasn't supposed to die, you know. He was only supposed to pass out so we could get it. She promised us no one would get hurt." She looked up at her husband. "Tell them, Alex. She promised and Wilson died and now she's gone and the curse is on her."

"Shut up, Clarissa." He pulled her by the arm, all the tenderness gone from his voice. "Just shut up."

"Did Elizabeth take the memory card from the safe, Clarissa?" Maureen asked. "Is that what happened?"

The woman nodded, rubbing her arm, moving away from her husband. "It was all her idea anyway. Alex would grab the memory card from Conrad's camera and Elizabeth would figure out how to get the tablet. We were supposed to work together. Now she has the card and the tablet and all of the pictures."

Frank Hubbard spoke into his phone. "Get out an APB stat. Elizabeth Mack. She's driving a twenty-twenty black Lexus with 'Haven House Inn' lettered on it. Get the license number from DMV. She's wanted for questioning regarding breaking and entering, theft, and possibly murder." He put the phone down and faced the Morgans.

"You have the right to remain silent . . ." he began.

Chapter 39

Things moved fast after the confrontation with the Morgans in Elizabeth's office. Alex and Clarissa lawyered up right away. It took a while to locate Elizabeth. She'd left her phone behind, so there was no tracking her that way. An alert citizen discovered the Lexus in the Amtrak parking lot up in Sanford, Florida, and police were on hand to arrest her when she got off the train in Virginia. All three suspects were scheduled for hearings at the county courthouse in Clearwater.

Clarissa's statement that Elizabeth had both Wilson's memory card *and* his tablet had been a surprise. It turned out that in addition to the three-way bottle switch, there'd also been a tablet switch.

Examination of the repair estimate Maureen had seen revealed that before turning over all of Wilson's electronics to the Haven police Elizabeth had acid-wiped clean the hard drive on her own tablet, then to be sure it was completely destroyed had it checked by a professional before she exchanged hers for Wilson's. Sam had actually seen Elizabeth "pour something onto a tablet," but that information didn't win him that thousand dollars from Zamora. It was, however, of interest to the police.

Clarissa had been correct. Elizabeth had keys to not only

the rooms but the room safes as well. Instead of sharing the money from Wilson's unearthly photos. Elizabeth had planned to keep it all for herself. The police now had custody of both the memory card and Wilson's own special tablet, which—if Gert was right about Wilson's talent with machines—was capable of showing the ghost pictures.

Who was the rightful owner of card and tablet? Were there really pictures of Haven's ghosts on them? Maureen had a feeling that between court proceedings, book contract litigations, and murder-trial evidence custody, the question wouldn't be answered for a long time.

Nora said Hubbard had told her that the bottle he'd fingerprinted in the kitchen—the bottle that had prints that didn't belong there—revealed a partial set of prints belonging to Penelope Josephine Gray. But since Penelope was already dead when that bottle appeared on the bar, it had to have been the one from Maureen's suite. He'd also confided that in his opinion the very idea of a camera that took pictures of ghosts was "total nonsense."

For Maureen, the most important aspect of all of these revelations was that with the arrests of Elizabeth and the Morgans, she was no longer a suspect in Conrad Wilson's death—and, not so incidentally, neither was Ted. She was free to pursue her plans for improving the Haven House Inn—including promoting the dining room as well as updating the general appearance of the place—and some of these welcome happenings had taken place in time for Haven's Halloween celebration.

With carpets newly shampooed, windows sparkling clean inside and out, and new pale green draperies replacing the heavy fern-patterned ones, the dining room ambiance was much improved. Maureen had indulged herself in de-pinking her own bathroom—with pale gray walls and navy accessories. She'd also replaced all of the inn's old-style light bulbs.

She hadn't taken time to buy a costume, and Lorna's island

girl getup was certainly out of the question. Penelope Josephine Gray's costume was still in the dry cleaner's bag, hanging in the now-ghost-free closet in suite twenty-seven. "I remember it," Ted told Maureen. "She called it 'Queen of the Night.' It was really pretty. At least try it on."

Ted was right. It was pretty, tight bodiced and full skirted, and sequin stars seemed to float within layers of soft organza in blues and blacks. The wand that George had described was silver, tipped with a golden crescent moon. A silver-and-crystal tiara completed the look.

Maureen modeled it for Lorna. "It looks as if it was made for you," the spirit declared. "If I wasn't wearing Glinda the Good Witch's ball gown, I'd be jealous."

The appraisal of the contents of the warehouse was well underway. Mr. Crenshaw had already separated what he referred to as "the wheat from the chaff." Most of Penelope's hoard had fallen into the "chaff" category, but it wasn't entirely worthless. Hundreds of beach towels, boxes full of beach toys, assorted articles of clothing, sneakers, sandals, sunglasses, and flip-flops were all deemed salable. Some of the suitcases were of good quality, but Maureen was disappointed to find that the cases marked MR. AND MRS. JOHN SMITH were empty—apparently Trent's parents had used them as props for their illicit rendezvous. Kids' toys and games, along with assorted holiday decorations, proved to be a good source of "wheat." There were several vintage Barbie dolls, a few desirable Matchbox cars, and some wonderful Christmas decorations dating back to the 1940s. The guest registers on the top shelf of the bedroom closet—with all those famous signatures—proved to be so valuable that several museums were bidding on them. All in all, it appeared to Maureen that selling the hoard would not only free up the money being paid for the rental of the locker but also easily pay for painting the outside of the inn.

"We have a long way to go before Haven House Inn becomes a paying proposition," Maureen told Ted as they studied the menu for that night's Halloween celebration. "But I'm glad we can at least keep our favorite four old-timers on the payroll."

"Naming the suites for the famous guests who've slept in them was a brilliant idea," he said. "Jake's article on Haven House says that the proposed Babe Ruth suite already has reservation requests."

"True," Maureen agreed. "And the Lucille Ball and Desi Arnaz one does too. Speaking of names, we need to come up with a new name for Elizabeth's."

"Later," he said. "Right now, we have a full house for tonight."

"That's a good thing."

"Mostly ghost hunters," he said.

"Afraid so," she agreed. "There's probably no way to get around it. Haven has its ghosts."

"I thought you didn't believe in them."

"I didn't."

"What changed your mind?' he asked.

"Maybe someday I'll tell you all about it," she said, "but for now, I'm going to put on my Queen of the Night costume and mingle with the guests. See you at the party."

Maybe someday I will *tell him about Lorna and John Smith and Crenshaw's opera singer and the rowdy bunch of ghosts who gather at the L&M Bar,* Maureen thought as she climbed the stairs to the penthouse, *but not yet. And I've decided to tell Trent and Pierre what John Smith said. All of it. Well, maybe not Lorna's part in it. One ghost at a time may be all they can handle.*

Finn, looking slightly embarrassed wearing a formal doggy tuxedo and bow tie, greeted her at the door. "Oh, Finn. You look so handsome," she told him. The golden looked up at the almost-smirking cats, perched at the top of their tower. She'd tried to dress them in cute costumes too, but—catlike—

they'd have none of it. "Never mind what they say," she told him. "They're just jealous because we're going to the party tonight and they aren't."

Finn followed her through the kitchen and into her bedroom, where the costume hung on the closet door. "I guess this'll be a tradition," she said. "I'll wear it every Halloween, and the rest of the time I'll keep it in the closet in suite twenty-seven, along with that mysterious picture of me that Penelope had, and the framed pictures of famous guests I'm going to use in redecorated suites, and the Halloween candy buckets." The golden tilted his head to one side. "You know, if we gather up enough stuff, enough information, maybe someday we'll figure out why Penelope Josephine Gray gave us this place." Finn tilted his head to the opposite side. "Yeah, I know. I'm starting my own hoard, aren't I? Never mind. I know what I'm doing. I promise, it'll never get out of hand."

> *With a message from the dead*
> *On a journey you've been led.*
> *Another message from a stranger*
> *Holds an answer, comes with danger.*
> *A riddle, a puzzle in plain sight.*
> *An answer, a vision in black and white.*
> *You'll know the where but not the why.*
> *Beware the place one comes to die.*
> ZOLTAR KNOWS ALL

"Maybe I'll put that Zoltar card in the closet too," she told Finn. She tossed her lucky coin in the air, caught it, smiled, and zipped herself into Penelope Josephine Gray's Halloween costume. At that moment, the future looked good. "We're going to be just fine, Finn," she promised.

"Woof," the golden agreed.

There was a tiny *ding* from the push bell, followed by a silvery laugh and a whispered, "We'll see."

Acknowledgments

First of all, thanks to the friendly ghost who haunted a house I once lived in in Gloucester, Massachusetts, and made me a believer.

Several of Florida's off-the-beaten-path, blessedly preserved small towns inspired my fictional locale of Haven. Thank you, Florida, for keeping it real—with a special nod to Cathy Salustri for her book *Backroads of Paradise: A Journey to Rediscover Old Florida.*

RECIPES

MOLLY'S APPLE-RAISIN PIE

1 recipe plain two-crust pastry

For the Filling:

⅔ cup raisins
6 tablespoons water
½ teaspoon lemon juice
¼ cup light corn syrup (Karo)
1½ teaspoons all-purpose flour
1½ teaspoons sugar
2 tart apples (Granny Smith)
¼ cup brown sugar
½ cup sugar
¼ teaspoon cinnamon
½ teaspoon ground nutmeg
1½ teaspoons cornstarch

For the Icing (Optional):

1 cup powdered sugar
2 tablespoons water
1 tablespoon butter, softened

Preheat the oven to 400 degrees F and line a 9-inch pie pan with a rolled-out crust. To make the raisin filling put raisins, water, and lemon juice into a heavy saucepan over medium heat. Bring to a boil, then lower the heat to medium low, and cook, stirring occasionally until raisons are plump (about 15 minutes). Separately combine the corn syrup, flour, and sugar. Mix well, then add to the raisins and continue cooking and stirring occasionally until thick and syrupy (about 20 minutes). Remove from heat and cool until just warm.

Peel the apples, cut them into thin wedges, and pour them into a large bowl. Separately, combine the sugars, cinnamon, nutmeg, and cornstarch, then add to the apples and stir until evenly coated. Spread the apple mixture in an even layer into the first rolled-out crust; then spread the raisin mixture over the apples.

Brush the rim of the crust with water, cover with the second rolled-out crust, seal, and flute the edges. Cut several slits on top. Bake for 40 to 50 minutes, until golden brown. Cool on a wire rack.

For the frosting, mix sugar and water and add butter. Mix until smooth and spread over cooled pie before serving.

ASTER'S SHORTBREAD COOKIES

½ cup plus 2 tablespoons sugar
1 cup softened butter
2½ cups *sifted* all-purpose flour

Mix the sugar and softened butter together thoroughly with hands. Stir in the flour and mix some more. Chill the dough for at least one hour. Roll it out to ⅓ to ½ inch thick. Cut into rounds. (Aster always makes her cookies round because that's the way Peter liked them, but she says you can cut yours into any shape you like. Leaves, ovals, squares, whatever.)

Place the rounds onto an ungreased cookie sheet. Bake at 300 degrees F (slow oven) for 20 to 25 minutes. The tops do not brown during baking, nor does the shape of the cookies change. The recipe makes about two dozen 1 inch x 1½ inch crisp, thick, buttery cookies.

TED'S BLACKENED GROUPER

(It would be nice to say that Ted invented this recipe, but it's really from the late, great Pappas' Restaurant in Tarpon Springs, Florida.)

Use a 2-pound fresh grouper fillet, preferably ¾ to 1 inch thick. Salt and pepper to taste.

For the Blackened Grouper Sauce Mixture:

2 tablespoons finely chopped garlic
1½ tablespoons finely chopped fresh parsley
1 tablespoon Lea & Perrins Worcestershire sauce
1 teaspoon dry basil
1 teaspoon oregano
¼ teaspoon thyme
½ teaspoon cayenne
3 ounces fresh lemon juice
2 teaspoons salt
4 ounces drawn melted butter

Mix all ingredients in blender, except for butter. Blend at medium speed for 20 seconds. After blending, mix with butter, place in 10-ounce jar with lid, and shake.

Ted cooks his grouper in a very hot skillet (cast iron is the very best). You can use either a grill or a skillet heated to 450 to 500 degrees F. Pour a thin layer of the sauce on the preheated skillet. Lay fish on top of sauce immediately. Then add more sauce on fillet as it cooks. Allow to cook about 5 minutes, depending on thickness of fish. Then turn fillet over and repeat with more sauce.

Grouper blackens as it cooks and may create a lot of smoke. Be sure it is done throughout.